Dedication

For me, this book has been has been a gift from God. For this, and the many wonderful people and things in my life, I thank Him.

This book is also dedicated to my family: Dad, Mom, Dana, Heber, Jay and Mackenzie, who always believed in, and encouraged me, despite having put up with many years of my hair-brained schemes.

And finally, to Gloria Patterson, the other Mom.

WHERE LEGENDS ROAM

THE KODIAK BOOKS
Where Legends Roam
Lee Murphy

DEFINING MOMENTS
P.O. Box 7037
Van Nuys, CA 91409

Library of Congress Cataloging-in-Publication Data
Murphy, Lee
Where Legends Roam/Lee Murphy
99-75269
ISBN 0-9667704-4-7
Printed in the United States of America
First Edition

Edited by Mariana Malkoskie
Cover design by Mike S. Compter
Book layout by Kathryn Louyse

Acknowledgements

I cannot assume credit for this work on my own. There are many wonderful friends who gave of their time and offered up their best ideas for this project. At best, I was smart enough to listen to them. Because all of their contributions are equally important, I have listed them alphabetically. This is because they are all the best. If there is anybody I have failed to mention, I apologize.

Michael Bernstein, Tim Bovard, Chris Buccowich, Beverly Burwald, Arlene Busey, Caryl Castleberry, Joe Cocke, Dr. Martin Dinnes, DVM, Charles Fischer, J. Richard Greenwell, Chris Hardt, Dr. John Hartwick, DVM, Scott Johnson, Don Lanning, Jacquie Leger, Carsten Lien, Rosella Linder, Kathryn Louyse, Dr. Roy P. Mackal, Mariana Malkoskie, Michael Martin, Michael Meaker, Steve Melendrez, Stefan Miles, Ronald Miller, Pasquale Moscatello, Cyrena Nouzille, David Patterson, Sam Pitassi, Robert Reid, Christine Richard, Alexis Skriloff, Renee Tedesco, Heidi Wiss.

THE KODIAK BOOKS

WHERE LEGENDS ROAM

Lee Murphy

Foreword

by Dr. Roy P. Mackal

This tale, *Where Legends Roam*, is a novel, a great adventure novel. It is fiction, of course, but very special in a number of ways. The storyline is gripping and fast-moving, and it carries the reader to the very end with a sense of excitement and anticipation for the next page. But many stories have this quality, and they also exhibit a high level of literary skill. This was all I expected when I read Lee Murphy's story. To my amazement and delight, I found much more in the manuscript.

I found that it was a tale about cryptozoology with a cryptozoologist as the chief protagonist. Cryptozoology is a new name, but not a new science. What is cryptozoology in reality? It is the investigation of, search for and study of unknown living animals which are unexpected in (1) size or shape, or in (2) time or place. The discovery of animals surviving from the past, thought to be extinct since evidence for them ends in the fossil record thousands or millions of years ago, is cryptozoological. Hans Schomburgk's discovery of a species of pygmy hippopotamus in Liberia in 1912 is cryptozoology. As I previously stated, this was part of what zoologists did in the 19th century. No eyebrows were raised, nor was anyone (whether scientist or layperson) vilified due to such activities. Then the cultural climate changed: reports of the Loch Ness Monster, the Yeti (or Abominable Snowman) and Bigfoot appeared. A tabloid atmosphere developed: serious cryptozoology was categorized as pseudo-science engaged in only by kooks and flakes. Those who dared to persist were ridiculed, tenure was denied to academic younger career scientists, and even scientists with established reputations and the best of credentials were labeled as having lost their senses.

As a scientist engaged in cryptozoology, I am happy to report that this situation has at least been partially modified. A key factor in this happy improvement was the founding of the *International Society of Cryptozoology* at the Smithsonian Institution in Washington, D.C., in 1982. I was the co-founder of this organization which consists of about 1000 members, approximately evenly split between scientists and non-professionals. The purpose of the Society is to disseminate accurate, serious, non-tabloid cryptozoological information in a peer-reviewed journal and in four annual newsletters. No longer need people interested in the discovery of new and strange animals rely on cloud-cuckoo land publications.

Why have I digressed to bring this information about the science of cryptozoology to you, the reader? The reason is that Lee Murphy has incorporated into his exciting adventure novel a true sense of what real cryptozoologists really do, what they feel, their hopes and fears, their successes and failures, their sacrifices, and their rewards, all encased in a marvelously entertaining adventure story. This achievement cannot fail to bring much enjoyment to the reader; it may even result in some readers pursuing cryptozoology in the real world, from an armchair or in a jungle, in ocean depths, or in lost worlds on mountain top plateaus.

Roy P. Mackal, B.S., Ph.D., D.Sc.

Hong Kong
1935

goat was loose in the marketplace. It had chewed through the rope that tethered it and was wending its way between the legs of shocked patrons, whose stunned faces elicited laughter from the other people who were milling about.

Voices here were loud, but not angry, as people bartered for food and other wares, while vendors took chickens from their holding pens and decapitated them in routine fashion without regard to cruelty, or for that matter sanitation, as the severed heads were left in bloody piles at their sandaled feet.

All along the street cleavers dropped in rhythm to the music of street musicians, as all varieties of animals were butchered for selective patrons. Skinned dogs hung from meat hooks, while across the way a vendor expertly peeled the skin from a cat in one deft, fluid move. Other tables offered a selection of body parts: piles of chicken feet, dog heads, pig ears, and even ox entrails. Nothing was wasted of any animal.

As foreigners were a rarity in this part of the world, a lone Dutch scientist turned many heads as he maneuvered through the ebb and flow of jostling peasantry. He was a short man, not much taller than the people around him. Preoccupied with other matters, he was oblivious to the excitement his presence was causing, merely because his skin, hair, and features were different from theirs.

People pointed at him, gesticulating excitedly as though they might be trying to ward him off, while others came up to him boldly, brandishing their goods; hand-crafted jewelry and various wood items, all beautiful and fetching, but of no interest to him. He simply pressed on through the barrage of faces, waving them away with a polite smile and nod. Looking past the curiosity seekers, his eyes scanned the buildings, deciphering the Chinese characters on walls and signs for one specific place.

A large following had formed around him when he noticed a peculiar item in the front window of a building that was otherwise indistinguishable from the rest. As he walked over to it, another vendor reached into a wooden barrel and proffered two handfuls of squirming live eels that brushed against his khaki shirt. The Dutchman ignored this as he shaded his eyes with his hand and pressed his face up against the glass to reduce the daylight glare, so he could get a better look at the mummified orangutan's head that was on display.

This was the place.

He went inside where the late afternoon sunlight filtered through billions of airborne dust particles, giving the room an ethereal quality. Wind chimes made of delicate sea shells tinkled in the warm breeze, and the room smelled of incense and tea that brewed in another room. But the Dutchman's senses were more attuned to the smell of rock and bones – the very things that attracted him to this apothecary where potions, powders, and various extracts were derived from thousands of organic materials.

Hundreds of small ceramic bottles filled with dried mushrooms, flowers, herbs, and roots covered the back wall of the tiny store. Animal pelts hung from the ceiling, their internal organs pickled in glass jars to remain fresh, or dehydrated to be pulverized at a later time, depending upon their usage.

These apothecaries were also wonderful sources of material for people like this Dutchman, who had come here in his search for the origins of humankind and to look for as yet undiscovered species of prehistoric life. The Chinese were notorious for excavating thousands of tons of fossils, calling them dragons' bones, and grinding them into powders that would serve as medicines and aphrodisiacs.

On this particular day, though as yet unaware of it, the Dutchman was about to make such a discovery.

He'd been through dozens of these apothecaries in places like Java, Borneo, and Sumatra, and it was in the Philippines that he discovered the first fossil orangutan teeth. When he inquired as to their place of origin, he was directed to this place in Hong Kong.

During his initial search through the deep, dusty drawers and massive wooden cases that filled the shop, he found the same things he had encountered in other apothecaries: more orangutan teeth, some pieces of a tusk, and the partial skull of some long-extinct rodent. He found some pieces from the jaw of *Ailuropoda*, the giant panda, and the teeth of *Stegodon*, an extinct elephant. There were even teeth from *Homo erectus*, the earliest hominid known to have existed in Asia.

He gingerly continued to go through the loose piles of fossils that had been dumped without care, not wanting to miss anything of significance, when he came upon something *extraordinary*.

It looked like a human tooth, a molar, but was more than six times the size of any human tooth previously known to exist. Upon closer examination, he saw that it was flatter than a human molar, with low crowns and thick enamel ideal for grinding heavy vegetation like bamboo. Was this the tooth of an ape? If it was, it belonged to an anthropoid ape far more gigantic than any known species – even the recently discovered mountain gorilla of Africa.

His heartbeat accelerated with the thrill of a new discovery as he took the tooth out of the drawer and held it into the light for a better look. It was a lower third molar, and the yellowish deposits within its pulp cavities indicated that it was originally found in some cave or fissure that had protected it from the harsh tropical elements.

He visualized what such an animal must have looked like. The American film *King Kong* had only been released two years earlier, and the screen image of that monster ape seemed a-not-so-unrealistic analogy. Of course, the animal this tooth had once been a part of was no monster. It had lived alongside the panda and the orangutan, peacefully filling the niche nature had intended it for. A monster only in size, and perhaps in appearance – at least to the simpleminded – *majestic* was how the Dutch scientist would have described this animal.

In his mind's eye he could imagine a dozen family groups feeding in a field of bamboo, their black fur shining under the Asian sun, with the big males intently watching the females and the young as they play and explore. They were just like gorillas, only twice the size of any known species of that great ape.

To have become extinct, as this species had, could only have been at the hands of early man. Cognizant thought had given the human species an unequaled advantage; the ability to form ideas that made the human animal a cunning predator. A single specimen of this large ape would provide a tribe of humans with plenty of meat and fat, as well as a thick pelt to protect them from the elements.

The Dutchman spent the next several hours on an exhaustive search, going through all the other drawers and cases of bones hoping to find another one of these magnificent teeth, if not something more. But he was unable to find anything that compared to the tooth which he assigned to this unknown primate of magnificent proportions.

Finally, he went over to the open doorway and held the fossil between the thumb and forefinger of his left hand, letting the sun glint off its ancient brown surface like some priceless jewel.

His name was G.H. Ralph Von Koenigswald, and he had just discovered the first evidence of the largest ape to have ever roamed the earth.

He had discovered *Gigantopithecus*.

The Cryptozoologist

G eorge Kodiak was born and raised in Hell. Hell, Michigan, to be exact.

One hundred and thirty-five feet down in the lake behind his house, a two hundred-foot sink hole bore the fossil remains of animals from the Pleistocene and Miocene epochs, more than ten million years ago.

His attention was fixed on a fourteen-inch circle of yellow light that shone from the lamp atop his head, upon a jagged limestone wall that was blanketed under a layer of slimy algae that whipped and danced with each languid wave of his hand.

In the center of the wall, an eye socket large enough to house a cantaloupe protruded through the slime. Twenty inches below that, a shattered stump was all that remained of a mighty tusk that had long ago disintegrated after this animal had died and become entombed in the rock. After more than three months of excavating by hand with various tools and dental instruments, the Mastodon skull was still more than two-thirds buried in the rock.

This was the most recent of hundreds of animal fossils the sink hole had yielded that included several species of extinct deer, saber-tooth cats, and giant sloths. He had even found the mummified remains of an early Asian immigrant who had been buried beneath a limestone shelf when this sink hole was still above ground before the ice age.

This was as much a home to him as anywhere else in the world. Not so much the depths of this sink hole, but the time in history which it represented. The Mastodon and the other animals down here were familiar to him as individual beings— friends from another life. But they had all gone on to the next dimension, and he was still trapped in this world, a stranger disconnected to other human beings in ways he never fully understood.

George Kodiak was something of a celebrity, albeit a reluctant

5

one, having become famous for a series of books he had written on his field of expertise: *cryptozoology*, the study of hidden and unknown animals. His books were all internationally famous, each based upon his experiences searching for such creatures as the Sasquatch, the Loch Ness Monster, and dozens of other animal anomalies reputed to exist, but denied by the scientific community at large.

Peace and solace were found in solitude. The only sounds now were the hiss of the air regulator in his mouth and the roar of bubbles that were expelled in the continuous rhythm of his breathing.

Kodiak checked his pressure gauge and saw that he had enough air left to allow for decompression. It had been a long day, and the water was getting steadily colder. Despite a physical body that could still serve him exceptionally well, there could be no doubt that he was getting old. Soon his joints and the old cracks in his bones would ache like hell and remind him that he was not a young man.

❧

Wayne Monroe had never been to Hell, and trying to find it proved to be far from simple. All he had to go on was that it was a small town with a population of less than a thousand people, located some forty miles northwest of Detroit. Ann Arbor was roughly twenty miles closer in the same direction, but nobody he spoke to in either of those cities had even heard of it. He ended up buying a map when he rented the BMW coupe at Detroit Metropolitan Airport, and in less than an hour he was stopped at a badly weathered and bullet-ridden city limits sign that read:

HELL
MICHIGAN
(aptly named)

Wayne was a five-foot, six-inch-tall cowboy born and bred in the heart of Texas, with a pushbroom mustache, lamb chop sideburns, and a gold and jeweled belt buckle that, on him, looked like it was

6

the size of a dinner plate.

"Just how well do you know him, anyway?" Ron Pearl had to holler to be heard over the car's engine, which had been poorly treated by previous renters and was in dire need of a tune-up.

Wayne had one of those sonorous voices that he didn't have to raise to be heard above the engine's din or the rushing wind. He had spent the last twenty-three years working in New York, but he never lost the trademark drawl that made words like "fine" sound like "fahn." "Not all that well, really. George is a good enough guy, but anybody who ever really knew him is dead."

Hell was not an altogether bad place; a rustic town that was spread along a five-mile stretch of road among open, rolling hills. They passed one bank, two service stations, various diners and private businesses. Pearl thought they played the devil thing up a bit much, as it was a common caricature that was used all over town on signs and painted on storefront windows.

Wayne Monroe was Kodiak's literary agent. And the fact that Wayne was naturally gregarious and business-minded didn't leave a great deal for the two men to have in common. Except for the books. Despite their differences, they were good for each other's careers. Kodiak even had a major following, in spite of himself. He rarely gave interviews, and not many people even knew what he looked like, except when his picture showed up on the cover of *Discover* magazine. His picture never appeared on any of his book jackets, and all his bios ever said about him was that George Kodiak was born and raised in Hell, Michigan.

They drove through a thickly forested area two miles outside of town and turned onto Von Koenigswald Road, which was little more than a glorified dirt path named for the discoverer of *Gigantopithecus*.

"How much farther is it?" Pearl asked, sounding like a petulant child.

"Don't know," Wayne said, thinking he'd really like to smack this guy, even if Pearl couldn't help the irritating quality of his voice. "From everything I've heard about the house, it shouldn't be difficult to find. It's a three-story Victorian set on an oxbow lake."

Wayne drove up a hillock covered with wild grass and spotted a multi-crowned rooftop just beyond the rise. The house looked like something out of a nineteenth-century *Daguerreotype* photo; a

7

massive, archaic building taller than the biggest trees around it, majestically set before the rippling black water of a lake that was surrounded by dense forestation.

Wayne described what he knew of its history.

"It was built during the years between 1921 and 1926 by George's father, Harold, for George's mother, Claudette Harris Kodiak. She grew up among Detroit society, the privileged daughter of an automobile company executive who could offer her everything in terms of material wealth. But when she took up with this lowly Indian half-breed, a man physically, mentally, and spiritually beneath her people – at least in the eyes of her family – well, that's when they disowned her.

"George is one-quarter Athapaskan Indian, the same lineage that produced the Apache and Navajo tribes. And the original family name was not Kodiak. In 1913 George's grandfather, John, left his tribal home on the Aleutian Islands to find a better life for his wife, who was the daughter of a white fur trader, and their thirteen-year-old son, Harold, George's father. John chose a career in the American military, but upon his induction into the Army a simple-minded clerk was unable to spell John's last name, so he substituted the name of John's birthplace – the island of Kodiak. John chose not to make a fuss about it, and the name stuck."

Wayne drove up the cobblestone driveway and stopped the BMW in front of the garage. The house's overall exterior had fallen into general disrepair. The grounds were unkept and overgrown with dead grass and weeds. The white paint was peeling and looked more like the color of weak urine. Still, the profile of the estate hinted at a glorious past.

He knew this was the right place when he saw the *Dimetrodons*: two carnivorous, lizard-like animals that existed thirty-eight million years before the dinosaurs. They were each ten feet long, and recognizable by the tall sails of skin that adorned their backs, and reptilian smiles that bore mouths full of long, sharp teeth appropriate for tearing the flesh off of their prey. The *Dimetrodons* were set on the front porch much the way other people would place concrete lions. Wayne did notice the evil-looking sentinels were a little too life-like for Pearl, who averted his eyes as he stepped up between them to the front porch.

Nobody answered the door when Wayne knocked, so he waited

a few minutes and knocked again. Pearl wondered if the delay wasn't a sign from Above to get away while they still had a chance. But Wayne reached for the door knob. Ordinarily, he didn't like to enter anybody's home uninvited, but it was nearing dusk, and the breeze off the lake was chilly. Besides, he could tell that his companion had had enough of standing between the two hungry-looking *Dimetrodons*, even if they were only made of fiberglass. The door was unlocked, and as Wayne opened it, Pearl muttered, "Please, God, don't let him have a dog..."

"George?" Wayne stuck his head inside, and his heart skipped a beat at the sight of the place before him. "Wow..."

Inside, the house was enormous; eighteen feet from floor to ceiling. It was a wide open space that made use of hand-carved support beams rather than walls, that lent a feeling of openness to the house.

They came inside and walked down a set of steps into a living room that was littered with bones. Most of these were casts of fossil skeletons Kodiak had purchased from various museums, and were either still in boxes, partially assembled, or just scattered haphazardly about the furniture. Wayne was not up on fossils, so he wasn't able to figure many of them out as he walked through the living room.

As the sun set beyond the lake, its red light reflected off the surface of the water and filled the house with bouncing phantoms of light. Wayne half-expected to hear the lonesome echo of a harpsichord playing from some wing of the house that had been uninhabited for years.

The place was also cluttered with books – hundreds of them. Books on prehistoric life and natural history, comparative anatomy and zoology, as well as several dozen books on unexplained phenomena. What didn't fit on the wall shelves was stacked into dusty piles on the floor and on the furniture. Kodiak had even used four piles of books to support a makeshift coffee table in front of a sofa.

On the walls were hung original artworks by Charles R. Knight, a turn-of-the-century artist famous for his classic reproductions of the prehistoric world.

They walked across the living room to a huge fireplace that was constructed of rocks bearing the fossil skeleton of a *Mosasaur*; an aquatic reptile that looked something like a thirty-foot crocodile, with large flippers in the place of its legs. And mounted over the mantle was the six-foot *Coelacanth* fish Kodiak had caught off Madagascar fifteen years earlier.

Wayne turned on a chandelier light over the dining room table when he heard Pearl gasp.

Erected next to the stairs, where Kodiak had removed a section of the second floor for additional space, was the partially re-constructed skeleton of a forty-eight foot *Tyrannosaurus rex.* Nearly the entire body was put together except for several bones still in crates on the floor.

They stared in awe as they walked underneath the Tyrannosaurus, absorbing its almost unreal dimensions. Its vast rib cage loomed eight feet above their heads and was large enough to encase three adult horses. Wayne shuddered as he imagined the horror this thing's prey must have known in those last few seconds of life, and he solemnly thanked God for its extinction. He also thought to ask Kodiak about letting him bring his nephew out here for a look sometime.

"This place is like a vampire's house." Pearl placed his hands on his hips, clearly impressed. "I'll bet *National Geographic* would love to do an article on this guy."

"Get in line," Wayne replied. He cupped his hands around his mouth and hollered, "George!" His voice echoed throughout the house, but there was no answer. "Of course," Wayne said, turning to face Pearl, "there is no reason for him to have expected us, since we did show up unannounced."

"You didn't call him?"

"He chooses not to have a telephone."

Pearl was flabbergasted. "What kind of person doesn't have a telephone? How does anybody get a hold of him, especially in this day and age!"

Wayne sighed. "I don't imagine he could be far. The lights are on. And the furniture looks comfortable enough. All we have to do is move a couple boxes of bones and maybe a stack of books out of the way and wait for him to show up. But first, something to drink."

જ્જ

Kodiak stopped at the mouth of the sink hole, thirty-five feet below the surface to decompress. Compared to the jagged, rocky walls of the two hundred-foot well beneath it, the bottom of the lake was smooth and sandy, with a few rocks and plants, but no fish.

When he was finally able to break the surface and wade ashore, he saw the figures of two men watching him from the edge of the water. He recognized the short one with the Stetson hat and the lit cigar as Wayne Monroe, who said, "What do you say, George? This here is Ron Pearl."

Pearl nodded. "How ya' doin'?"

Kodiak didn't say anything as he hoisted the air tank off his shoulders and removed his face mask.

Wayne said to him, "You might wanna do something about that booger you got hanging from your nose. Looks like you got a damn banana slug climbing down your face."

❧

Kodiak took them to the Hell Hole, a place that boasted the finest dining in all of downtown Hell. It was a dark hole-in-the-wall, with the odor of stale smoke heavy in the air and on the red naugahyde furniture. The decor of the place was tropical and gaudy, with towering South Pacific demons carved from lava rock, and wooden tiki masks adorning floral-papered walls. Again with the devil stuff, Pearl thought, as he followed Wayne and Kodiak over to the bar.

One object that caught Pearl's eye was the plaster cast of an eighteen-inch footprint mounted on the wall behind the bar.

"It's the one thing everybody's got an opinion on," the bartender told them about the Sasquatch print Kodiak had given him several years ago.

"More for or against?" Wayne asked him.

The bartender shrugged. "That usually depends on what that particular person thinks of George." He laughed, and Kodiak smiled.

"Obviously more against. Thanks, Jack." Kodiak took a pitcher of beer and three glasses, and led them to the back of the tavern where they could speak in private.

They slipped into a booth and Ron Pearl was able to take a good look at George Kodiak. His impression was of a wolf. A big alpha male who was getting on in years, but could still take on any

11

adversaries who dared challenge him. He was slower with age, but one slip or miscalculation on the part of his opponent, and the consequences would be swift and merciless. Pearl had heard many stories about George Kodiak that would confirm the need for caution. Yet, here he was in person, and he seemed pleasant, even amiable when he said, "I don't get many visitors. What is it that brings you boys to my little slice of Hell?"

Pearl let out a breath, composing himself, then said, "Well, George, if I may call you that, I'm sure you're familiar with Emory Pittman?"

"Passingly." Kodiak was being facetious. Emory Pittman was a billionaire land developer who got his start building tract homes in the 1950's, to now owning some of the largest buildings in the world. His picture had been on the cover of almost every magazine at one time or another, including *Mad*.

Pearl was embarrassed. "You're right, of course. It was a stupid question."

Wayne poured the beer into the glasses and passed them out.

Pearl continued. "I work for Mr. Pittman. I represent his interests, so to speak. Mr. Pittman is a philanthropist who has been instrumental in serving as something of a diplomat on behalf of the United States to countries where we might otherwise be denied an audience, so to speak."

Kodiak said, "The same kind of thing Armand Hammer did with the Soviet Union."

"Exactly." Pearl continued. "Mr. Pittman has become aware of your desire to arrange a joint American/Vietnamese paleontological expedition. It turns out he has some interest in the subject and is giving serious consideration to financing the trip. Mr. Pittman has, of course, financed previous expeditions between the two countries, but those were to search for the remains of American MIA's. This is an entirely different project – in the spirit of scientific cooperation." Pearl held up a large paperback book titled *Hunt for the Living Gigantopithecus*. It was one of Kodiak's books. "This book has convinced Mr. Pittman that the Sasquatch is a reality, and he's particularly interested in the *Gigantopithecus*-Sasquatch theory. Correct me if I'm wrong, but your father was something of a paleontologist, wasn't he?"

"Paleoanthropologist, yes," Kodiak stated. "I learned most of what I know from him and others. He was a personal friend of Ralph Von Koenigswald."

"The man who first discovered *Gigantopithecus*. Is that how you came to consider that animal as a possible candidate for the Sasquatch?"

Kodiak told him, "More than fifty years after Von Koenigswald discovered that first tooth in Hong Kong, some fifteen hundred *Gigantopithecus* teeth have been found, as well as four fossilized jawbones – but nothing else. I want to go to Vietnam to try and find a complete *Gigantopithecus* skeleton. I'm hoping a complete skeleton might finally solve the Sasquatch riddle."

"So, why Vietnam?" Pearl asked. "In this book you state that some of the richest Giganto deposits found so far have been in southern China."

Kodiak answered him. "The Chinese sites have been badly stripped of fossil material by the apothecary industry, and the Chinese don't readily welcome ventures of this nature. While the Vietnamese have no serious interest in the fossil trade, they are most anxious to make a connection with the West. Why would Emory Pittman want to be involved in all this? It seems odd that he would be associated with such things as unknown animals."

Pearl shrugged and took a dainty sip of beer, as though he were trying it for the first time and did not know whether or not he would like it. "I have known Emory Pittman for more than thirty years, Mr. Kodiak, and I probably know less about him now than I did back when he first hired me. Who can ever figure the idle rich?

"All I know for certain is he would like you and Mr. Monroe to come out to his place in Arizona. If you're agreeable, he can have his private jet at Detroit Metropolitan first thing tomorrow."

Hunt for the Living Gigantopithecus

ildred Hunnicut lived in Washington State's Olympic National Forest for thirty-seven years, where her late husband had built their home. He had worked as a forest ranger for thirty years and was retired only one year when he died of a massive heart attack. While she missed him as much as any human being could miss another, living alone in this beautiful wilderness never bothered her.

Until two nights ago.

She had settled in for a quiet evening of reading by the fireplace when she heard peculiar noises outside and went to investigate. Raccoons had been getting into the garbage lately, attracted by the smell of discarded cat food cans. This irritated her, because she always washed the cans out and wrapped them in plastic before tossing them in the trash. She wouldn't mind them going through the rubbish, if they didn't make such a mess for her to have to clean up the next day.

She sneaked outside and looked around the corner to see what was rummaging through her trash. Her heart nearly stopped cold when she saw a man bent over her garbage can, looking through the refuse. Then her eyes adjusted to the moonlight, and she really didn't believe what she was looking at. No more than twenty-five feet from where she was standing a *Sasquatch* was foraging in the rubbish.

In all the years she lived here she had never once seen one. She heard stories about these unusual animals roaming the Pacific Northwest, but even Steve, in all his years as a ranger, only saw footprints, and that only happened twice.

She didn't know what to do. Ordinarily, she probably just would have watched, fascinated, as it went about its business. But there was the story last month about that trailer park on the other side of Lake Crescent that was supposedly attacked by one of them. The

14

rangers said it was really a bear, but she was scared nonetheless, and went as quietly as she could back into her house, locked the doors and windows, and shut out all the lights.

The next day she felt a little foolish, having realized that she was probably not in any danger. Besides, the creature she saw wasn't anywhere near as big as they were usually described. This one stood a little over five feet tall, covered with short, black hair and looked rather spindly, like it might have been a juvenile. She was relieved that nobody from the ranger station in Red Fern bothered to come and investigate after she had called them the previous night.

Two days later, after there was no further evidence of her mysterious night visitor, she felt it was safe enough to feed her cat on the front lawn while she sat on the porch swing to watch the sun set behind the Olympic Mountain Range.

The shadows of the forest grew long across the front lawn and overcame her small gray tabby as it fed on the plate of canned food that was labeled *Chunks & Stuff*. Whatever the *Chunks & Stuff* really were didn't seem to concern the cat.

The cool air felt good as Mildred rocked back and forth on the swing, lulling herself into a drowsy state. This was her favorite time of year, as Summer would be winding down soon and Autumn would be here. She didn't know if she had actually dozed off, but when she looked back at the cat, it was gone – and so was the plate.

Mildred sat up, suddenly very alarmed, and looked wildly around, fearing something happened to her cat. "Kitty-kitty-kitty!" She got up from the swing and looked around. The cat was very good about staying away from wild animals and remained close to the house, but she always feared there might be a time some predator would come along and snatch her pet. She heard the cat hissing from under the porch and bent down to investigate. The cat was there, backed up against the wall, its eyes open wide and its ears pressed against its head. It was looking at the woods beyond the yard and kept hissing.

Mildred looked in the same direction that the cat was looking and saw the plate lying on the grass near the trees, discarded. She walked over to pick it up and froze; twenty feet from where the dish lay she saw two large yellow eyes staring at her from behind the bushes. She blinked once and they were gone.

Three days after her first sighting of the animal, Mildred was visited by two men she had never seen before. They were both young men in their thirties, stocky, with ruddy, sun-tanned features. She figured them for lumbermen, and they neither confirmed nor denied this. One thing was certain: they bore an intimidating demeanor and made no bones about what they wanted. "We hear you're claiming to have seen a Sasquatch?" The one who spoke stood only inches from her closed screen door and looked like he was poised to come barreling in at any second. The other man stood only a couple feet back and glared at her without saying anything.

For the first time since living here, Mildred was scared. "I thought I saw something, yes. Why, may I ask, is that any concern of yours? You're not rangers."

The closest man ignored Mildred's question, and said, "We don't take this kind of nonsense lightly. Your misguided effort to report this can draw an unwanted element to these parts. We take this very seriously and won't tolerate any attempts to invite the kind of trouble this can bring. Do you understand me?" The man seemed to take this personally, and Mildred got the very clear impression he could be dangerous if provoked.

Still, she didn't like the idea of being threatened and told them so. "Young man, unless you can show me some legitimate reason for your coming out here and harassing me, I will report you to the rangers. My husband is a ranger."

The first man looked at his companion, who took a couple steps closer to the porch. The first man stared at Mildred, increasing the element of intimidation and said, "Your husband's been dead for six years." Having made their point, the two men left, and Mildred locked herself in the house, too scared to report them for fear of a reprisal.

⁂

Looking tough but comfortable in well-worn blue jeans, a denim jacket, black T-shirt, and suede boots, George Kodiak cut an imposing figure as he walked across the drizzle-soaked tarmac of Detroit Metropolitan Airport. With his Army duffel bag slung over his shoulder and his hair pulled back into a ponytail, he always drew suspicious looks from security personnel, because he just looked like trouble.

He came around the main terminal building and saw an unusual plane set alone on the tarmac, away from the commercial airliners. It was a 747 that was painted gold with a blue stripe running its full length. Inside the blue stripe was the name PITTMAN INTERNATIONAL.

"Good morning." Ron Pearl was approaching him from the direction of the plane with two other men. They were dressed in dark suits and sunglasses, giving the impression of government agents.

Kodiak stopped. His back stiffened and his muscles tensed in anticipation of a confrontation as they came over to him.

Two of the men stood on each side of him as Pearl stood in front of him and extended his hand. "It's good to see you again." Pearl was cordial, even friendly, but his sunglasses bothered Kodiak, especially since the weather hardly warranted wearing them.

Pearl said, "We have to go through a brief security check before boarding the plane. So, if you'll hand Mr. Wieben – to your left there – your bag, while Mr. Utenidge checks your person for any concealed devices... Strictly procedure."

Kodiak handed his duffel bag to Wieben, who set it on the ground and went through its contents, trying to keep everything close to how it had originally been packed. His bag only contained more jeans and shirts, essential toiletries, and an extra pair of boots. Wieben took the extra pair of boots and turned them upside-down to see if anything was hidden inside.

Utenidge asked Kodiak to raise his arms so he could frisk him, and Kodiak said, "Let me guess. Strictly procedure?" Utenidge ignored him and proceeded to feel him up. "Don't bother with the prostate. I had a physical a couple weeks ago." Utenidge ignored this remark, too, and asked Kodiak to empty and then turn out his pockets. He took out a dollar eighty in change, a comb, and from his back pocket a deck of playing cards that appeared to be marked.

Utenidge handed Kodiak back the items from his pockets, and Wieben zipped up the duffel bag. Pearl said, "Thank you, Mr. Kodiak. Now, if you'll go up the ramp, we'll be taking off shortly."

Kodiak picked up his duffel bag and walked up the ramp to the plane.

When he reached the top step, Wayne Monroe appeared before him, working on what must have been his eighth double Brandy Manhattan. "Wayne, you are the butt-ugliest stewardess I have ever seen."

"George... George, you are not gonna believe this. Wait till you check this stuff out. It makes Virgin Atlantic look like... like the Wright brothers." Wayne grabbed Kodiak's jacket sleeve as much for balance as to lead him into the plane. The interior had been completely renovated. Having eliminated the standard interior design for this type of aircraft, Pittman took full advantage of the space now available.

They stood in a spacious and comfortable-looking dining room where the table was large enough to accommodate a dozen people. Each chair was attached to a swivel arm and was anchored to the table which allowed them to move freely without toppling over while the plane was in motion.

Wayne nodded to a closed door at the head of the dining room and said, "There's a fully stocked kitchen back there. It's got everything – including a chef. I'd show you, but he damn near bit my head off the first time I looked back there. I'll tell you this, if I'd have had my buck knife with me, there'd be a secret ingredient added to the soup and he'd be singing soprano."

From the dining room Wayne led him down into the salon; posh, opulent space furnished with leather recliners and sofas, with coffee and end tables finished in black lacquer. There was an entertainment center against the far bulkhead that boasted a big screen television and a DVD player. There was a library of more than a hundred DVDs that ranged from all-time classics, to pornography, to pirated copies of films that hadn't even been released yet. Next to this was a state-of-the-art stereo system. Wayne had put on a compact disc of chamber music that was playing at a comfortable volume.

"And this..." Wayne took a remote control from a drawer in one of the end tables and pushed a button. The floor opened up in front of the television and a hot tub came up. Wayne laughed like an excited child at Christmas. "Isn't this great? This guy's even richer than me!"

"We also have six bedroom suites, each with its own bathroom, as well as two private offices, a conference room, a sauna, and a gym, which is really just a Universal weight machine. How do you do? My name is April, and I'll be your flight attendant." April looked like a sixteen-year-old. She walked over to Wayne and pushed the hot tub button a second time, and it went back under the floor. "Once we're in the air, you can use whatever you like." She took Kodiak's bag. "May I put this away for you?"

"Thanks."

"Would you like something to drink before we take off?"

"Canadian Club, straight."

"Mr. Monroe?"

"Maybe later, thanks. When will we be taking off?"

"It will be at least another twenty minutes." She smiled and left them.

Wayne turned to Kodiak. "You believe this? That Pittman's got some imagination. I am going to try that hot tub. Even if I have to go in naked!"

Kodiak said, "I hope this thing comes with parachutes."

April came back with Kodiak's drink. "Once we're in the air, lunch will be served."

Wayne asked, "What will we be having?"

"Australian lobster tails, broiled. Prime rib, served with New England clam chowder and a Caesar salad, with shrimp cocktail appetizers. If you need anything else, just push the call button on this console."

❧

The plane landed at Emory Pittman's estate in northern Arizona. When Kodiak and Wayne disembarked, they were met by Mark Dubbins, a tall, cadaverous-looking fellow who must certainly have been in his seventies. He was dressed in a conservative tweed suit that looked a size too big for his slight physique. "Mr. Hodiak?"

"Kodiak."

"Like the bear," Wayne added.

"I'm Mark Dubbins. I am Mr. Pittman's personal assistant." Dubbins spoke in a simple monotone that was mildly clipped with the vaguest hint of a British accent. He made none of the gestures customary of an introduction and his eyes were hooded by ancient, wrinkled lids, giving him more the look of an automaton than a human being. "I trust your flight was pleasant?"

"Very nice, thank you." Wayne was still giddy from the trip and all the toys he got to play with and all the liquor he got to drink.

Dubbins escorted them to a Range Rover that was mounted with a plexi-glass top for unobstructed observation. "If you gentlemen will allow me to take your luggage..." The mechanical Dubbins took their bags and placed them in the back of the Range Rover, while Kodiak and Wayne got in on the passenger side. Dubbins closed up the back and got in the driver's seat. "It's Mr. Pittman's wish that you be given a tour of the estate, after which you will be brought to the main house to meet with him."

Kodiak noticed several distinct scars on and about Dubbins' lower face and neck that weren't blatantly obvious, but the sun highlighted their shiny-smooth surface.

Dubbins drove the Range Rover half a mile from the airstrip to an open range surrounded by hills that reminded Kodiak of some of the places he had worked as a forest ranger. "Mr. Pittman has recreated the environments from several of the earth's continents in order to properly house his collection of wildlife specimens. If you'll look to the right, you will see the buffalo."

There was a large herd of buffalo grazing lazily upon the thick grasses of the range. They paid little attention to the Range Rover as it cruised past them and across a small creek, heading up to hills that were richly forested with a variety of spruce, cedar, and other pine trees, many of them close to a hundred feet tall, having been planted over thirty years ago. This forest, representative of North America, boasted an abundance of wildlife forms indigenous to the United States and Canada.

They didn't get to see many of the animals Dubbins told them existed here, because the habitats were far too expansive to see in a single afternoon. The animals they did see included gray timber wolves, grizzly and black bears, and mountain lions.

From the back seat Wayne chuckled, and said, "So when do we get to see the Dinosaurs?" Kodiak and Dubbins ignored him.

At the end of the North American habitat they went through an underground tunnel that ran a thousand feet. When they came out, it was like they were on the other side of the world.

"Mr. Pittman's most proud of this habitat. It's an engineering marvel. He's almost perfectly re-created a polar landscape in Arizona."

The temperature had dropped considerably, so Dubbins turned the heater on.

Dubbins' bland, unemotional voice gave the impression of

reciting poorly rehearsed material as he prattled on. "He's imported several varieties of penguin, as well as other Arctic birds, walruses, seals, musk ox, and polar bears."

"Polar bears?" Wayne wrapped his arms around his torso while waiting for the Range Rover to warm up, and looked around excitedly.

This landscape was in a deep trench of a canyon that was five miles long and one mile wide. Nearly one-third of this canyon was cut into a granite mountain, which allowed ice to be built up and spread outward, where huge refrigeration coils kept the ground cool from beneath. Massive walls of ice were placed strategically about this part of the landscape to separate the animals that might otherwise attack and do harm to each other.

There was a lake with several icebergs floating in it, and Dubbins headed in that direction, where much of the action was located.

The area beyond the lake was temperate and surrounded by gigantic granite walls. On the far side of the canyon musk ox were grazing in a field of vegetation.

They came to a place where two sections of ice appeared to have smashed together creating a series of ridges and towers. A large bull walrus was sunning himself atop the highest perch that was capable of sustaining his tremendous weight, while several females and younger males lazed on the ice beneath him. In the lake the young played with each other, diving in and out of the water.

Beyond them Kodiak saw the dorsal fins of a killer whale pod that was cruising by. He couldn't imagine Pittman not having some kind of underwater barrier to keep the whales from getting to the other wildlife, and Dubbins seemed to read his mind. "These whales are not the southern variety that are so well known for their voracious appetites and their attacks on other sea-going mammals. These are of the northern species that feeds solely on fish. This lake, as well as all the rivers and lakes throughout the estate, are well-stocked with salmon and trout."

About fifty yards away, a huge polar bear spotted the car and started moving after it at more than a casual trot. "My God, look at the size of that thing," Wayne marvelled.

Dubbins brought the Range Rover through another tunnel, shorter than the first, where a steel gate blocked their passage halfway through. When they stopped, the bear quickened its pace to a full run, and Kodiak watched it with mounting concern. If they did not get through this gate fast, the bear may very likely attack. As the polar bear was one of the deadliest predators in existence, it could easily smash through the plexi-glass canopy and slaughter them. Wayne said, "I remember reading somewhere that if you lie perfectly still a bear will think you're dead and won't attack you. Anybody for giving it a try?"

An electronic eye detected their presence, and the gate opened, closing behind them, locking the curious bear out.

Ten minutes later they emerged in a field of bamboo, beyond which trees stood tall against the blue Arizona sky. In those trees dozens of orangutans were swinging on lianas, and leaping from branch to branch at distances that would make an Olympic gymnast shudder. For such awkward, clumsy-looking animals, they were truly at ease in the trees, where they were agile and graceful.

These were among Kodiak's favorite animals, though he couldn't help but feel a kind of sadness whenever he saw them, because he knew their ultimate demise was only a matter of years. Their habitat in the wild had radically diminished from most of mainland Asia to a few small islands, as they were relentlessly hunted for zoos and scientific studies. Sometime over the next century, he knew man will have wiped them out.

Kodiak felt a sense of appreciation for what Pittman had created here. This wasn't so much a zoo as it was a wildlife sanctuary, where many endangered species could thrive in environments that mirrored those in the wild.

When they entered the clearing, they saw giant pandas feeding on the bamboo. Pittman had to have some *major* political connections, because not only did he have a mating pair of adult pandas, but he possessed *two* mating pairs, and there were several young feeding alongside the adults.

They drove through thirty minutes of winding Asian wilderness trails without seeing another animal. Then they came upon the ruins of an ancient Buddhist temple standing among palm trees that swayed in the temperate breezes. A Bengal tiger was lying on the front steps, its body stretched completely out under the sun. Wayne looked up through the plexi-glass top and hoped the tiger wouldn't spot them and suddenly decide on a midday snack. But the tiger didn't seem to care, and as they passed the huge cat simply rolled onto its back, putting one great paw out as if it were reaching for the sun.

They crossed a series of creeks and bridges that took them to a simulation of the East Indies where they saw a variety of life from that part of the world. Most notably were the saltwater crocodiles, cobras, and Komodo dragons. Dubbins pulled over so they could watch as two ten-foot dragons went to work wrenching hunks of meat from the tattered corpse of a goat that was suspended from a tree. From another tree, three smaller dragons were also watching, waiting for the bigger ones to finish gorging themselves so they could have their turn at the carcass.

Dubbins drove on.

Once they were clear of the Asian territories, Dubbins took them through an area the size of a football stadium, which was still under construction. There were men operating earth-moving equipment and clearing the area out.

Dubbins explained, "This is going to be a saltwater lake. Not unlike the one in the polar habitat, but this particular lake is going to house a great white shark. When it's finished there will be observation windows on all sides."

Kodiak was doubtful. "A lot of people have tried to keep great whites in captivity and failed. What makes Pittman think he'll have better luck?"

"Mr. Pittman hopes his will be the first to survive. He believes he knows where all the mistakes were made."

They drove up the earthen hillside that would someday be under water and came to a ridge that overlooked an African savannah. Dubbins brought the Range Rover down to the flat land, and they watched a herd of elephants lazily making their way across the plain. Even at the distance from which they observed them, these animals seemed majestic and graceful in spite of their bulk.

Dubbins turned down a road behind the hill, and they lost sight of the elephants. In this small valley a den of lions was resting beneath an acacia tree with the bloody skeletal remains of a recent kill scattered about the ground.

Wayne asked, "Surely he doesn't let the lions roam with the other animals he's imported?"

"Not at all. The animals are kept separate by a series of well-hidden electric fences, and deep rivers and lakes. The carcass you saw was a cow. We turn several of them loose among the various predators so they can plunder them at will."

Wayne cringed. "Charming."

The lions ignored them as they passed within fifty feet and drove on. Farther along the savannah they passed the first electric fence.

There were greater numbers of animals in the next compound, animals that were compatible within the same boundaries: giraffes, rhinoceroses, ostriches. Two ostriches were engaged in pursuing a rhino as the Range Rover entered. Dubbins said, "The rhinoceros have developed a nasty habit of sitting on the ostrich eggs. This infuriates the ostriches who attempt, in vain for the most part, to avenge themselves."

Kodiak thought he noticed the glimmer of a smile on Dubbins' face, but then it was gone.

They came to a river where the elephants were now wading. There were also hippos, as well as several large crocodiles sunning themselves on the sandy bank.

Dubbins drove parallel to the river another mile and then headed toward the woodlands at the base of the next hill, where they saw zebras, wart hogs, and wildebeests roaming about the foliage. They went deeper into the woods where the plant life became more tropical, but was still open. Kodiak spotted an Okapi. This animal was an ancestor to the giraffe, but looked more like a caribou without antlers. The Okapi was thought to have been extinct some twenty to forty million years until it was rediscovered in 1903. It was declared a living fossil and was adopted as the official emblem for the *International Society of Cryptozoology.*

The Okapi suddenly seemed distracted, but not by the Range Rover. It looked northward, then darted into the brush. None of the others noticed it, but Kodiak sensed something was about to happen.

Dubbins cruised through the woods at a steady ten miles per hour.

Suddenly, something let out a blood-curdling screech and hurdled across the hood of the Range Rover. Dubbins hit the brakes, but whatever the thing was, it was gone, having left a streak of blood across the hood.

"What the hell...?" Wayne leaned forward to see what had happened when more animals ran in front of the Range Rover and gathered in a clearing to their left.

Three adult male baboons circled a leopard and were moving in for the kill. This was the aftermath of an earlier fight, as the leopard was already injured and bleeding, and two of the baboons were suffering from serious retaliation attempts.

The big cat crouched low to the ground, its ears plastered back against its head, screaming at its enemies.

The three baboons spread out so the cat would be unable to watch them all at the same time. They snarled and lunged at the cat, making a sound that was uniquely their own; something akin to a barking-roar.

The leopard was hopelessly outnumbered, especially since the baboons matched him in size and ferocity. But the cat would go out fighting.

Inside the Range Rover, the three men had a ringside seat to the fight, but neither Kodiak nor Wayne wanted to see this. "What happened to the million-dollar security that's supposed to keep these animals apart?"

The animals had come to a clearing that was enclosed by fencing, which made driving the Range Rover in to break up the fight impossible. Kodiak was looking over the dashboard and asked Dubbins, "You have a radio or something we can use to get a hold of Pittman? I don't think he's gonna want to lose these animals."

When Dubbins didn't reply, Kodiak was shocked. "Dubbins, these animals are going to rip each other to pieces. If we can't get a hold of Pittman, then we need to break this up. Do you have a tranquilizer gun, or anything we can use?"

Dubbins just looked down. "There's nothing I can do, Mr. Kodiak."

Kodiak grabbed Dubbins by his collar and pulled him over to the passenger side. "You'd better do something to stop this, or I'm gonna throw you out there with them!"

"George..." Wayne sounded like he was going to be sick.

Kodiak turned to him, still holding Dubbins, who did nothing to protect or even stand up for himself.

"George, there's nothing he can do."

Kodiak looked out the window.

The fight was on. One of the baboons made a biting lunge at the leopard's haunch, and when the leopard turned, another baboon went for its throat.

Kodiak released Dubbins and tried to open the glove compartment. It was locked, so he smashed his fist into the glove compartment door and tore it off. He found a twelve-inch flashlight and got out of the car.

Wayne called after him to get back inside, but Kodiak ignored him. He took aim at what he assumed was the alpha baboon and shouted, trying to distract them. This ploy failed, so he hurled the flashlight and struck the baboon's head. The animal screeched, but did not turn away from the leopard.

There was a blur of motion as all four animals got into it. The leopard screamed. The baboons roared.

"George!" Wayne passed Kodiak a tire iron from the back of the Range Rover, and Kodiak heaved it at one of the baboons. He connected – a perfect blow to its shoulder. But it was too late to stop the bloody frenzy.

The baboons backed off. One crawled away, holding its paw to its throat which had been sliced open by the cat. It would be dead in minutes.

The mouths of the other two baboons were clotted with blood, and the leopard's belly was torn wide open. It remained crouched down, screaming at its adversaries as a pool of its own blood formed beneath it.

The two baboons pounced again. Their screaming reached a crescendo, and then the fighting stopped. The two surviving baboons began tearing the leopard to pieces.

Kodiak could do nothing more than stare at what remained of this mess. Finally, as he prepared to get back inside the car, a glint of light caught his eye – something in the tree above the fenced-in area. It was a camera. There was another directly across from it, covering another angle. It dawned on Kodiak what was really going on here. These animals didn't get loose on their own. This had been staged. This was a rich man's cock fight.

Inside, Wayne was looking at the floorboard. He didn't want to see what had happened.

Kodiak glared at Dubbins, debating whether he wanted to beat the hell out of him, or save it for Pittman, who had orchestrated this fiasco. He looked at the scars, and thought about the way Dubbins hadn't even tried to defend himself. Dubbins was obviously an abused person.

"All right, the tour's over. Take us to see Pittman. *Right now!*"

The Need to
Own Nature

Following the incident in the African woodland, Dubbins took Kodiak and Wayne directly to Pittman's house; a Scottish castle that was shipped, a section at a time, to this place in Arizona and reconstructed almost exactly as it had been originally built.

The castle was built of granite blocks and boasted several hundred-foot towers that rose above the battlements of the main structure. A line of dragons, linked head to tail was sculpted in relief beneath the battlements. The castle's huge stained glass windows looked muddy without any interior lights to make them shine.

The trip took over half an hour, because they had to go through a South American rainforest that was located beside the African rainforest, with a three and a half mile section of Amazon River that came down from the hills and acted as a moat for the castle.

The river was stocked with Amazon River dolphins, manatees, black caimans, frogs, turtles, and several species of piranha.

Dubbins drove the Range Rover across the drawbridge, past the high stone arches of the gatehouse where they waited while the main gate opened at an arthritic crawl.

Wayne noticed two men standing on a twenty-foot platform that was erected over a separate pond within the castle grounds. "Hey, George." When Kodiak turned to him, Wayne nodded toward the activity at the pond.

The two men pulled a live chicken from a bag and were struggling to hold it still. One of the men cut off the chicken's head, and they both got soaked with blood as its wings flapped and its legs kicked, until they got a better grasp and dangled the body over the pond, shaking it to get the blood to rain down on the water.

SNAP!!! A gigantic green form exploded from the water and came within grabbing distance of the two men. Wayne thought they must have nerves of steel, because they didn't even flinch. They simply released the chicken into the thing's mouth as it descended back into the pond with an explosive crash and was gone.

The gate was open, but the three men were still looking at the pond. "That's Mark Anthony. Mr. Pittman's most prized possession. He is the largest American alligator known to exist, coming in at twenty-one and one-half feet," Dubbins said with some pride before stepping on the gas and pulling into the courtyard.

When they got out of the Range Rover, they were grateful to finally stretch their legs after the long and emotionally distressing ride.

Kodiak and Wayne followed Dubbins into the castle and down a long gallery where hundreds of original art masterpieces hung on the walls. Wayne turned in circles as they walked, trying to look at all the paintings.

One concession Pittman made to modern technology was to install an elevator that Dubbins used to take them four floors up to the inner sanctum: Emory Pittman's private quarters.

There was a steel vault door across the hall from the elevator on the fourth floor, and next to that an intercom where Dubbins pressed a receiver button.

"Dubbins, is that you?"

"Mr. Kodiak and Mr. Monroe to see you."

"Good. Let them in, pronto." The voice sounded ancient. It had an unearthly quality that was more than just distortion from the speaker.

Dubbins placed a card key into the vault door, and it jarred open. He pulled it wide enough for them to pass through. "Gentlemen..."

Wayne went in first, followed by Kodiak. Dubbins remained outside and closed the door behind them. There were several audible clicks and electronic hums as the door automatically locked.

Pittman's bedroom was a penthouse apartment that was constructed on the very top of the castle. It was split level, complete with a kitchen and dining room, game room and entertainment center. Two of the walls were made entirely of glass, allowing a view of the surrounding grounds. From here they could see the elephants and giraffes on the African savannah.

Emory Pittman was sitting up in the middle of a kingsize bed. He looked even older than Dubbins, with a face like a desert scape that was bleach white and pocked with tiny scars and huge liver spots that went to the top of his bald head. He had startlingly clear blue eyes that were in stark contrast to his aged face.

Under the white, wrinkled skin, he was a powerfully built, very well-muscled man, like somebody who had worked out all his life. When he smiled his large white teeth and sharp blue eyes gave him the look of a human skull reanimated with some malevolent life force. "Mr. Kodiak, what a pleasure it is to finally meet you!" He leaned forward with obvious discomfort and extended his hand, holding a paperback copy of Kodiak's book on the Sasquatch; *Hunt for the Living Gigantopithecus.* Pittman placed his hands on his lap and said, "Forgive me for this impertinence on my part, but I broke my hip in a riding accident last month, and I'm going to be laid up for a while. It's had a hell of a time healing." Perhaps this was the source of the smell Kodiak picked up. It hit them like a wave when they came into this room; a dirty, cloying smell that was more than a mere lack of personal hygiene. It smelled like Pittman's injury had gone septic and the reek had permeated everything. "So tell me, what did you think of my little collection?"

Kodiak was reluctant to answer, unable to understand why Pittman would allow the baboons and the leopard to get together. But looking now at this pathetic, bed-ridden, probably mentally unstable old man, all he could think to say was, "I saw it."

"And?"

"And, I suppose if one feels the need to own nature, it's an impressive undertaking."

Pittman sighed with mild exasperation. "And it's not finished yet. I'm going to collect specimens of every animal known to exist. I'm even having a saltwater lake built for a great white shark."

Kodiak couldn't repress a skeptical grin and said, "Don't you think that might be a little unrealistic? Even for you?"

Pittman ignored the remark. "How did you like my little performance with the baboons and the leopard?" Pittman leered, anticipating a reaction.

Kodiak said, "I don't know why I should be surprised you know about that."

Pittman laughed. "You shouldn't be, since I'm the one who arranged it."

Wayne said to Pittman, "You're as bad as those jackals back

home, who raise domesticated lions and elephants so's they can be hunted by money counters who like to play big game hunter!"

Pittman found this amusing and smiled at Wayne. "Whoa, hold on, Old Paint. You got me all wrong." He turned back to Kodiak. "Looks like Uncle Cornpone here may have some cajones after all." Pittman laughed and picked up a remote control and pointed it at the large screen television opposite his bed. "Here, look at this..."

They watched a video tape of Pittman walking through a petting zoo of baby animals that had been assembled in the castle's courtyard. This footage had been shot before his accident, with Pittman in the middle of a large swarm of handicapped children. He was carrying a little girl with Down Syndrome in his massive arms, laughing and playing the part of Grandpa to the underprivileged. He said to Kodiak, "This was last year. I do this thing every year. You know, let all the little retards come and gawk at my pets. They love it, and it doesn't look too bad for me, either." He chuckled.

Kodiak and Wayne looked at each other. There were definitely some weird angles to sweet, lovable "Grandpa" Pittman. He seemed to have a passion for life and a love of nature that was contaminated by his need to own and ultimately degrade the things he made a part of his life.

There was something intrinsically familiar about Pittman to Kodiak; something ugly that made him vaguely uncomfortable and caused him to dislike the old man without knowing why.

Pittman seemed to become melancholic. "Of course, this place will never be as good as it used to be. Not really. Forty years ago I owned a tribe of Asmat head hunters from New Guinea. Kept them penned up where that white shark lake'll be. Had 'em fenced in with electric fences and twenty-four hour surveillance cameras. I recreated their whole village, too. They were my favorite acquisition, until several of the bucks got loose and slaughtered my groundskeeper and his family. Then I had to send them back. You know they even reproduced while I had them." Pittman told this story with the same pathos one remembers a favorite pet. He shut off the television.

Kodiak felt sick as he watched the old man. And that stink wasn't helping. "What was it you brought us out here for, Mr. Pittman?"

Pittman smiled, his shining eyes looking surreal on his skull-like face, and he said, "Tell me about Vietnam. I understand you intend to find a complete *Gigantopithecus* skeleton?"

"Yeah, I think there's a good chance. And it might answer the question whether *Gigantopithecus* was a quadruped or a true biped."

"I've read this book of yours," Pittman said, holding up *Hunt for the Living Gigantopithecus*. "You make a compelling argument in favor of the this thing's existence. Be honest with me now. What do you suppose the odds are of one ever being captured?"

Kodiak shook his head. "There have been literally hundreds of expeditions to find one of these animals over the past several decades. You heard of Tom Slick? He was another millionaire who financed several expeditions for both the Sasquatch and the Yeti. Even after all his efforts, he came up empty-handed. In the more than twenty years I've been looking, I haven't seen one yet. That's why I want to go to Vietnam. I think the odds are greater of finding the fossil skeleton than a live specimen."

Pittman quietly considered this for what seemed like minutes. "So, what would it take for you to forget Vietnam, and consider capturing for me, for my zoo, a live *Gigantopithecus*, or Bigfoot, or Sasquatch, or whatever the hell they're calling it this week?"

Kodiak and Wayne looked at each other again, and Kodiak said, "Just like that?"

"Just like that."

"You make it sound easy."

"For you, I think it would be. Even if you'd never admit it."

"You know," Kodiak said, "you could have saved yourself the couple of hundred thousand dollars it took to bring us out here. If you really did read that book, then you know as much as I do on the subject."

"Don't be a smart-ass, Kodiak. If all I was interested in was reading about you making plaster casts of footprints and putting Bigfoot crap in a baggy, I wouldn't be wasting your time. More importantly, I wouldn't be wasting my time. I thought you were supposed to be smart. Maybe you're too smart for your own damn good."

Kodiak walked over to the nightstand and picked up a deck of playing cards and shuffled through them while Pittman went on. "I want to back an expedition, to be led by you, not to Vietnam for fossilized bones, but to Washington State, to capture a living specimen and bring it back here to me."

"What makes you think you'll be any luckier than anybody else?"

"I happen to know some people who also believe these animals exist. People associated with the timber industry in this country. They're very good at keeping track of these creatures. They have to be, and I think you understand why. They have sent me some pertinent information regarding the best location for a probable capture. And I have you," Pittman said.

Kodiak didn't know what to say. He thought Pittman was crazy.

"Of course," Wayne cut in, "there is the matter of George's fee. Not to mention exclusive book rights, and first shot at writing the article for any publications that may be interested."

"There's five million dollars in it for you, tax free, under the table in a foreign account of your choice, just for trying. And if you're successful, I'll double it. Not only that, you will have unlimited access to the animal for study on my land. The only string being that *you cannot publicize the capture.*"

"Why me?"

"You're just the first one I'm approaching. I've been studying you for over a year now. You and others like you. Roy Mackal and Peter Byrne, to name a couple of your buddies.

"As I told you, I'm looking to stock my zoo with specimens of every living animal." Pittman laughed.

Kodiak was truly perplexed by this man. He had always liked the idea of a competent expedition, but after what he had witnessed earlier with the baboons and the leopard, he could not in good conscience even consider working for Emory Pittman.

Pittman continued. "I should think you'd be sympathetic to my plight. In fact, I think there's a lot of good I can do for you and the people involved in your field of endeavor.

"Jamie Montagna's downstairs in the library. He's the one who first brought your work to my attention, although he was a little miffed when I sent for you. He was under the misguided impression that I would simply contact you for advice while he led the actual expedition. So, I'm letting him sign the checks and call the shots. But when it comes down to the actual hunt, Kodiak, you'll be giving the orders." Pittman watched Kodiak with bemusement, then was distracted by something he saw on the nightstand. Kodiak had set the playing cards down, but there was a single card, the queen of diamonds, sticking out of the wood by its corner, like a knife.

Kodiak and Wayne got into the elevator and headed for the first floor. Wayne asked, "So what do you think?"

"I don't know. I sure as hell don't care for the idea of Pittman's having this animal as a personal possession. I think it does far greater harm than good to the species in general."

Wayne chuckled. "So, you gonna go on this expedition?"

Kodiak said, "I can always use five million dollars."

"I thought he was offering you ten?"

"That was for a capture."

It then dawned on Kodiak why he disliked Pittman so much. In 1951, three months after his mother died, Kodiak found a stack of letters she had written to her father in Detroit, all of which had been returned unopened. She kept them all, burying them in a trunk in the attic. Although he never knew his maternal grandfather, these unanswered letters made him hate the useless old bastard, and he wanted to do something to rub the old man's face in the pain he had caused his own daughter.

The family estate had been a huge mansion he had never before seen, nor been invited to. One night he searched for and found the estate and, at well after midnight, when the last of the house lights had been off for at least an hour, he had cut the telephone lines and scaled the outside wall to the master bedroom suite, where Dorian Harris slept like a baby. Kodiak turned on the light and barricaded the bedroom door so nobody would be able to come in when the old man started screaming for help.

But the old man didn't scream. He had simply sat up in his bed and glared at Kodiak with hate-filled eyes.

"I'm not here for your money."

"I know who you are," Harris said.

"The hell you do."

But Dorian Harris had known who the intruder was. There wasn't any family resemblance between the two of them. They really looked nothing alike. What the old man had recognized was the same inner core of cold, almost cruel hardness that existed within himself. It almost filled him with good humor to see that this ugliness that had driven him to become the person he was now had been passed on to someone he considered a lesser human being, who would probably be destroyed by it. "You're Harold Kodiak's kid."

Kodiak had repressed a shudder when he also recognized the steely glimmer of cold rage he so often saw in his own reflection, and he hated this man even more. "I'm also your daughter's son."

The old man had only grunted, glaring at him from the bed. A bed he was in alone. "Speak your piece."

"I imagine you already know she's dead. Hell, you had a hand in killing her." Kodiak crushed the letters in his fist that trembled with rage. He pulled a chair up beside the bed and opened the first letter. It was three pages long, telling the old man about the house Harold was building for her. Kodiak had removed the picture she had originally enclosed with the letter, not wanting the old man to have the satisfaction of seeing the house.

He had read for over an hour, letters about his birth and growth over the years, birthday wishes for her parents, dozens of Christmas and Easter cards, and a sympathy card when her mother had died, all unopened by him.

Kodiak had read them all, and the old man sat stoically against the headboard, totally unmoved. Kodiak had to pause from emotion twice during the letter about his own father's lingering death from cancer, which had been the last letter she wrote to the old man.

Finally, he had gotten up and tossed them all on Dorian Harris' bed. "That's it. I'm finished. You can call the cops now."

The old man had sat still, staring at the lifetime of unanswered correspondence. Then he had lifted his right hand from under the blankets and pointed a .45 automatic at Kodiak's head. "I could blow your head off, and nobody would do a thing about it. You have ten seconds to get the hell out of here. And if I ever see you again, I swear I will kill you."

Kodiak was sickened. Not from the old man's total lack of compassion for his own daughter, nor by his threat to kill him. What had made him so sick was that, looking at this hateful creature, he had finally seen a glimmer of himself in another member of the family. A hard heart was all he inherited from his grandfather.

He left that night by unblocking the door and walking past confused staffers who rushed to Dorian Harris' side.

Kodiak had figured that was the end of it, but six days later he got an invitation from Uncle Sam to serve in the United States Army. His grandfather had used his connections in Washington to get him drafted into a combat unit serving in Korea at the height of the war.

Kodiak and Wayne came out of the elevator and walked across the hall to the library where Jamie Montagna was standing beside a wet bar, pouring himself a drink. Montagna was a middle-aged man with a pug nose and leering eyes that gave him a smug, self-absorbed air. "Kodiak. What're you drinking?"

Kodiak walked over to the bar and poured a shot of Canadian Club.

Montagna studied Kodiak with a mild smirk. "No ice. That's got to go down like gasoline."

Montagna rubbed his hand across his bald head and said to Kodiak, "Pittman talk you into tagging along?"

Kodiak took a sip from his drink. "Yeah, I think so."

"Good." Montagna went over to the leather sofa near the fireplace and sat down. He smiled, but it was a flat, humorless imitation of a smile.

Kodiak said, "Pittman tells me you turned him onto my work. What line of work are you in, Jamie?"

"I've always been a kind of armchair cryptozoologist, myself. I've read all the literature, gone on a few expeditions in Washington State looking for the Sasquatch. But on a more personal level, I'm sort of a liaison with the State Department." Kodiak did not like Montagna. There was something greasy and intangible about the man that meant trouble. He said, "The State Department. What exactly is it that you do, Jamie?"

Montagna shrugged. "You might say I'm involved in research and development. Obviously I can't go into too much detail, but I get ideas for things, and Uncle Sam gives me enough free reign to follow up the details as I see fit."

"And how does Pittman's Sasquatch hunt fit into your plans?"

"It's kind of a mutual thing. Like I said, I can't go into too much detail, but I think we have a real shot at a capture." Montagna raised his glass to Kodiak and finished off his drink.

Montagna's evasive answers were a clear indication of his resentment towards Kodiak's involvement in this endeavor.

Norm

ildred Hunnicut went outside an hour before sunset and placed a huge mound of cat food in the middle of her yard. She didn't know if this was going to work, but she had to try, just in case the visitor did come back.

She didn't think it would make its appearance until after dark, so she went back into her house and watched the plate of food from the kitchen window. Naturally the cat ate first, but Mildred anticipated this and placed more food than usual on the plate. After the cat finished, the bait drew out a few crows and small animals that made the nearby woods their home, but they hardly made a dent in the small mountain of food.

It was almost nine o'clock when the sun began its evening descent. Mildred went back outside and took a position behind a row of shrubs that separated her property from the road that branched off of the 101.

In fifteen minutes it was dark, and she soon regretted the crouching position she had taken. But before she was able to get up to relieve the cramps in her legs, she saw the Sasquatch just beyond the trees that bordered her place.

She got a much better look at the animal this time. It was about five feet tall, as she remembered, and wiry, like a basketball player. She couldn't make out any facial features except for its large, wide eyes that reflected the orange light from her porch. It reminded her of pictures she had seen of baby gorillas, but if this was a baby, she thought with some amazement, God only knew how big the adults were.

When it stepped into the open yard, she could see the blue-gray of its face, and the black, inch-long hair that covered its sinewy body. It was cautious, but looked twice in her direction without seeing her. It walked upright, like a human being. Although its arms were longer than those of a man of comparable size, the length of its legs made it obvious this animal was not prone to knuckle-walking.

The Sasquatch walked over to the plate of cat food, paused to look around again, then crouched down and lifted the plate to its face, sniffing the contents. After another brief pause it started shoving the cat food into its mouth with its hand.

The cramps in Mildred's legs finally became too much for her to bear, and she had to change her position. It seemed that even before she moved, the animal sensed her presence and stood up, dropping the plate and looking right at her.

She tried not to move, but was unable to remain balanced and fell backward to the ground. The creature hissed and took a step toward her.

Oddly, Mildred did not feel threatened, but was more worried that the animal would run off before she had an opportunity to get back on her feet.

The animal, on the other hand, did feel threatened. It bared its teeth at her and screeched.

She got back up and took a step forward, almost stumbling because of the numbness in her legs. Her mind raced with emotions and thoughts about what she was seeing. Despite the very presence of the Sasquatch, she still couldn't totally accept what it was, that it was real. She caught herself looking for signs of a hoax; that it was only somebody in an elaborate costume.

The creature bent in a half-squatting position, like a linebacker about to move in for the tackle. It made a deep, throaty growl, but didn't move.

Mildred stopped ten feet from the Sasquatch, maintaining steady eye contact with it.

The creature stood upright, hissed again, screeched, and then ran back into the woods.

Mildred was shaking, as much from elation as from the rush of adrenalin. She was also a little disappointed that it had run off. Ridiculous as she told herself the idea was, she actually hoped to make some kind of connection with the animal.

She walked over to the plate it had cast aside and picked it up, looking toward the woods where the creature had run. She hoped it had stayed nearby and was watching her now. But in the distance she heard it screech again.

When George Kodiak first laid eyes on Norm Cocke, old Norm was picking his nose. Norm was a friend of Montagna's who lived in Seattle and was at the airport to pick them up. He spotted Montagna among the dozens of people getting off the plane and wiped his hand on his pants before approaching his friend. "Jamie!" Norm walked over to them, laughing with something akin to a smoker's hack-bellow.

Montagna and Norm embraced, and Kodiak stood behind them, making sure he carried his duffel bag with his right hand and kept his left in his pocket so he wouldn't have to shake Norm's hand.

Montagna stepped back for a good look at his friend. "You look good, buddy."

Kodiak almost laughed out loud when Montagna said this, because Norm Cocke was one of the ugliest people he'd ever seen. He was about Kodiak's age, with long, greasy gray hair that hung in front of beady, black pig eyes. He had big, horse teeth that looked too big for his mouth, and he had the facial structure reminiscent of a Neandertal man. He even walked with a slight forward slump to his shoulders that intensified his protohuman appearance.

"It's good to see you, Jamie. I got your cable only this morning, and I ain't had much time to get everything together, but I came through."

"I knew you would. Got somebody I want you to meet." Montagna stepped aside to introduce Kodiak. "Norm Cocke, this is the man I told you about, George Kodiak. *The* George Kodiak."

Norm smiled, clearly impressed, and being familiar with Kodiak and his work, he said, "Born and raised in Hell. I like that!" He was making reference to the bios on the jackets of Kodiak's books. "You all have any other luggage you got to get before we haul ass?"

Montagna held up his suitcases and said, "Just these. Pittman's having a load of equipment shipped to the lodge after we get there."

"Good enough. Come on, I'm parked in the loading zone."

They walked outside and Montagna and Norm continued to bask in the glow of rekindled friendship. "Letitia coming with us on the trip?" Montagna asked.

Norm spat. "Hell, no. Who needs her tagging along? She'd just ruin our good time." Then he smiled like a devil and said, "But

Ruthie is!"

Kodiak had no idea who these people were that they were talking about, but he noticed as soon as Norm mentioned this Ruthie, Montagna became a little quieter. He even looked pale.

Norm changed the subject. "You're not gonna believe this one, Jamie. Couple of months ago I'm in small claims court because this guy I hired to replace some windows took my money without doing the work. So I take this guy to court to get my money back, right?

"Well, as you know, my name's pronounced Coke, like the cola, but it's spelled C-O-C-K-E. The O is long. Wouldn't you know it, the fart-head I'm suing happens to be a guy named Steve Trojan.

"So what happens is, when my case comes up, this stupid bailiff calls out 'Cock versus Trojan!'"

Montagna laughed as Norm shook his head in dismay. "I was so embarrassed."

Norm's car was a twenty-five-year-old International wagon that looked like it had never been washed. The paint was so badly faded it wasn't even white; it was a non-color. The tires were balding, and the windshield had a large spiderweb crack on the passenger side that looked like it was caused by a bullet. Norm opened up the tailgate so Kodiak and Montagna could toss their bags in the back, where Kodiak saw a bumper sticker that read: *I brake for beer!*

"Norm, you get a hold of those people I asked you to call?"

Norm was not pleased with this part of the deal, and said, "If you're talking about Tyler and his merry band of goons, yeah, I called them."

Inside the International the upholstery was cracked and smelled of sun-hardened foam rubber padding and urine. Kodiak got into the back seat and rolled down the window. It only opened halfway, but that was enough for the fresh air to dispel some of the rank odor inside the vehicle.

Norm and Montagna sat up front.

"Jamie, why do you want these fart-holes coming along on this trip? They're just a bunch of rank amateurs."

"Tyler's a friend. I owe him a favor. Besides, his band of rank amateurs are familiar with the territory and have been tracking these animals for years."

"And that's supposed to qualify them?"

"Norm, I used to be one of those rank amateurs."

Norm said, "I still say they're gonna be a waste of time. What do you think, Kodiak?"

"We can use the extra hands, I suppose," Kodiak said with little interest.

"Besides," Montagna added, "they're not getting any of the money. When will they be meeting us?"

"They'll be at the lodge tonight."

"Good." Montagna turned to face Kodiak in the back seat. "I told you before, I've always been something of an armchair cryptozoologist. I've even been a member of the *International Society of Cryptozoology*, on and off. I'm mostly into the Sasquatch thing. Especially that case in Russia from several years back, you know, the one where those mountain men captured that female Sasquatch and had sex with her."

This intrigued Norm. "No kidding?"

Kodiak said, "You mean Zana?"

Montagna said, "Yeah, Zana. That's it. She was supposed to have given birth to some hybrid children. I even went to Russia after the Soviet Union fell apart to follow up some leads. Of course, I can't talk much more about that."

Kodiak looked at the two idiots up front and wondered if this Tyler and his band of merry goons were anything like them. He had Montagna pegged as a member of the "lunatic fringe"; bizarre, sometimes dangerous people who appeared on the doorsteps of legitimate investigators of the paranormal, with their own twisted ideas concerning the identities of whatever mysterious phenomena they chose to observe. These people had fantasies, as Kodiak considered them, of capturing the Sasquatch, or other unknown animals by whatever means were available. One such person even suggested a plan to drop poison gas over Washington State's Ape Canyon to see what might turn up.

Norm took them to his place; a rustic outpost that looked like a survivalist camp outside of Seattle. The house was a single-story building constructed of gray concrete blocks and sheets of corrugated tin for roof covering. Kodiak knew this was the house, because there was a carport attached to it.

Thirty yards from the house, down a small hill, was a longer building that was similarly built. Kodiak figured that was where Norm kept the teenage boys he kidnapped and chained to the walls in nothing but their undershorts.

Norm plowed up the front path at fifty miles an hour, deliberately aiming for some chickens that were scratching the ground around the carport. The chickens scattered, narrowly avoiding the balding tires as the wagon skidded to a halt. The three men got out, and Kodiak was very relieved to finally be free of that urine smell.

Norm said, "Just leave your stuff in the car. Letitia's got some grub waitin' on us. Then we'll shoot some targets before heading out."

The front door, indeed the only door to the house, was solid steel with three locks, which Norm opened, and they walked in. Norm stood in the open doorway and then roared, "That doesn't smell like steak!"

A moment later a small, rotund woman stepped out of the kitchen. She seemed rather sheepish and was covered with old bruises on her face and arms. "There wasn't going to be enough, so I made stew."

Norm looked at the floor, molding his rage like an artist molds clay. "I told you I wanted steak. I don't want stew. I got company here who don't want stew."

Kodiak decided to speak up. "Actually, Norm, stew sounds pretty good about now."

Montagna turned to him. "Just let Norm handle this."

Kodiak could have killed Montagna at that moment.

Norm pointed to the kitchen. "In there, now." Letitia complied, and Norm turned back to his guests. "Help yourselves to some brews. I keep a couple of sixers of Old Milwaukee in the mini-fridge next to the sofa." He followed Letitia into the kitchen.

Kodiak stared at the closed kitchen door, wanting to go in and intervene on Letitia's behalf, but he knew his interference would only make things worse for her later on.

Montagna nudged him. "Brewskies." He opened the three-foot refrigerator beside the sofa and took out two cans of beer.

Kodiak took one and looked around the room. The place was a toilet. The couch was the only piece of furniture in what barely passed for a living room, and it looked older than the car outside. There was a new television set on a dining room chair, with a videotape machine on the floor beside it, which looked out of place with the rest of the junk. The throw rug under the sofa was covered with pee stains and the only decorations were nude centerfolds taped to the cinder block walls.

Montagna sidled up to him, also looking around. "Norm's not a rich man, but he's a hell of a good guy. You know he served in Korea, too."

From inside the kitchen they heard Norm's voice rise in anger, followed by a vicious slap, then Letitia whimpering.

Kodiak said, "Which side?"

Montagna ignored the remark. "You don't know what Norm has to put up with from that useless sow. She starts lipping off about one damn thing or another, so old Norm whacks her a good one across the mouth. Sometimes that's the only way to keep them in line. Like you never struck a woman?"

"So what's the story on this Ruth you were talking about back at the airport?"

Montagna took a sip of beer, hesitating. Then he said, "She's Norm's mother-in-law. And I don't mind telling you, she's bad news. Norm's crazy about her, but to tell you the truth, she scares me."

"Does she know how Norm treats her daughter?"

"Does she know? Ruth treated her worse than Norm ever has. You want to know how Letitia and Norm got together? Ruth *sold* her to him. He's forty years older than Letitia. It's like a psycho version of Fred and Ethel Mertz."

"And just what is it about Ruth that has you so shaken up?"

"Norm calls her Ruth-less. And that's exactly what she is. She's more animal than human, if you ask me." He took a hard drink of beer, like he was trying to rinse a bad taste from his mouth. "She's meaner than hell, Kodiak. She's just... I don't know. She's just..."

There was another slap from the kitchen, then Norm came out, his Neandertal face flushed, running his fingers through his greasy hair to get it out of his eyes, only to have it flop right back down. "Afraid we're stuck with stew." He took his place at the head of the dining room table.

Kodiak and Montagna joined him and waited in silence as Letitia came out and set before each of them a plate that was piled high with an incredible looking meal that made Kodiak's mouth water.

Kodiak was the only one to thank her as she served lunch. She simply nodded, holding a bloodied napkin to her nose. When she finished serving lunch, she went back into the kitchen not to be seen again. As they ate, Kodiak secretly hoped that she would come charging back out, brandishing a butcher's knife and bury it deep into old Norm's chest. Hell, he thought, I'd even hold him for her. But Letitia remained hidden as per Norm's orders.

When they finished eating Norm farted, then took the plates one at a time and threw them against the wall, shattering them. "Let's go, gents."

They went outside and headed toward the second cinder block building – the one where Norm kept the teenage boys. Halfway there, something lunged at them with startling ferocity. Had it not been chained to a tree, the Pit Bull would have jumped on Montagna and ripped his throat out. Montagna and Kodiak jumped back, and Norm laughed out loud.

"I see you still have Goliath." Montagna's voice trembled, making Norm laugh even harder.

The dog was bred strictly for fighting; its face and body were mangled from old wounds, and its right hind leg was bent and atrophied, almost sideways.

"Old Goliath's been retired, I'm afraid. He went after some woman a couple months ago and tore her leg up pretty good. She was threatening to sue me and have him put to sleep."

Montagna seemed genuinely stunned by this news and said, "What did you do?"

"I threatened right back. I got a couple buddies to drop in on her uninvited like." Norm started laughing again. "They sodomized her old man right in front of her and told her they were both gonna die if she didn't drop the suit. Guess what? She dropped the suit." Norm kept laughing as he walked over to the second cinder block building and opened the steel door.

He flipped on a light, and Kodiak saw that this was an armory. The wall across from the door was lined with all sorts of automatic weapons. He wasn't up on the makes, but he knew that most, if not all of them, had to be illegal. They were displayed on the wall like trophies, all in mint condition.

On another wall there were posters of Adolf Hitler and red flags bearing the Nazi swastika. Beneath these was a workbench where

Norm did repair work and loaded his own ammunition. Over the bench were several framed photographs. Norm noticed Kodiak was intently looking at the shots, making Norm smile like a teenage boy looking through his first Playboy. "Memory lane, huh, Kodiak?"

These pictures brought back some ugly memories for Kodiak of his time in Korea. They were all black and white photos taken of Norm and his combat buddies standing over their victims. One picture was of young Norm holding a severed head.

There were more pictures on the wall; color photos from Norm's days with the ADC – *Animal Damage Control*. This was a government agency formed to hunt predatory animals that haunted ranches and threatened livestock. There were reports that the agency had been allowing hunters to go beyond just killing the occasional mountain lion or coyote, as they were literally wiping out hundreds of these animals. A picture of Norm standing beside a small mountain of severed cougar heads attested to this.

A three-foot wall separated the workshop from a firing range that took up the rest of the building. Three paper targets of human silhouettes were hung from pulley lines at the opposite end of the range, in front of a twenty-four-inch-thick reinforced wall that would stop the high-powered rounds that were usually fired in here.

Norm walked up to Kodiak holding a large caliber machine gun. "This is my new baby. German MG-32, the first version. When I got her, she was missing a few parts and the firing pin was bent, but I had a go at her and now... care to give her a try?"

Kodiak looked at the way Norm cradled the weapon in his arms and said, "You fondle that thing like somebody who's never had a girlfriend."

Montagna grunted, holding back a laugh, and Norm glared at him.

"All right. How's this for somebody who's never had a girlfriend?" Norm pointed the machine gun at the targets. Kodiak plugged his ears and stepped back from the barrel, which was right next to his head.

Norm fired at all three of the targets, making a straight line where all their throats would be. Two of the targets were cut off and fell to the floor. He lowered the weapon and glowered at Kodiak. "Beat that."

Kodiak took the gun, felt its weight, then spun around, the barrel suddenly aiming directly into Norm's stunned face. Norm stumbled out of the way, and Kodiak fired at a poster of Hitler, blasting away all of Der Fuhrer's face, leaving only his ears.

Norm and Montagna took their fingers from their ears and squinted to see the poster through the gunsmoke. When it cleared, they were speechless.

Kodiak tossed the gun back at Norm. "You're right. It's a hell of a weapon."

Norm didn't say anything. He just put the machine gun away.

Kodiak saw several leather collars with radio transmitters attached to them hanging over the retaining wall. He recognized them from his days as an agent for the Department of Fish and Wildlife. They were worn by animals that had to be tracked for various reasons.

Norm saw him looking at them and said, "A few years ago the government was getting freaked out that poachers were gonna wipe out the black bear population. They attached these radio collars to the bears so they could keep tabs on them. The damnedest part was, all we had to do was home in on the same frequency to track 'em down and blow 'em away!" Norm and Montagna both laughed.

Kodiak was familiar with the black bear poachers. These bears were usually killed for the same reasons any big game animal is hunted; for their pelts and for trophies. But the big money came from selling their gallbladders to Korea for their supposed medicinal and aphrodisiac value. There were twelve collars hanging from the ceiling, representing a dozen murdered bears.

They got back into Norm's urine-smelling International wagon and drove to the Bremerton Ferry in downtown Seattle. Once they were on board, Norm pulled out a six pack of Old Milwaukee. He and Montagna stayed in the car to drink, but Kodiak had to get some fresh air, so he went up on deck.

It was a little after two o'clock, and the sun was still high up in the sky. The cool breeze off the water felt good, so he leaned up against the forward gunwale and breathed in the fresh, salt air.

After fifteen minutes he had to turn his back to the wind, but he wasn't ready to get back in the wagon with Montagna and Norm. There were five other people on the deck; a family of four that looked like they were tourists from out of state, and a woman who was standing by herself, looking out at the ocean, oblivious to everyone else.

She was beautiful; fairly tall and lean, with long auburn hair that cascaded down past her shoulders and shone in the sunlight. She wore a loose-fitting wind-breaker, with khaki slacks that fit snugly around her shapely hips and thighs. She was turned too far away from him to make eye contact, but he wasn't bold enough to approach a woman he didn't know, so he just leaned back and admired her this way until she went inside the cabin.

ॐ

When the ferry docked, Kodiak got back into Norm's wagon and they took Washington Interstate 3 to Interstate 106, which took them to U.S. 101. That circled around the Olympic Peninsula and took them to the town of Red Fern located seven miles south of the Strait of Juan De Fuca, on the outskirts of Olympic National Park.

In order to keep up with changing times, the town of Red Fern was undergoing a face-lift. Much of the town was under reconstruction, expanding to accommodate the large numbers of people who were coming out this way every year.

The Red Fern Lodge was one of the few places in town that was, so far, being left as it had originally been built: a redwood building that boasted fifteen modest and inexpensive motel rooms. But its main attraction was the Red Fern Tavern, a bar, grill, and dance hall that was all part of the same structure. It was also the only source of nightlife for miles around, so the locals, tourists, and lately, the dozens of construction workers contracted to rebuild the town, spent all their evenings there.

Kodiak, Montagna, and Norm arrived at the lodge a few hours before sunset and checked into their rooms. Kodiak's room was sparse in furnishings with one twin bed, a dresser and nightstand. The basic decor was circa 1949 western, complete with a yellowed painting of a cattle drive hung over the bed.

After a hot shower and a change of clothes (the urine smell of Norm's wagon had permeated his clothing), he decided to call Wayne Monroe in New York, where it was after midnight. But Wayne wouldn't care, as he was up till nearly three every morning.

"Hello?"

"Wayne."

"George, how was your trip? Are you at the lodge?"

"Yeah, we got here half an hour ago."

"And?"

"So far, no good."

"What's wrong?"

"You'd love this guy Cocke. He makes Montagna look like a solid citizen."

"Oh, no..."

"Yeah. And now I'm supposed to go over to the tavern and meet three more of them."

"You still want to hang around?"

"I think it's better if I stick with this. My overall feeling is that these guys are too stupid to catch anything more than a good dose of the clap. But just the same, I want to make sure they don't get lucky. I'll give you a call when we get back."

"There is some good news," Wayne added.

"What's that?"

"Pittman's check cleared. You're four-point-five million dollars richer."

Kodiak smiled and said, "Do me a favor, Wayne. Deposit it in the Loch Ness account." Then another thought came to him, something that had been bothering him all day. "There is one other thing, Wayne..."

"Name it."

"This Cocke's got a wife just outside of Seattle. Actually she's little more than a sex receptacle. Anyway, he's got her beaten down pretty good, and unless something is done to get her out of there, he's either gonna kill her, or she's gonna do him and spend the rest of her life in prison."

Wayne's concern for this was apparent in his voice. "What do you want me to do, George?"

"With Cocke out here with us, that will give you a few days to see this woman. Her name's Letitia. Go and see if you can't do something to get her out of there before he comes back. It will be at least a week. Take fifty-thousand dollars and put it into a special account just for her. See if you can set her up someplace safe."

Wayne said, "That's noble, George. And I'll be happy to do it. I'll set out first thing tomorrow."

"Thanks, Wayne. I owe you."

The Red Fern Tavern was almost as dark inside as the night was outside. Creedence Clearwater Revival performed *Born On The Bayou* full-blast on the juke box, and the place was extremely busy with people both on the dance floor and in the lounge. The floor was covered with sawdust, and the redwood walls were decorated with animal trophies that included the heads of bear, buffalo, moose, and full body mounts of fish, racoons, and rattlesnakes.

Kodiak came in and made his way past the bar that divided the dining area from the sunken dance floor, and could barely hear Montagna when he called to him from a booth on the far side of the tavern.

There were five people in the booth, talking and having drinks. When Kodiak walked over they all stopped talking and looked up at him. Norm and Montagna were here, with a large bearded man who looked something like a pissed-off Santa Claus, a younger man in his twenties, and the auburn-haired woman from the Bremerton Ferry. The pissed-off Santa stood up and extended his hand. "George Kodiak. This is a real pleasure. I'm Ben Tyler." Santa actually seemed like a nice guy in spite of the natural scowl of his features. "Did you hear Bugs Bunny admitted to being a homosexual?"

"What?"

"Oh, no." The woman hung her head, obviously having heard this one before.

Ben smiled at her, then looked back at Kodiak. "Now we really know what's up Doc!"

Everyone laughed, and Kodiak shook Ben's hand. Montagna said, "Ben is the head of a local Bigfoot awareness organization..."

Ben interjected, "The Sasquatch-*Gigantopithecus* Resource and Information Center."

Montagna continued, "Ben and his people spend their weekends and vacations looking for something that might lead to positive proof of the Sasquatch's existence."

Tyler was still standing when he turned to the others in his group and introduced them. "This is Dave Bovard," he pointed to the young guy, who nodded, sizing Kodiak up with juvenile hostility.

Tyler then pointed to the woman. "And this is Cyrena

DeVarona." She stood and shook Kodiak's hand. "How do you do? I've read some of your books. I think they're very interesting."

"Thanks."

Tyler sat back down and scooted over, making a space for Kodiak. "Sit down, please. What are you drinking?"

There were two pitchers of beer on the table that everyone had been drinking from except Cyrena, who was drinking iced tea. "Beer's fine."

Tyler poured Kodiak a glass and set it down in front of him.

Kodiak looked at Montagna and Norm. Montagna had maintained his phoney air of being just one of the boys, but Norm was sullen, clearly unhappy about these people having joined the expedition.

Cyrena looked at Kodiak and smiled. She was even prettier up close, and had an infectious smile. Her auburn hair had some silver in it that caught the light like it did on the ferry and gave it a radiant quality. She was probably in her forties, and had obviously lived right. Her eyes were her most captivating feature; they were wide and the same shade of green as ripe grapes. She was coolly appraising him with those eyes, and he could see she was also capable of great compassion and humor.

Kodiak said to Ben, "How long have you been in this business?"

"Twenty-three years, on and off. I don't make a living at it, since we're a nonprofit organization. I run a small print shop in Seattle, and I operate our headquarters from there."

"You ever seen one?"

Ben's eyes took on a dreamy quality as he seemed to look through Kodiak. "No. God, would I love to. The closest I ever came was about ten years ago. I was actually tracking Cripple-foot."

Cripple-foot was something of a legend in Sasquatch lore. Its footprints had first been seen in Bossburg, Washington, in 1969. A set of footprints was discovered measuring seventeen inches in length, making them some of the largest such prints ever photographed or cast in plaster. What made these prints particularly spectacular was that the right foot was deformed. According to physical anthropologists who studied the casts, it was determined that the foot had probably been injured in the animal's youth, and it was a deformity that would be very difficult to fake without expert knowledge of the foot's anatomy. Cripple-foot's prints had reportedly been seen in years since, in some instances as far as a hundred miles from Bossburg.

Kodiak was impressed. "I take it you cast the prints you came across?"

Ben sat up a little straighter, smiling with pride. "Of course."

Kodiak said, "I've got some of the original Bossburg casts back home. Maybe after we get back we can compare them."

Ben nodded. "I'd like that."

Montagna said to Ben, "In the meantime, what have you been able to dig up about our quarry?"

"We're in a hot-bed of activity. There have been several sightings in and around the Olympic National Forest over the past couple years. So much so, it's unprecedented. Did you hear about the trailer park?"

"I heard that was a bear."

Kodiak asked, "What trailer park?"

"There's a trailer park on the other side of Lake Crescent that was attacked by one of them. At least, that's what they claim."

Montagna shook his head. "I think it's crap. If it wasn't a bear, it was bull. I heard because of the newer facilities opening up on this side of the park, the guy running the trailer park needed some gimmick to bolster business. That's one thing Bigfoot activity's always been good for."

"It can't hurt to check it out, anyway," Kodiak said and took a drink of beer.

"Well, either way," Ben said, "this is definitely the place where we're going to have the best luck. Now I figure our friend George can go with Jamie and myself tomorrow and start checking out some of the more recent reports."

"Why not me?" Norm sounded resentful and petulant.

Montagna answered him, "Norm, Pittman's shipping the equipment here tomorrow. I want you to be here to handle the unloading of it. It's gonna be an all-day job."

"I still think it's crap." Norm belched and poured himself another glass of beer.

Cyrena looked at him with disgust and shook her head.

Ben continued. "About all that leaves for us to take care of is renting the horses. We'll need a dozen of them."

"Can I do that?" Cyrena was looking at Kodiak. "I've had some experience with horses, so I think I'd know what to look for."

"That'll be fine," Montagna answered.

Ben turned to Kodiak. "Looks like that's it, then. Who knows, maybe you'll even get another book out of this."

Kodiak took another drink and looked at Norm, who was still brooding.

The Fourth Great Ape

W hile George Kodiak was getting better acquainted with the other members of the expedition at the Red Fern Tavern, eighty-five miles away Mildred Hunnicut was hiding behind the same bushes she had taken cover behind the night before. She was hoping the Sasquatch would return. Instead of cat food, this time she put out a large bowl of fruit. Things like mangos, pineapples, and watermelon. She peeled and sliced them, hoping their aroma would draw the animal out.

She didn't bring a chair or anything else that would make her comfortable, because she had no intention of remaining hidden. Tonight she was going to get as close to the animal as it would allow.

She didn't have long to wait.

She saw the porch lights reflected in its eyes, and then she witnessed its entire form emerge from the woods into the open yard. It seemed to have thrown its previous caution to the wind, as it went right for the fruit, resting itself on its haunches in the middle of the yard and eating.

She debated whether or not to approach the animal. It seemed to be enjoying the meal so much that she hated to scare it away. It suddenly struck her as peculiar that she never once thought to bring out her camera and get a picture of this spectacular creature. It would be so easy right now to get a picture of the Sasquatch and finally lay all the rumors and myths to rest, but that wasn't what Mildred wanted. She had lived long enough that she didn't have anything to prove to anyone to find pleasure from her private encounter.

The animal chewed with its mouth open, looking around as it ate. When Mildred finally decided to stand up, the creature looked right at her and froze, a big chunk of mango clenched between its teeth.

Mildred came out from behind the bushes slowly, being careful not to stumble or make any sudden moves that would frighten her Sasquatch, as she now thought of it.

The animal rose to its feet and made a deep, throaty growl, still holding some pieces of mango in its paws.

Mildred approached the animal slowly, getting within fifteen feet of it. She stopped, keeping her hands at her sides. She felt giddy, not at all scared, which was probably foolish, but nobody ever told Mildred Hunnicut what to do.

The Sasquatch swallowed its food and hissed at her, baring its teeth and crouching as if to lunge. But instead, it took two steps back.

Mildred took one step forward.

The animal screeched, but still it did not take off. It looked so much like a gorilla, with its pointed head and wide, flat nose. She wished she could remember some of the things Dian Fossey had done in that movie, *Gorillas in the Mist*.

She knelt down beside the bowl of fruit and picked up a chunk of pineapple which was dripping with juice, and she began to chew on it, keeping a constant eye on the animal.

It watched her intently, still in a semi-crouch and making that throaty growl.

She took another piece of pineapple and set it out before the Sasquatch. Then she took several steps back.

The animal slowly accepted the fruit, still watching her. It hissed again and then stepped back toward the woods.

Mildred felt this could be her last chance to gain a little of the Sasquatch's trust, so she took a piece of mango from the bowl and extended her hand toward the ape. It stopped and turned toward her, studying her for several minutes, never moving towards the offered fruit, but eyeing it longingly. It finally turned, and with its wide, hairy back to Mildred, wandered back to the safety of the woods.

Mildred listened as it trundled away until she couldn't hear its footsteps anymore. She would try again tomorrow night.

❧

At eight o'clock the next morning Kodiak met Montagna and Ben Tyler for breakfast at the Red Fern Tavern. Kodiak had a cup of black coffee. Montagna had two eggs, sunny side up, a side of hash browns that he called "hashish browns," and coffee.

In all his life Kodiak had never seen anybody put away a breakfast the likes of which Ben had: two orders of pancakes (because they only came four to a stack), three sides of bacon, two slices of ham, four eggs (two scrambled, two over-easy), and coffee – decaffeinated.

By nine-fifteen they had finished breakfast and walked over to the ranger station at the south end of town.

The ranger on duty was Jim Crichton, a big, middle-aged linebacker of a man. He was bigger than Ben, but all muscle. He was used to people coming around and asking questions about Bigfoot, especially after that incident at the trailer park. He had even dealt with groups of Bigfoot hunters before. He considered them all to be crackpots.

Crichton had heard of Ben through the newsletter Tyler's organization put out, and he'd also heard of George Kodiak, and even though he didn't believe there was such a thing as Bigfoot, he saw no problem in talking with these people.

"That's right, Mr. Tyler, we have indeed received more sighting reports than is usual for us."

"You think you could give us the names and addresses of some of these people?" Ben asked.

Crichton thought about it. "I don't suppose that would be a problem. Whether or not they'll talk to you is another matter entirely. Most folks aren't real anxious to be called psychos or liars."

"That's okay," Ben said. "Our investigation's strictly confidential."

"You don't have to tell me. Why don't you gents help yourselves to some of that coffee while I get the information you want." Crichton got up and went into the back office.

≥▲

At ten-thirty a U-Haul truck pulled up to the Red Fern Lodge with the supplies that Emory Pittman had promised to deliver. Norm came out first to check everything out. He was wearing the same clothes he had on the day before, and his breath smelled from a combination of beer and not having brushed his teeth. The driver gave him the inventory list and took off for the tavern, leaving

Norm to do the work of unloading the truck.

Norm was looking the list over when Dave Bovard came out and patted him on the shoulder. Norm glared at the kid like he was going to smack him, but Bovard didn't notice.

There were seven backpacks and sleeping bags, four igloo tents, two self-inflating CO_2 rafts, and a dozen sealed boxes that contained other provisions. And lying to one side of the cargo was a stack of titanium struts that would be assembled for the Sasquatch cage.

"Good morning."

Dave and Norm turned to see Cyrena standing behind them. She was wearing blue jeans, hightop tennis shoes, and a flannel shirt. "Isn't it beautiful out?"

It was a beautiful day. The sun was shining bright in a cloudless blue sky, and the mountains that surrounded the town were covered in the kind of brilliant green discernable only to the naked eye. It was something that could never be captured on film or in a painting.

Bovard smiled and gaped at her ample chest, at which he was always trying to cop a peek.

Cyrena heard a strange grinding sound, and when she looked at Norm she thought he was growling at her. As Norm stared at her the deep, grinding noise in his throat had risen to his mouth. He then tilted his head back, hawked up a loogie and spat straight up into the air. He opened his mouth and *GLICK!* He caught the ball of mucous and swallowed it again.

Cyrena gagged and turned away, but Dave laughed like he'd never seen anything so funny in his life. This pleased Norm, who smiled at the kid and said, "Liked that, huh?"

Between laughs Dave said, "That was funny as hell!"

"Well then, what say we off-load this crap, then you and me can go suck down a few brews for lunch? You are old enough to drink?"

"Sure am, Mr. Cocke."

"Just one thing. My name's Norm. Only my wife calls me Mr. Cocke."

❧

In all, Ranger Crichton was able to supply them with the names and addresses of seven people who were involved in, or had witnessed, some kind of Sasquatch activity. He took the time to screen out the nonsensical reports. Two of the remaining reports had to be discounted when they were proven to be bears, and two others were written off because the witnesses involved were from other states and had gone back home.

That left three people with whom they could spend the day interviewing about Sasquatch activity.

Their first stop was to the cabin of a local named Dutch Gipson. He had lived and worked in Seattle most his life as an insurance broker and came to live in his cabin in Olympic National Forest after retiring.

Gipson was a friendly, open person, as most people living in these parts were apt to be. He did seem a little self-conscious to talk about his experience at first, but loosened up when it became obvious that they were going to take him seriously. "I never believed in it much, one way or the other. At least, not until three weeks ago when I saw one of the damn things myself..." He laughed a little uneasily.

"What did it look like?" Ben was inquisitive without being challenging.

Gipson described the creature he saw. "Well, it looked a lot like the one in that film. You know, the one where you see that Sasquatch walking across the creek. It obviously wasn't the same one, but it looked a lot like it. It was about eight feet tall. I know this because it was standing in an orchard of sapling fruit trees I planted. They're only five feet tall, and this thing towered way over them."

"Was this day or night?"

"Broad daylight. He was just eating the leaves off the branches nice as you please. He was covered with shiny black fur, with some silver on the back. At first it looked like a man in a gorilla costume, but I could see the muscles moving under the fur, and it just looked too real. I only saw him from behind when I came out and spotted him. After a couple minutes he headed back into the woods."

Kodiak said, "Would you mind showing us where this happened?"

Gipson took them to the tract of land behind his cabin he had turned into a fruit tree orchard. The ground was freshly tilled around the sapling apple, walnut and peach trees. The little orchard was about half an acre and ended at an open meadow that was within a hundred yards of the edge of the woods.

Gipson pointed across the meadow. "He just walked across the field and into those woods."

Kodiak stepped into the orchard, studying the ground for any sign of footprints.

Gipson continued. "We had rain a couple days last week. But I took some plaster casts of his footprints after he left."

Gipson invited them back inside and showed them ten separate casts of footprints in successive steps the animal took to get across the orchard.

Ben measured them. Because each one represented a different stage of the animal's walk, they varied slightly in shape and space between the toes. The complete length of the foot was sixteen and three-eighths inches. Ben looked at Kodiak and said, "There's no way of knowing for certain, but if the ground outside is comparable to when this thing walked across that orchard, then it outweighs us by a couple of hundred pounds, at least." The footprints left by Kodiak, Ben and the others barely penetrated the ground half an inch. The Sasquatch prints were closer to two inches deep.

Kodiak asked Gipson for a magnifying glass, and Gipson obliged. The footprints were typical of the kind usually associated with these creatures; thus, the very reason for the name "Bigfoot". They were generally human in shape, though obviously much larger than the average human print. The soles were thickly padded, with no arch, bore a double ball, a long, wide heel, and five toes that were almost equal in size.

Kodiak scanned the surface of the cleanest cast with the magnifying glass and found what he was looking for. "Here we go."

Ben leaned close to Kodiak and scrutinized the plaster cast. "What is it?"

"Dermal ridges."

෨

After Norm, Dave, and Cyrena finished unloading the U-Haul, the driver left. Then Norm and Dave, since they had become buddies, took off for an early lunch, leaving Cyrena to deal with putting the stuff away.

The waitress who served them, a slender, dark-haired girl of southern heritage, brought them their first round; a beer for Dave, and a beer and a shot for Norm, who made a depth charge by dropping the shot glass into the beer glass and guzzling half the drink down. He wiped his hand on his sleeve and belched.

Dave took a couple chugs of his beer and smiled at Norm.

Norm leaned back in his chair, shot a loogie four feet into the air and caught it in his open mouth. He looked back at Dave. "So, kid, what's the story on Miss America?"

"You mean Cyrena? She's all right. I don't know her all that well. She likes to hang out with our group and go on hikes and stuff."

"I thought she got a little uppity when we were joking around."

"I guess. Why do you want to know about her?"

Norm shrugged. "I don't know. Being as we're all gonna be out in the woods together, I just want to get to know everybody."

"If you want to get to know her, why don't you just ask her?"

"Kid, when you want to get to know somebody, I mean *really* get to know them, who they are, what they're about, you don't ask them. You ask somebody you trust will give you the lowdown. And I trust you're the man for the job."

Dave looked away, his face flushing from the suggested flattery.

Norm finished off his drink, then called across the tavern to the waitress. "Sweetheart, couple more Old Milwauks and a shot for me. Thanks." He turned back to Dave. "You ever get any action?"

"With Cyrena? I told you, I don't know her all that well."

"What's to know? She's got a hole, don't she? Besides, I seen the way you're always gawkin' at her." Norm smiled, his wide, ape mouth and horse teeth making him look like the Cheshire Cat's ugly brother.

"She does have a nice pair of jugs, especially for an older lady. I saw her once in a T-shirt. They're a little banana-shaped, but they got a lot of bounce."

Norm laughed. "That a boy!"

The waitress came back and set their drinks on the table. Then she took Norm's emptied glasses.

"Thank you, darlin'." Norm studied her long and hard as she walked away. Then he said, "Yeah, old Cyrena's definitely got them. Listen, it's not like I think there's gonna be any trouble on this trip, but I kind of got a problem with this Kodiak."

"Oh, yeah?"

"He strikes me as a real 'holier than thou' type, you know what

I mean? I got a real feeling he don't much care for the way I do things, either. Jamie's so in love with the guy he refuses to see that Kodiak thinks he's trash, too."

Dave nodded. "Yeah, I kind of got that impression last night, especially the way Ben worships him."

"Now, we're all here to have a good time, maybe catch a Squatch, make history. But I need to know who my allies are should, say, anything happen to make us take sides."

"What do you mean?"

Norm leaned forward in a conspiratorial manner, looking around so as not to be overheard and said, "Jamie and me, we're tight. We're like blood brothers, you know? And this Tyler, Jamie likes him, and he strikes me as being somebody who goes with the flow. He don't make waves. But I got a real bad feeling about Kodiak. He's gonna try to ride roughshod over this whole thing, because he's the Bigfoot expert.

"So, I guess I'm asking, kid, should things get hairy, who's side you gonna be on?"

This made Dave uncomfortable, and he fidgeted in his seat before saying, "What makes you think there's gonna be any trouble with Kodiak?"

Norm shrugged. "Suppose the hunting goes a little slow and nothing turns up? We might as well get something out of this trip, don't you think? Maybe you, me, Jamie, and maybe even old Tyler might wanna have a go at Miss Cy-rena."

Dave smiled, his eyes wide and unbelieving, but also hopeful. "Are you serious?"

"Hell, she strikes me as the type who might even enjoy it. After all, you said yourself she likes to hang around groups of men in the wilderness."

Dave's smile got bigger. "Count me in."

Norm bellowed his sickening hack-laugh and made another depth charge.

&.

The next stop for Kodiak and the others was an RV park located some thirty miles south of Gipson's place, which was run by a middle-aged former biker named Billy Harvey. Despite his surly, unkempt appearance, and a body that rivaled Ben's for the walking-natural-disaster-award, Harvey was friendly and seemed eager to tell them about his encounters. "I say encounters because it happened more than just one time."

Kodiak started the questioning. "What happened more than one time?"

Harvey told him, "Late at night, something kept cruising into the camp grounds and stirring things up."

Ben stopped him. "Before you give us a rundown on the specific goings-on, would you mind if I taped this?" He took out a pocket-size dictation machine and set it on the coffee table between them. He then nodded to Harvey. "Go ahead."

Harvey continued. "Basically, the whole thing started about, I'd say, two months ago. In the middle of the night we heard something screaming, way the hell out in the woods. But in these mountains it carries real good and scared the crap out of most my guests. Especially the kids. Hell, who am I trying to kid? It shook me up pretty bad, too."

"What kind of screams?" Ben asked. "Can you describe them?" Harvey considered it, the pensive look seeming out of place on his fat, hairy face. "Well... it almost sounded like somebody imitating an ambulance siren, or doing a slowed-down version of Curly." They all laughed, then Harvey continued. "But it sounded creepy. It was so loud, it got all the dogs around here barking like crazy."

Ben interjected, "There was a case just like this in Puyallup, back in the early seventies. You mentioned it in your book, George."

"Back in '72," Kodiak said. "Some people even managed to record it. I heard it myself a couple times, and I have to admit it was unsettling. Of course, there wasn't anything to link it specifically to Sasquatch activity of any kind."

Then Harvey continued. "That's where my story differs. For three nights this screaming goes on. It gets to where my guests finally start to pull up stakes and go home.

"Then it stopped. For two nights there was nothing.

"But the following Sunday night, we hear what sounds like a bear rummaging around. It gets a little upset and starts making noises I don't normally associate with bears, like grunts and screeches, even whistles. Finally, it flings a portable barbecue across the camp, and it leaves.

"The next day we see these footprints all over the place. Big footprints."

Kodiak asked, "Did you make any casts?"

Harvey said, "No. The ground around here's real hard pack. The tracks were only in the surface dust. But it doesn't end there, because our mysterious visitor must have had a real bug up his hairy butt. Three nights later he comes back and attacks a Winnebago!"

Montagna said, "We heard something about that." He sounded skeptical.

Harvey either didn't pick up on Montagna's tone, or chose to ignore him, when he said, "Yeah, it was big news all last month. Knocked it on its side. The family that owned the camper was pretty badly shaken, but nobody was hurt, thank God. And the entire area around the camper was covered with those tracks, same as before. I measured one, and it was fifteen inches long!

"But here, let me show you the tape from the local news." Harvey got up and took a video cassette from on top of his television and played it for them.

The picture on the screen was a daytime shot of a local reporter standing in front of the exposed underside of the overturned Winnebago. "It looks like Bigfoot's back, and this time the Paul Bunyon Trailer Park's got him. Behind me is an overturned Winnebago camper belonging to Eric and Michelle MacDonnell, who were vacationing here in Washington from Los Angeles, when they became the recipients of a most unwelcome visitor."

The picture cut to Eric and Michelle MacDonnell standing in front of Billy Harvey's office. MacDonnell was pale and looked very uncomfortable as his wife leaned into his shoulder and cried. Eric MacDonnell continued the story. "We were sleeping when we felt something slam into the left side of the camper. When it started rocking back and forth we thought it was an earthquake, but earthquakes don't roar.

"Just as everything started crashing all around us, I could hear people outside hollering things like, 'Look at the size of that thing!', and 'It's a monster!'. All I remember is after the camper fell over, we had to climb out through the side windows."

The reporter asked, "What will you do now?"

"We're insured, and everyone's okay, so we're gonna head on home and try to forget this whole nightmare," MacDonnell said, sounding more tired than scared.

"Do you believe in Bigfoot?"

"Hell, yes!"

The shot went back to the reporter standing in front of the Winnebago wreckage. "Rangers never actually saw any of the alleged footprints the animal left behind, and because it was dark, they believe what the witnesses really saw was just a large bear that had been causing some problems in this area looking for food."

Billy Harvey shut off the tape. "Bear, my eye! Now, I didn't see it, but I did see those footprints."

"Did you photograph them?" Kodiak asked him.

"No, but other people did."

Kodiak was beginning to lose faith in anything Billy Harvey had to tell them, but still asked, "Any of them still around here?"

Harvey shook his head. "No. But I can give you their names and addresses."

ॐ

Cyrena really didn't mind doing the inventory alone, because she had gotten sick of the constant jokes about female genitalia. There were six pages of inventory to match with the equipment, and she did that in Kodiak's room, since his was the closest. He had provided her with his key that morning for this purpose before he took off with Ben and Montagna.

When she decided to break for lunch, she knew that Norm and Dave would be in the tavern, so she took a walk down the street to the only other restaurant in town; a small corner coffee shop with lots of booths and big picture windows that looked out at the green mountains.

She was tired from all the lifting and carrying of boxes and supplies, but the air outside refreshed her as she stretched, closing her eyes and feeling the full force of the sun on her face. The pine smell was so strong in the air that she didn't want to stop inhaling.

There is a sound indigenous to mountain areas throughout the world: the constant rumble of far-off rivers and waterfalls that carries through the canyons like a hundred thousand voices all whispering in unison. She stretched her arms back as far as they would go and arched her back, standing on her toes for added leverage that renewed and invigorated her body.

She took her time walking down the street, enjoying the little town of Red Fern. She lived in Washington all her life, but had never been here before. She had never even heard of Red Fern. She was enjoying the walk down Main Street smiling and waving to people who seemed equally happy to return the gesture. Naturally, some of the construction workers were very eager to get her attention with whistles and cat-calls. She was a very attractive woman, but she never gloated on it. Even though she knew their attempts to catch her eye were just good-natured fun, it still made her uncomfortable, so she picked up her pace and went into the coffee shop.

The old guy who ran the place was standing behind a cash register at the front counter and smiled as she walked in. "Most folks are gone fishing, hiking, or some other outdoors activity, so things are a little slow. Why don't you go on ahead and take a seat wherever you please." He handed her a menu and gestured to the empty cafe.

She took a corner booth with an unobstructed view of Main Street where she could also keep an eye on the Red Fern Tavern. She wasn't a person easily given to paranoia, but she didn't like the idea of Norm cruising down this way when she couldn't see him coming. She hated feeling like this, especially in such a beautiful part of the world where people should feel the most free. But Norm Cocke gave her the creeps like she had never known. The man was openly slimy, looking her up and down, feeling her up with those dark, beady eyes, staring at her breasts and crotch.

The old guy came over to her table and set a glass of water down for her. "Eating alone today?"

"Yep."

He set a paper place mat down with some utensils. "Are you ready to order, young lady, or would you like a few more minutes?"

"What do you recommend?"

"My wife whipped up a heck of a beef brisket last night, and the leftovers make a terrific sandwich. That and a side of cole slaw and potato salad would sure hit the spot."

She nodded and handed back the menu. "Tell you what, throw in a large glass of iced tea, and you've got a deal."

"Fair enough." He winked at her and went into the kitchen.

Cyrena looked back out the window.

Dave Bovard was sure hung up on Norm. What could he

possibly see in that walking ball of pus that he would want to emulate? She had known Dave for three years, but he was always so shy around her, at least when he wasn't acting like a punk. He could be smug, belligerent, and cocky. She'd even caught him looking at her breasts, but at least he tried to be covert about it. He was a little old to be acting like a teenager, but she always thought he'd outgrow it. But hanging around Norm, God only knew what that was going to turn him into.

The old guy brought her a tall glass of tea with a slice of lemon floating in it. He set it down, nodded and left again.

She poured some sugar into her tea and stirred absent-mindedly while she kept looking up the street. She thought about Kodiak. She couldn't understand what it was about the guy that had Ben and Jamie Montagna fawning all over him, but she knew it wasn't really his fault if they wanted to make asses of themselves. He even seemed uncomfortable with the mantel they placed upon him.

The first time she saw him wasn't in the Red Fern Tavern.

She recognized him from the ferry out of Seattle, standing by himself on the deck. She didn't know who he was at the time, but she had to admit she was impressed by what she saw. He was very good-looking, tall and muscular, aged just right. But she wasn't the type to approach a total stranger, especially one who looked like he might knock your teeth down your throat if the mood struck him.

Ben was quite taken with him, too, which she found odd. In the six years she had known him, Ben Tyler was a natural leader, the type of man others looked to for guidance and protection. This was a good sign, however, because Ben was good at reading people. She could trust his judgement, which meant Kodiak was probably okay.

The old guy brought her lunch over and set it down. "Here you go. I gave you two pickles. Enjoy."

She returned his smile. "Thank you." She wasn't sure she could eat all the food he had piled upon her plate, but she was willing to try.

The bell over the coffee shop door jingled, and Cyrena looked up to see an old woman come in. She had to be the strangest-looking person Cyrena had ever seen. She appeared to be Native American, and she could have been over a hundred years old. Her skin was very dark, and her eyes were difficult to see under the precipice of wrinkles that formed upon her forehead. She had no lips, as age had drawn them back over toothless gums, like a mummified cadaver. She had long, dark gray hair that cascaded well past her shoulders from under a dirty red bandanna, and she wore a loose-fitting work shirt that hung oddly from her bony, humped frame. Her arms looked like weathered twigs, all angles, that ended in long, dirty claws that were her hands.

The old guy offered her a greeting, but the hag ignored him and took a seat at the counter. After several seconds she sensed Cyrena's eyes upon her, and she turned to stare back.

The old woman's scowl was extremely menacing, so much so that it made Norm seem like a harmless clown in comparison. Cyrena continued to look at the hag, embarrassed to be staring, but unable to look away. She noticed several peculiar-looking pelts that were hanging from the old woman's belt, each with a hand-crafted silver tag attached to it. Next to the pelts she wore a formidable Bowie knife in a leather sheath.

Cyrena finally forced herself to look out the window and eat her lunch. But she could still feel the old woman's menacing gaze like warm, greasy fingers running through her hair on the back of her head. God, she thought, what is this trip turning into?

ૐ

Three men were standing at Mildred Hunnicut's front door asking her about the report she had made to the Red Fern Ranger Station regarding her Sasquatch sighting. She regretted making that call the day after the first encounter, especially after her visit by the two mysterious lumbermen, and she was reluctant to talk. Her initial impression of these three did not help loosen her tongue, either. The one in the front looked like Kris Kringle's evil twin, the second one looked like one of those wimps with a chip on his shoulder and a taste for persecuting the less fortunates of the world, and the third one looked like a fugitive from *America's Most Wanted*.

"I was mistaken. What I saw was a bear. I couldn't see it very well, because I didn't have my glasses. But it came back the next night, and I saw that it was just a bear."

Ben nodded. He didn't want to be aggressive, because he knew what they must look like to her, but he could also tell she was hoping to get rid of them quick. "You didn't let them know at the ranger station that it was just a bear?"

"Young man, those rangers didn't believe me when I called the first night, so I just didn't bother."

Montagna spoke up. "Which direction did the bear come from?"

Still anxious to get them to leave, she pointed to the woods on the far side of the house, where she kept the garbage cans. "There. Both nights."

Montagna nodded and headed in that direction.

Kodiak knew she was lying. He could pretty much guess that Ben knew, as well. He respected Mildred's desire not to subject the animal to outside interference, but she made two major mistakes. The first was letting them know that the animal had come back the following night. The second was pointing out from where it entered her property. Ben was no dummy, but Kodiak had to try. "We're sorry to have wasted your time, ma'am. Should anything come up, please contact us at the Red Fern Lodge. You can ask for George Kodiak or Ben Tyler."

She nodded and closed the door.

Ben was completely dumbfounded. "Are you crazy? If she wasn't lying through her acrylic teeth, then I'm going on a liquid diet!"

"Take it easy, Jabba. I know she's lying."

"Then why'd you cut it short?"

"Ben, I know you have the same appreciation for these animals as I do. I know more than anything that you'd be perfectly happy just to see one in action, maybe get some film, or something to capture the moment. But that's not Montagna's trip. You know as well as I that fool's in this for the long green, and I hate him for it. Him and that idiot Cocke."

He was getting through to Ben. But Ben was still vacillating. His desire to actually see a living Sasquatch, even to be involved in a capture... But he was willing to listen. "What do you suggest, then?"

"We may have a repeat visitation going on here. Maybe the old lady's gotten to where she doesn't want anybody screwing with it so she can enjoy it. So I say we get Montagna and Cocke lost on some wild goose chase, then you, Cyrena, Dave and I can come back and convince her that we just want to observe it without interference."

Ben stroked his beard, thinking it over. "Think we can convince her?"

Kodiak smiled and said, "With your natural charm? It'll be a piece of cake."

Montagna went around the back of the house and scrutinized the soft dirt where the lawn stopped and the forest started. He found what he was looking for: a partial footprint. He couldn't tell how long it was, but it belonged to an animal about the same size as a man, probably a juvenile Sasquatch.

He figured the old bag lost her fear of the thing and started feeding it so it would keep coming around. As he stared at the footprint something on the lawn caught his eye, and he saw Mildred's gray cat cleaning itself.

Mildred watched Kodiak and Ben from inside her living room as they continued to debate the matter. They finally turned and headed back towards their car. She breathed a sigh of relief.

Her cat let out a sudden cry of pain, and Mildred ran for the kitchen. Midway through the dining room she saw the other man, the balding wimp, standing in her kitchen, holding her cat by its tail, threatening to smash it against the wall. His hand was bleeding from where the cat had scratched him.

"Let's talk turkey, Mama."

"You!" She started for the kitchen, but Montagna drew back to swing, and the cat howled. She stopped. She was shaking as she debated screaming for help, but the only people who would hear were those two men he came with.

"Tell me about the Sasquatch."

"It was a bear."

"Mama..." He gestured to the cat with his head.

She hesitated.

The cat mewed in pain.

She relented. "You're right."

"Uh-huh..."

When Kodiak and Ben got to the jeep, they looked around for Montagna. There was no sign of him, so Kodiak said, "Piss on him. It's a nice day for a walk."

"You know, George, I get the impression you don't think too highly of Jamie."

"You're a perceptive guy, Ben." They both laughed and headed back to the lodge without Montagna.

ঽ⁂

Cyrena was almost finished with lunch. She had no idea whether or not she liked it, because her attention was on the street outside. Not so much to keep an eye out for Norm, but it was the only way she could keep from looking at the mysterious hag who she knew was watching her.

The entire time the old bat was in the coffee shop all she had to eat were three hard-boiled eggs dipped in horseradish, and she had to put her dentures in her mouth to eat them. Cyrena watched as she took a bottle from her baggy shirt and struggled with the cap until it finally came off. She took a single white pill from the bottle and shoved it under her tongue. Probably nitroglycerin for a heart condition.

When she was finished, Cyrena left a tip for the old man and left as quickly as she could without seeming too eager to get away from there, even though she was. Ten yards outside the coffee shop she heard the bell jingle over the front door, and she knew the old woman had come out behind her.

In spite of the hag's appearance of infirmity she kept up with Cyrena, who stepped up her pace. She made her way up Main Street trying to figure out who this old woman was and what she was going to do if the old hag followed her all the way to the lodge. Of course, she could also have had a room there, but what were the odds of that? Then there was the business of those pelts, and the very large knife. God, she felt like such a wimp, scared of a hunch-backed old woman who was probably crippled with arthritis and osteoporosis. But Cyrena couldn't shake the feeling of danger that came from the old witch, and that was enough to make her want to stay well away from her.

As she got within the vicinity of the lodge, she saw old Norm standing out front, leaning against a wooden railing and sipping a beer. Her heart sank at the sight of him. He was looking right at her and smiling, and it was not a "hello, how ya' doing" kind of smile, either. Great, she thought, now I'm trapped between two of them.

Norm started walking toward her, still smiling...

Cyrena stopped cold, frozen with shock and dread as Norm walked right up to her... and brushed past, ignoring her completely.

Relief washed over her as she turned to watch Norm walk to the hag and grab her in a bear hug.

The miserable bat let out a sickening groan that could have passed for an elephant reaching climax. Cyrena guessed this was a sound of pleasure. Coupled with Norm's coughing hack-laugh, they sounded like two asthmatic pigs.

Norm stepped back to look the old hag over. "Ruthie, it's sure good to see you!"

The hag grunted in agreement, and they embraced again.

Cyrena shook her head and went inside the lodge.

❧

When Kodiak and Ben got back to the lodge, there was a message from Mildred Hunnicut asking one of them to call.

"Mrs. Hunnicut, this is George Kodiak."

"Mr. Kodiak, I'm afraid I lied to you earlier. It was a Sasquatch."

"I see. May I ask what brought on this sudden change of heart?"

There was a long pause before she answered, "I was afraid people would think I was crazy. An old lady living alone... Anyway, after hearing about what happened at that trailer park, I just got scared."

"You were adamant it was a bear. If anything, you seemed more frightened of us..." Then it dawned on him. "Mrs. Hunnicut, is somebody there with you?"

Montagna took the phone from her. "I suppose you think it was real funny leaving me behind, huh, Kodiak? Get everyone together and get all the gear over here before sundown. We're going after this one."

Kodiak flushed with anger. He hissed into the phone, "What did you do?"

"You're paranoid, Kodiak. Just do what I say. We got work to do." Montagna hung up.

Kodiak suddenly had a sinking feeling in his stomach as he realized the luck he was certain would elude them may come through after all.

Deepening the Lines of Dissension

They had to take two vehicles for the hour-long trip to Mildred Hunnicut's house, which was located just outside the Queets Valley. There wasn't enough room to fit all the boxes of supplies in Norm's wagon. Kodiak was grateful for that, as he couldn't stand the thought of another ride in Norm's International with that piss smell. He rode with Ben, and Norm followed with Ruth in his wagon.

Ben asked him, "So, what do you think of that Ruth?"

"You mean Satan's ex-wife?"

"Why do you say his ex-wife?"

"Because even he's not mean enough to put up with her for very long."

They both laughed.

"She's definitely a weird one," Kodiak said. "Even Montagna's got some reservations about her."

This surprised Ben. "No kidding? Maybe I should lay down the law about her coming along on this trip."

"Ben, you see that knife she carries? I don't think I'd want to be the one to tell her she's got to hit the bricks. Besides, I don't think old Norm's going to sit idly by and let you tell her where to get off."

"Actually, I wasn't planning to. I was gonna ask you to do it." Ben laughed again.

"Thanks."

Ben's laughter trailed off. "He's something, too, isn't he?"

"Who?"

"Old Norm."

"I was under the impression you knew him?"

Ben shook his head. "Never met him before now. But it doesn't really surprise me that Jamie likes him."

"Why's that?"

"Don't get me wrong, Jamie's an all right guy. I never had any problems with him. But I also know better than to screw with him."

Kodiak hardly knew Ben, but he couldn't shake the feeling that he was about to get a sermon.

Ben went on. "I can see where Jamie could be bad news if he wanted to be. His being friends with this guy Cocke is one aspect of his personality."

"How long have you known Jamie Montagna?"

Ben thought about this as they turned off the 101 to a forest road, with Norm right behind. "Ten years, give or take. He caught my ad in a magazine and joined us on one of our weekend excursions. He was a regular for about five years, then his participation started to dwindle. I hadn't even seen him for four years until yesterday."

"Do you know what line of work he's in?"

Ben shook his head. "No. You?"

"Something to do with the government. State Department, I believe. But I prefer to avoid any unnecessary conversation where he's concerned."

Ben smiled. "I noticed. I also noticed that he knows you don't like him. He acts like he doesn't get it, but he does. And you can push him too far, you know."

"I'm not particularly concerned about having my back to him," Kodiak stated.

"Yeah, I noticed that, too. You see, I've never had any trouble with Jamie, because I don't push his buttons. Now, I know you don't like the way he toadies up to you, because that pushes your buttons. But I'll tell you, George, I hope to God it never comes to blows between you two, because it's gonna be a bad mess for whoever loses."

"Oh?"

"In a straight fight it's obvious Jamie would probably end up in an iron lung. But it's not as simple as that, because Jamie's not above fighting dirty."

Kodiak didn't say anything.

"I'm good at reading people. I can accurately size somebody up ten minutes after meeting them. That's why I'm able to get along so well with most people, because I can see where to tread softly, and where not to tread at all.

"I may even be making a big mistake right now by telling you, but after meeting you, I can see you've got a serious mean streak in you."

Kodiak raised an eyebrow in mock curiosity, but said nothing.

"It's obviously not something you chose to be born with, and it certainly doesn't make you a bad person. In fact, it's because you're generally a good person that you've gone through a lifetime of hell trying to control it. And of course, the harder you try, the worse it gets."

Kodiak just continued to look out the window.

"But I'll tell you this, George. God help anybody stupid enough to think they can cross you and walk away in one piece."

❧

There was a private stable fifteen miles northwest of Red Fern where Cyrena and Dave went to rent the horses. They were going to need twelve altogether; seven for the riders, and five more to carry supplies.

The owner of the stable, Andy Paul, suggested they use llamas as beasts of burden as they are more suited for such work than the horses, especially at higher altitudes. It was also clear that Paul was taken with Cyrena the moment he laid eyes on her. Dave felt an ugly surge of jealousy, but couldn't act on it because he had no business being jealous. After all, Cyrena never paid much attention to him, because he was just a kid in her eyes, and she would never take his romantic overtures seriously. Paul was closer to her own age and was a big, robust Oklahoman who looked like he could whip his weight in wildcats. And he strutted around like he knew it.

"I understand you folks are plannin' to do some Bigfoot huntin'?" Paul asked with a grin.

"Word certainly spreads like wildfire around these parts, doesn't it?" Cyrena smiled back at him.

The big cowboy took off his Stetson and ran his fingers through the thick, curly red hair that covered his head. "Actually, Jim Crichton over at the ranger station's a buddy of mine. He told me you folks'd probably be coming my way."

"We're not looking to kill anything. We just want to see what we can find out there. I hope that won't affect whether or not you'll rent us some horses," she said with natural diplomacy.

"Little lady, that's none of my business, just so long as my animals are well cared for. Anybody ever mistreats one of my horses, there'll be hell to pay." Paul cast a suspicious eye at Dave, who was walking behind them. At this, Dave decided he hated the stupid cowpoke.

Paul took them across the lot to a corral where three dozen horses were ensconced. They were beautiful animals; differing hues of gray, black, brown, with two buckskins that stood out among the rest.

"Where are you folks from, anyhow?"

"Most of us are from Seattle, but we have a couple out-of-staters riding with us."

"That so? How many of you altogether?"

"Seven."

"Well, it sounds like y'all will be having a pretty good time. I almost wish I was going with you," Paul said, and Dave noticed a slight leer to his smile. "You strike me as somebody who knows horses, so I'll just let you peruse the stock and decide for yourself." Paul opened the corral gate and stood aside for Cyrena to enter, enjoying the view from behind, Dave noticed.

Cyrena moved casually among the horses. She had a genuine affection for them, and it showed in the way she touched and patted them, the way she spoke to them, holding one still to look at its teeth. She knelt down and checked the shoeing on another and checked its hooves for thrush. She looked them over for swayback and saddle sores. When she came across one she really liked, she made a careful examination of its legs to see if they were spavined, or had bowed tendons. All the horses were in excellent condition.

She didn't know nearly as much about llamas as she did horses, but felt sure they were probably in just as good a shape. She turned back to Andy Paul and said, "I believe we can do business."

Paul took Cyrena to his office to finalize the deal, and Dave was told to go with one of Paul's assistants to help get the animals ready.

As he went through the motions of handing saddles to the assistant, all Dave could think about was what they were going to do to Cyrena once they got her in the woods. It was different now than when Norm was talking to him in the tavern. When he and Cyrena came here from the lodge she talked to and treated him as an equal, as somebody she actually cared about and was interested in. Not just as Dave, the kid who was good for lugging baggage through the woods while everyone else hung out together. Of course, he always liked her looks. That was nothing new. But as they talked and he got to know her as a person, he liked her and felt a pang of dirty guilt for all the times he masturbated, thinking about her nude body pressed up against his in a hot shower, both of them slick and shiny with soap suds.

The assistant asked Dave for a bridle and Dave gave it to him, clearing his throat, then he looked back toward the office. Cyrena really was a nice person. She had even asked him about his hobby of model boat building, asking many pertinent questions that proved she was paying attention, even recalling specific details he had mentioned earlier. She even told him that she might go to one of the regattas that he entered.

Something else that surprised him about her was that she collected reptiles. She had three snakes – two pythons and a boa constrictor – and several pet lizards, including her favorite, an iguana. She was unlike any of the girls he had ever known, and this turned him on in ways his filthy thoughts couldn't.

The office door opened, and Cyrena came out followed by the idiot Paul. They were laughing about something, but she looked at Dave and rolled her eyes.

Paul said, "Everything ready?"

Dave and the assistant finished loading the horses and llamas onto two long trailers for the drive to Mildred Hunnicut's place. Paul escorted Cyrena to the first truck where they both got in, and Dave rode in the second truck with the assistant.

They took Interstate 112 to the 101 following the outer perimeter of Olympic National Forest.

About twenty minutes into the drive, Paul was looking out at the forest and said, "You know, that's a shame. Truly, a rotten shame."

"What do you mean?" Cyrena asked with some trepidation. She thought Andy Paul was nice enough, but he came on a little too obvious, like some of the boors she knew back in Seattle who were always hitting on her at work.

"Well, you can't tell it now. But not so many years ago this place was full of Douglas firs nine and ten feet across. All cut down and shipped to the mills. Many of them over a thousand years old. They got them in the park, too, where it's supposed to be against the law to cut them down."

Cyrena looked at the surrounding woods, which looked very much like untouched virgin forest. "How could they log the park if it was illegal?"

"They were what was called 'danger trees'. For whatever reason the bureaucrats could dream up, certain trees were sold off because they constituted some kind of 'threat to public safety', I guess."

The Olympic Mountains were the last large wilderness area to be explored in the continental United States. The Olympic National Monument was first established to be a wildlife refuge for the endangered Olympic Elk, which had been indiscriminately slaughtered nearly to the point of extinction by 1903.

The elk filled the most important ecological niche, as far as these lands were concerned. Where they dwelled in large numbers the forest remained free of an over abundance of undergrowth, wide open with panoramic vistas in all directions.

"As the elk became sparse," Andy Paul explained to Cyrena, "the undergrowth would take over completely. Why, hell, when the elk were almost gone, the Ozette Forest was virtually impenetrable, and remains just like that to this day.

"Of course, as the largest game animal in the United States, the elk were irresistible prey for hunters who took only those parts considered worthy of trophy status, leaving the rest of the bodies to decay throughout the forests."

ès

Ben pulled his jeep into Mildred's driveway, and Norm brought his wagon up behind it. Montagna heard them from inside the house and came out carrying a cup of coffee. "Norm." He walked over to Ruth's side of the wagon and helped her out, as she was only capable of clipped, arthritic movement.

Kodiak looked at the house and saw one of the curtains being pulled closed. He felt guilty for their intrusion into Mildred's life, and he hoped there would be some way he could make amends. But he doubted it.

Ben got out of the jeep and said, "Think we should start off-loading some of this stuff?"

"We might as well wait till Cyrena gets here with the horses."

Montagna came over to them and stood on Kodiak's side of the jeep. "I see you brought everything. Good. I don't want to make any more of a commotion than is absolutely necessary, just in case our friend comes back tonight. And there's a good chance he will."

Ben decided to play dumb. "So it really was a Sasquatch she saw?"

"It sure as hell was."

"How'd you get her to fess up?" Ben asked Montagna.

"It took a little sweet-talking, but she ultimately succumbed to my natural charisma. Listen, it might be a good idea for somebody to wait up the road for Cyrena and Dave so we can stash the horses someplace away from here."

Kodiak volunteered for this, and Montagna studied him for some indication of an ulterior motive. "All right. Then when you're finished you can come back here, and we'll plan our strategy for the capture."

"Jawohl." Kodiak clicked his boot heels together then turned and headed up the road.

Montagna took Norm, Ben, and Ruth inside the house, which was totally dark except for the kitchen. Mildred came into the dining room and looked at them.

"Mama, I got some people I want you to meet. You already know Ben, and Kodiak's gone up the road to wait for the others. This here is Norm Cocke, and Ruth Trelane."

Norm laughed. "Mama? Well, I am pleased to meet you. I just hope you fixed us something to eat, because I'm good and hungry." Norm laughed so hard he forced up a lung oyster.

Ruth was back in the living room looking over a large standing cabinet made of teakwood and glass that was filled with ceramic knick-knacks. She ignored everyone else.

Mildred said nothing and went back into the kitchen.

Norm asked, "What's her problem?"

Montagna shrugged. "Who knows. She's got some cold cuts and stuff in the fridge we can eat later."

Half an hour after Kodiak and the others got to Mildred's house, Andy Paul's truck came to the place where Kodiak was waiting beside a granite boulder that stood fifteen feet on end. Cyrena thought it actually resembled him, and wished she could have gotten a picture of him leaning against it.

Paul pulled to the side of the road, and Kodiak came over to them as Dave and Paul's assistant started off-loading the animals from the trailers.

Cyrena made the introductions. "George Kodiak, Andy Paul."

The two men shook hands, but Paul seemed a little stand-offish.

Kodiak said, "We won't be taking the horses back to the house. There's a clearing in the woods a little farther back where we can keep them until we set out."

With the animals off-loaded, Dave walked over. He felt bad enough about Cyrena having to ride out here with that jackass, Cowpie Paul, but when he saw Kodiak, his heart sank. Especially when he saw the way Cyrena's face had brightened being near him.

Kodiak nodded at Dave. "How're you doing, Dave?"

Dave just grunted and looked away.

Cyrena said, "I picked out a horse for you. It's the gray one with the black rump."

Kodiak looked at the seven horses. "Is there supposed to be some correlation between me and a horse's ass?"

Andy Paul looked at Cyrena with admiring eyes. "Now, y'all be careful. I don't much believe in Bigfoot myself, but there are plenty of other things in them woods that can give you trouble."

She patted his gloved hand reassuringly. "We'll be fine. And we'll get your animals back to you in a couple weeks."

"Look forward to it." Paul then turned to Dave. "You keep an eye out for this little gal, son. Make sure she don't get hurt."

Dave nodded and said, "I'll do that." But he was thinking, I'm not your son, and she's not your wife, you sheep-sucking, cowpoke retard.

Paul smiled. "That a boy." He tipped his hat to Kodiak without making eye contact. "Mr. Kodiak." Paul and his assistant got in their trucks and went back home.

Kodiak untied his horse from the others in line, climbed onto the saddle and rode over to Cyrena, as she mounted a buckskin gelding. "Shall we?" He gestured toward the woods with his hand.

She smiled. "After you."

Dave followed on a brown mare, leading the llamas.

Kodiak led them through the woods, up a steep hill circumventing Mildred's house and came to a grassy clearing, where he stretched a steel cable between two pine trees. The cable was used so the llamas could not chew through it and escape.

Cyrena and Dave dismounted their horses and the three of them went to work chaining the twelve animals to the cable, leaving them enough chain to eat the grass.

Kodiak looked at Cyrena, surprised to find himself so taken by her. She was a beautiful woman, but not merely in the physical sense. Her beauty came from inside and radiated a warmth and kindness toward other people. She was one of those extremely rare human beings who by their very nature were innocent without being naive. He knew he would probably never see her again after this trip, and that made him feel more alone than he already was.

Dave was at the far end of the line, so Kodiak walked over to Cyrena and leaned close to her ear. "Having a good time?"

"Very good."

"I'm glad. Listen, I don't want to alarm you, but it might be a good idea to stay alert. Keep away from Norm and Jamie as much as possible."

She wasn't really surprised by this, but she didn't care for this confirmation of her earlier concerns. "Staying away from Norm'll be no problem. Him or Ruth. You think there's going to be trouble?"

He paused for what seemed a very long time, and just before she was about to speak up again, he said, "No."

ٮ

Jamie Montagna brought a shoe box-size metal container into the house from Norm's wagon. It contained tranquilizing equipment, and he laid everything out on the dining room table: two dozen darts, several large syringes, and two bottles of liquid chemicals. Next to these items he laid out three air rifles.

Montagna picked up one of the bottles and started measuring off some of the liquid into a syringe.

Old Norm was behind him, leaning against the kitchen doorway and sucking on a brew. "What is that stuff, anyway, Jamie?"

"Ketamine hydrochloride. It's a powerful tranquilizer commonly used on primates."

"How do you know how much to use?"

"The general rule is two-point-five milligrams per pound. Now, according to Mama in there, we're probably dealing with a juvenile, possibly two hundred, two-twenty-five in weight. I want to play it safe, so I'll use five hundred milligrams. That should allow for a safe

LB-50."

Norm made a sound of exasperation. "Let's pretend, just for a minute now, that I ain't no Nobel laureate..."

"Yeah, yeah, right. LB-50, that's our margin for error. That gives us a certain amount of leeway should we overdose the animal. That way, the amount of juice we pump into him won't be fatal."

"And what's in that other bottle?"

Montagna glanced at the second bottle, then continued measuring the tranquilizer. "Doxapram hydrochloride. That prevents respiratory failure should I miss-guess our LB-50."

Norm laughed. "You damn near got to be a rocket scientist to figure this stuff out, huh?" He took another swig of beer and belched.

While Norm watched Montagna prepare the darts in the dining room, Ruth was sitting in the dark living room, warming her aged bones in front of the fireplace. When she first came into the house, she spotted the gray cat and felt the urge to hunt it down and kill it, as she always did when there was a potential "game animal" around. The cat sensed her malevolence and went upstairs to get away from her. That didn't matter to Ruth. She would simply bide her time until she was ready; then the cat wouldn't stand a snowball's chance in Hell.

In the meantime she reached into her shirt pocket and took out her nitroglycerin pills. She slipped one under her tongue, closed her eyes and hummed an Indian song her grandmother used to sing to her.

❧

Ben met Kodiak, Cyrena, and Dave as they walked out of the woods and up the path to Mildred's house. He explained that he could no longer stand the atmosphere inside. Norm was being his usual obnoxious self, Mildred wanted nothing to do with any of them, and Ruth was giving him the creeps.

Kodiak said, "I was going to ask you to come with me to take the cars to where we stashed the horses so we could pack everything for the trip."

Ben leapt at the opportunity. "Hell, yes! Anything to get away from here. Of course, you'll be driving Norm's car?"

Kodiak shook his head in dismay. "And you say I've got a mean streak. All right, let's get it over with."

"You mind if I come with you?" Cyrena asked in a conspiratorial tone.

Dave had been morose ever since he saw how pleased Cyrena was to see Kodiak waiting for them on the road. What hurt most was that she didn't seem to notice, or even care about his dour mood. He didn't ask to come along and just headed back to the house.

ঽ⋆

Everyone had gone outside except for the old Indian woman, who sat in front of the fireplace, making animal cries of displeasure whenever the fire started getting low. Mildred didn't like her, but she was more frightened of her than any of the others, so when the old bat howled, Mildred went in and added another log while the hideous bag glared like the devil.

Back in the kitchen Mildred could hear the others through the open window. That creep Montagna was giving orders like he was the biggest turd in the toilet. And every time that Norm Cocke gagged up something to spit, Mildred had to suppress the urge to vomit.

Forty-five minutes after they had gone off to pack the horses, the one called Kodiak walked in the back door with several empty canteens. "Mind if I use your tap?"

Mildred just shrugged and turned away.

"Thanks." He went to the sink and turned on the water.

She listened to the metallic reverberation of the water as it flowed into the first canteen. This man seemed all right, and in some ways he even reminded her of Steve. Of course, Steve wasn't as tall, and was more stocky, but they both had that look of underlying moodiness that reflected in their features. But he was with those other people and that was enough to ensure that he was no good.

A couple minutes later the woman came in. She was very pretty and even seemed friendly. She tried to strike up a conversation with Mildred a couple of times, but Mildred chose not to get involved with her. She felt a little bad for that decision.

The woman said, "I see you have a friend." Mildred turned and saw Kodiak had picked up her cat. The cat was normally very scared of strangers, especially after Montagna threatened it, but now it was purring and chewing playfully on Kodiak's fingers as he stroked its head and belly. A lump formed in her throat as she watched them. Her emotions were so badly tangled from recent events that she was numb. She must have had a strange look on her face, because they were both looking at her, and the woman said, "Are you all right?"

Mildred was suddenly overcome and a tear ran down her face. "His name's Larry."

ê

The screen door slammed, and Montagna saw Kodiak heading across the front lawn toward him. "Kodiak, we have to talk about setting up our stake-out..." Kodiak grabbed Montagna by his shirt collar and nearly strangled him as he marched Montagna into the woods. Fifty feet through the brush Kodiak slammed Montagna up against a tree.

"I want to know what you did to get Mildred to tell you about the Sasquatch."

Montagna couldn't breathe. He clawed desperately at Kodiak's fist, but there was no give. If Kodiak expected him to answer, he was crazy. Montagna grunted and spittle ran down his chin. Kodiak felt the wetness on his fist and loosened his grip, but still held Montagna firmly in place. "Let... go... of...me..."

Kodiak only glared. Mercy was not part of the bargain.

Montagna gagged again, then said, "Nothing. Not a damn thing... nothing. Let go of me..."

Kodiak said, "All I've gotta do is pinch your weasely head off, and there will be no stake-out tonight. Not for you. Not ever."

Kodiak released Montagna, who slumped to the ground, taking in deep gulps of air and looking up at Kodiak through his watering eyes. "I'm in charge. Me. You got that?"

Kodiak said, "You're in charge of the check book! And when we go back in there, you're gonna write Mildred a big fat check, compliments of Emory Pittman. You'll also recall that Pittman put me in charge of the capture. He said something about you being a coward, and a screw-up."

Montagna spat, slowly getting up. Kodiak had dropped him on some ants. He swatted at them to get them off of himself. Finally he turned back to Kodiak. "You're in charge, huh? Well, you might want to be careful, because accidents can happen out here in the dark."

Kodiak reached for Montagna's collar. Montagna flinched, but Kodiak only straightened Montagna's shirt and wiped away a couple ants. "Are you threatening me, Jamie?"

"Just stating a fact." Montagna shoved past Kodiak and went back to the house.

Montagna was right. Kodiak had acted prematurely. He put himself in jeopardy after this confrontation, and it wouldn't be safe for him to be outside tonight.

He knew he could trust Ben, but Norm was Montagna's lackey, and he'd happily put a bullet in the back of Kodiak's head if it was what Jamie wanted.

ပ

Old Norm took a position on the roof of the garage, lying prone with one of the air rifles. It was mounted with a nightvision scope that would make the surrounding woods clear as daylight.

Montagna and Dave had the two remaining rifles and were positioned on opposite sides of the property.

Ben was on a hilltop overlooking the back yard, armed only with a pair of nightvision goggles. He was sitting on a tree stump with a perfect view of the back of the house and most of the front yard. He could see Ruth inside, curled up in front of the fire. He could also see the dining room, but he couldn't see Kodiak or the other women.

Earlier, he saw Kodiak grab Montagna and drag him into the woods. He knew he should have intervened, but didn't have the nerve to do so. He was tremendously relieved – and confused – to see them both walk out on their own two feet. But now Kodiak was in the house, and Jamie had become much more imperious when ordering the others around.

Ben saw Norm on the roof of the garage and wished he had one of the rifles, as he had a perfect shot at Norm's butt. He scanned across the roof and spotted Dave atop a telephone pole, looking back at him. After several minutes of staring at each other, Dave finally nodded and turned back toward the woods. Ben couldn't understand why, but he felt a strange malevolence coming from

Dave and thought if he could have seen Dave's face, he might not have liked what he saw.

Between the four of them they had most of the area under surveillance.

They maintained contact via FM band radio headsets that allowed them to keep their hands free. Montagna addressed the others. "The sun'll be going down in ten minutes. Do whatever you gotta do now; otherwise, be prepared to hold it in for a very long time."

Norm spat. He was having a contest with himself to see how far he could spit, but each of the projectiles he forced up from his throat landed in the same spot, forming a puddle. He was now working on making a shape of the puddle, which looked remarkably like Bob Hope's profile. "Hey, kid." Norm was talking to Dave over the radio, but everyone could hear. "By this time tomorrow the hunt'll be on, huh?"

Montagna cut in, "What's the matter, Norm? Don't you think we're gonna have any luck tonight?"

"I was just commenting how nice it would be if we got to take a trip into the woods. Ain't that right, kid?"

Dave said, "Yeah."

"Hey, Jamie, where's that Kodiak, anyway?"

Montagna sighed. "Who cares. It's a little late to worry about him. He's smart enough to stay inside now."

The sun was almost completely down. Montagna said, "All right, let's observe radio silence unless you see something. Over and out."

Ben suddenly had to go to the bathroom.

❧

Mildred made tea, and they sat at the dining room table. Cyrena stroked Kodiak's arm, trying to calm his rage after Mildred told them how Montagna threatened to kill her cat if she didn't fess up about the Sasquatch.

Mildred spoke just above a whisper so Ruth couldn't hear them. "I was scared when I called the ranger station, because I didn't know what it was going to do. But now I feel like a fool. After that first encounter I was paid a visit by two men who wanted to know about my sighting. I figure they got the information from the ranger station in Red Fern, but they chose not to enlighten me. They had mentioned something about how my reporting it could bring some sort of 'unwanted elements' to these mountains. They made it clear I would be wise to just keep my mouth shut about the Sasquatch—and them. Then when you people showed up today, I thought they were back with reinforcements."

Kodiak looked at her face. "You didn't do anything wrong. And nobody's going to bother you again."

Mildred nodded and sighed. Then she said, "I have heard of you. All those books you've written about strange animals. Have you ever written any fiction?"

"No. But I've been accused of it," Kodiak retorted, and they all laughed.

"What kind of animal is it, exactly? I don't think it's a gorilla, because they don't walk like people do."

"I believe it's *Gigantopithecus*. A higher primate that existed throughout Asia up to half a million years ago."

Mildred shook her head. "I'm sorry if I sound like a skeptic. God knows I have no business acting like one, but how could they have existed out here all this time without ever being found out? And how'd they get all the way over here from Asia?"

"They've been reported throughout much the world for more than two hundred years. You've heard of the Yeti? As for how they got over here, the theory is they crossed the Bering Strait land bridge, same as the Indians. Which is a pretty amazing feat, because no primate other than Man has been known to dominate as wide a range as this animal," Kodiak said.

Cyrena said, "I think you mentioned in your book several eye-witness accounts by American soldiers of large, bipedal apes spotted in Vietnam during the war over there."

"I still don't see how they managed to evade detection after all these years." Mildred pounded her fist on the table to emphasize her point.

"Nobody's looking. Not really. The plain truth is, the people best qualified to lead a legitimate investigation just aren't interested. They simply refuse to believe it exists. Don't get me wrong, there are legitimate scientists involved in some of these investigations, but their fields of endeavor usually have little, if anything to do with zoology. They're also in serious danger of censure from their peers in the scientific community. Of course, the best evidence regarding footprints and the animal seen in the Roger Patterson film has come from the dissenting voices of physical anthropologists from Russia, England, and the United States. But they're dumped in the same boat as the rest of us who are scrambling around, trying to figure this mystery out."

Mildred smirked. "I heard that film is a hoax..."

"A lot of people have heard that," Kodiak said. "And not many of those people know the facts behind that film.

"In the Fall of 1967, Roger Patterson and Bob Gimlin, from Yakima, Washington, encountered a large, female Sasquatch at a place called Bluff Creek, in Northern California. She was standing near the water's edge, and when she spotted the riders on horseback, she walked away from them at a brisk, but not panicked, pace.

"Patterson and Gimlin were searching that area for evidence of the Sasquatch for a documentary film Patterson was going to make. Sightings and evidence of huge footprints had been frequent around the Bluff Creek area for years. They still are. Anyway, when their horses saw the animal, Patterson was thrown from his saddle and had to scramble to get his sixteen millimeter camera out of the saddle bag before the creature got away. That's why the first several seconds of the film are so badly jarred – Patterson was running across the rocky ground trying to catch up with it.

"When the Sasquatch turned and glared at him, Patterson knew it was probably a good idea to stop, so he knelt down on one knee and continued filming. That's where you get the clearest shot of the animal. The whole thing lasted about fifty seconds before she disappeared among the trees in the background.

"Now, the reason so many people wrote the film off as a hoax is because the animal on the film walks upright like a human being, so it was purported to be a man in a costume. But that is the *anomaly*! Anthropoid apes, the gorilla, chimpanzee and the orangutan are all quadrupeds. The biomechanics of this animal's stride would indicate that its resemblance to a human gait is only superficial."

Mildred said, "You said the Sasquatch is a female. How do you know that?"

"She had breasts," Kodiak answered. "Large, pendulous breasts. The problem skeptics seem to have with this is that the Sasquatch's breasts were covered with fur, not something seen on 'real' apes. She also had a prominent sagittal crest on the top of her head, something that is commonly seen on gorillas – male gorillas.

"But we are talking about a species of ape heretofore unknown. None of the great apes look exactly alike. Chimps don't look like gorillas, gorillas don't look like orangutans. The idea that the breasts are covered with fur could be a logical adaptation, considering the cold climate in which these animals dwell. Besides, there is one other primate known to have developed chest hair: Man.

"Also, a sagittal crest is not a form of sexual dimorphism. That's where the jaw muscles attach to the skull. In gorillas the sagittal crest is more prominent in males because males have heavier mandibles than females. The creature in the Patterson film is much larger than even a male mountain gorilla. So a female of this species would have a tremendous mandible, requiring a high sagittal crest. The two female *Gigantopithecus* jawbones that have been found bear this out.

"Based on the fourteen-inch footprints that were cast at the time of the encounter, the Sasquatch was estimated to be six feet, six inches tall and weighing roughly five hundred pounds – that's a conservative estimate. The animal's height was determined by comparing its foot length to the foot-to-height ratio seen on the film, indicating that this animal had shoulders three feet across." Kodiak stood up. "I am six feet tall. No human being standing six feet tall has shoulders three feet wide. Their arms just couldn't fit into the costume."

"I know I said I don't want them to catch this one," Mildred said, "but isn't it likely that someday, somebody's going to catch one? And won't there be some benefit to mankind in the long run?"

Kodiak shook his head. "I'd be an idiot to think a capture isn't inevitable. Someday. But I don't want to go down in history as the guy who handed over the first sacrifice. And as far as there being any benefit to mankind, that argument just doesn't float. We already know there's very little benefit, certainly not enough in my opinion, to justify the current animal medical research that goes on. That leaves straight vivisection for a complete anatomical study of the animal, which offers nothing, and a big draw at the zoo.

"Pittman's very sharp to keep this whole thing on the Q.T. If and when the Sasquatch is proven to be a reality, the first thing that will happen is it will be labelled an endangered species. The species will have to be studied in-depth in order to determine the numbers in existence, and when you consider how difficult even sighting one of these animals can be, the process can take years. In the meantime, all logging will cease. All encroachment into the wilderness will cease. This includes building of roads, homes, et cetera. We're talking at least in the United States, but more than likely that will include all of North America. If you recall how protecting the Spotted Owl affected logging, just think about the impact this will have on the economy. And believe me, there are interested parties going to great lengths to monitor this situation. The more ridiculous they can make the whole Sasquatch business look, the less likely qualified scientists would be willing to risk their academic necks.

"Your mysterious visitors were probably affiliated with the timber mills. Emory Pittman has extensive financial interests in the lumber industry, which is why they'd be willing to cooperate with his little venture here. There's no conflict of interest.

"My personal feeling is the best thing for all parties concerned is to leave the damned things alone. Let people come out to the woods and observe them like Peter Byrne is trying to do. Or like Jane Goodall and Dian Fossey did with chimps and gorillas."

"I agree," Mildred said, "but that still doesn't explain how they managed to evade detection for so long."

"*Gigantopithecus* was actively hunted by *Homo erectus*, an early species of man that also took up residence in Asia. In order to have survived, these animals would have to know that Man is an enemy. And the evidence gathered so far indicates that the Sasquatch goes to considerable lengths to avoid any contact with human beings. Most of the sightings are by accident."

"It's just so amazing. I came so close to touching it, and I didn't feel the least bit threatened. Now, the animal I saw looked like an ape, but if it walks upright, and has human-shaped feet, doesn't that mean it's part human?" Mildred asked.

"Not at all. There is already a precedent for a bipedal species of anthropoid ape. *Oreopithecus* was an animal that existed in the Miocene epoch of Tuscany some fourteen million years ago and is known to have been fully bipedal, although its feet were widespread, with long, splayed toes. It was only the size of a chimp and wasn't capable of the strides the Sasquatch and Yeti are reported to have.

"As for the human-shaped feet, the truth is that contemporary apes, gorillas, chimps, and orangutans actually evolved their prehensile feet from the feet of primitive apes that were very much like our own. The footprints actually strengthen the case for a primitive species of ape."

❧

Norm was getting bored, and lying prone on the roof of Mildred's garage was uncomfortable. He had no idea how long he'd been up here, but it seemed like hours. He continued to pan the perimeter of the yard through his rifle scope for any sign of the Sasquatch. In his heart he wasn't really sure he could believe this animal was just going to come walking out of the woods and into their rifle sights.

Montagna was hunkered behind the same row of shrubs Mildred had hidden behind the last two times she saw the creature, and he was scared to death. The plan had been for Kodiak to be outside, while Montagna directed the hunt from inside the house – where it was safe. But that damned Kodiak assaulted him today, and blew everything to hell.

At least Kodiak had taken him into the woods, out of sight so nobody could see him on the ground, sitting in the ants, hoping he wouldn't have to defend himself against Kodiak. But maybe that's why Kodiak took him out there; so nobody would be around in case Montagna kicked his ass.

He felt nauseous, like he was going to vomit. He chose this spot because it had the quickest access to the safety of the house should the animal show up and turn out to be violently aggressive. What was worse, even that old lady, who was totally alone, wasn't afraid of it. He hated himself.

Montagna looked around again. His bowels cramped, and he was sweating. He didn't know what he would do if the Sasquatch suddenly showed up. Probably throw up on it.

Dave had the best view of all, nearly three hundred and sixty degrees, but every time another flash of heat lightning erupted across the sky he shuddered, feeling dangerously exposed atop the telephone pole. Montagna told him that he would be safe. He also made it very clear what would happen if Dave came down from his assigned post against orders. It would make getting struck by lightning seem like a vacation in Bermuda by comparison.

On the hill above the back of the house Ben kept his vigil with the nightvision goggles on his head. Whenever the lightning flashed he was blinded by green phosphorus, and the static it caused on the radio headset hurt his ears.

He thought about the possibility of actually seeing a living, breathing Sasquatch. For years – hell, the past twenty-three years – he trekked the woods of the Pacific Northwest, hoping and sometimes praying that he'd see one.

Then it became an obsession; every shadow, every hulking tree trunk had his pulse pounding, his eyes bugging with the thrill, the hope...

The worst part was the dreams. He had Sasquatch dreams. Ben would be lurking in the woods and suddenly, to his immediate left, no more than five feet from him, stood his quarry. It was always turned away from him, and he'd hear his subconscious mind urging him to see the face... You've got to see the face! He always woke up before seeing the face, feeling disappointed that it was just another dream.

After all these years of frustration and disappointment, he finally became capable of remaining objective about the search, but never doubtful. He knew this was probably his best shot at finally seeing the animal, seeing that elusive face. Deep down inside, Ben was praying: Please, God...

Half a mile away the horses and the llamas were becoming skittish. The lightning frightened them, but there was something else; an animal presence they could sense nearby that scared them even more.

The juvenile Sasquatch had been watching the horses almost since they were first tied down in the clearing. It was on its way to Mildred's place when it got distracted by the scent of these new animals and, remaining hidden, it observed them for over an hour. Its curiosity finally got the better of it, and it came down to the clearing for a closer look.

The horses snorted and tried to rear up to fend it off as it walked towards them, and some of the llamas tried to chew through the cable while others made plaintive bleating sounds. Their aggressive manner gave it pause, and it walked around them, maintaining a safe distance. It meant these animals no harm. Indeed, the Sasquatch was not nearly big enough to do more than frighten them by its mere presence. It had seen larger members of its species go after other animals, most often livestock, especially chickens, but sometimes pigs, or even the occasional cow. Dogs were a nuisance. If there were any natural enemies of the Sasquatch, it would be the canine variety. Dogs always reacted to their presence with fear, out of which they would either respond with hysterical barking, or outright aggression. In the few cases where a dog was known to have tangled with a Sasquatch, the outcome was gruesomely predictable.

ेॐ

"My husband, Steve, was a ranger. We came here thirty-seven years ago. My God, we loved these woods. I still do. I just don't know how much longer they'll be around. Just prior to our having come here, the Park Service had ended sixteen years of logging inside the park. They sacrificed well over one hundred million board feet of virgin, primeval forest to the lumber mills."

Kodiak nodded, then said, "The National Parks Association was against this park from its inception. They even tried to get President Roosevelt to veto the whole thing. The Park Service was big on preservation rhetoric, but when it came to down to brass tacks, they were AWOL.

"But we also have to remember who's at the root of all this. The timber industry's always had the Forest and Park Services in its back pocket. Through greed and avarice, they chose the people they wanted in all the decision-making positions. As is usually the case in this country, it took the people banding together to finally get the Olympic National Monument turned into a National Park. After the park became a reality, there was a public poll taken that showed Americans were disgusted with the lumber industry and the mindless greed that perpetuated their misguided belief that they were somehow entitled to these forests to do with as they pleased."

The conversation was warm and amicable. The like-minded threesome were bonding through underlying sincerity and common cause. Mildred had grown comfortable with Kodiak and Cyrena, and she was glad they were with her. She felt safer.

Cyrena shook her head, her brow furrowed in frustration. "Andy Paul had mentioned this. He also said something about danger trees..."

Mildred said, "That was a line of twaddle spewed out by the Park Service to accommodate their rape-in-progress. There was a clause in the Park Service act of 1916 which basically stated that any trees designated as 'danger trees' were eligible for logging. These so-called danger trees were listed as trees that were damaged by insect infestation, infection, or windthrow. You could not possibly imagine how many trees were suddenly discovered to have been suffering from insect damage!" Mildred laughed, but the vehemence in her voice made it more of a scoff.

"A favorite of Steve's was windthrow. Any trees that were subject to windthrow were fair game for the loggers. Of course, when you clear-cut an area, the surrounding trees suddenly become exposed to windthrow, so they got axed, too."

Kodiak said, "We should be careful not to give the loggers themselves too bad a rap here. The Lumber and Sawmill Workers Union were very much in favor of saving the forests of the Olympic Peninsula."

Cyrena got up and took Mildred's cup. "Let me get you some more tea, Mildred."

ॐ

The air turned more than a little cool, and Ben wrapped his jacket around himself for warmth. He looked at his watch. It was eleven-thirty. They had only been out here for an hour and a half, but it seemed like several hours.

Montagna's voice sounded as bored and tired over the radio as Ben felt. "How's everyone holding up? Ben?"

"Not a problem. All clear from my point of view. Over."

"Good. Dave?"

Ben looked across the roof of the house at Dave, who looked like an abnormal blob on top of the telephone pole. He moved a little, and Ben saw the barrel of his rifle. Dave answered Montagna,

"Nothing yet. Over."

"Norm?"

"I'm peeing."

Ben looked at Norm, who was standing on the roof of the garage and urinating on the ground.

Montagna protested, "Norm, you could be messing everything up! Get back down!"

"Wait for the shake... There." Old Norm zipped up his trousers and laid back down on the roof. "Sorry, Jamie, but some things just won't wait." He bellowed his hack-laugh that made everyone else who heard it want to gag.

Montagna was kneeling down with his head bowed between his legs. There was no question he was going to be sick. All that remained to be seen was from which end he would let go first. This was no different from what had happened in Libya and then Iraq. And it was in Russia that he and his two partners were captured by government secret police, who were really Russian Mafia, and in a bid for his own freedom, he sold out his friends and agreed to watch as they were horribly tortured. Maybe he was something of a coward, but he had one of the highest success rates of anybody in his field. Cowardice could be a tool, too.

That turd Kodiak must have known this. Pittman told him, so Kodiak made sure Montagna was left outside – with the Sasquatch. Montagna knew Kodiak was just as scared of that thing as he was, but Montagna wasn't going to crack.

The truth of the matter was he liked – or at least admired – Kodiak. He saw things in Kodiak that he liked to think existed within himself. Mainly, leadership skills and the ability to win people's respect through his actions. But Kodiak was also a threat. A serious threat to Montagna's leadership. And this would not be tolerated.

He swallowed the bile back down and took the tranquilizer dart from his rifle. It was time to show everyone what a phoney Kodiak really was.

᠎⁊

Kodiak finished his tea and shook his head when Mildred offered another cup. Cyrena was captivated by the history of

Olympic National Park and listened intently.

"In 1947 a watchdog group called the Olympic Associates had to be formed to protect the park from the Park Service," Mildred said, sighing at all the depressing memories this conversation had dredged up for her. "Of course, the Park Service toadies still found a way to get the trees out. They sent trail crews deep into the back country, where they'd log trees well out of sight of anyone who might do something about it. Then they'd simply roll the logs into the rivers, where they'd end up at the Crown Zellerbach Dam and be loaded onto the trucks and shipped to the mills. It either didn't occur to these jackasses, or probably they didn't care, that these logs were destroying the spawning beds of the fish indigenous to the rivers.

"Steve once told me about a boyscout troop that had come upon one of the clandestine logging sites at the North Fork Campground. They sent a letter of protest to the Park Service Director with pictures of the perfectly healthy trees being cut down on park land. They were naturally unaware of his complicity, and were stunned when they got a reply that stated the usual nonsense about windthrow, fire danger, and insects.

"Well, these boys were so incensed by this, they sent a sarcastic response that stated how they could not imagine how these pristine forests could have managed to survive all these millennia with so many wild animals and malevolent insects around to destroy them."

They laughed at this, then Mildred continued. "But that's not the best part. At the park Visitor Center in Port Angeles, there's an exhibit depicting life in a logging camp. And wouldn't you know, those damn fools built it out of wood logged from the park!"

The front door suddenly opened, and Montagna walked in. "Kodiak, catch!" He tossed something across the room and Kodiak caught it out of reflex. It was the tranquilizer dart, and the tip cut the inside of his middle finger.

Montagna smiled. "You should be more careful. That's filled with Etorphine."

Kodiak's heart skipped a beat and his throat caught. Etorphine was a powerful tranquilizer used on elephants, and it was deadly to humans. People had died by merely scratching themselves with a needle that touched this drug.

Where Legends Live

From his place on the hill, Ben could see everything that was going on inside the house. Montagna had tossed something to Kodiak, making Kodiak face off with him. Ben's blood turned cold when he saw the look on Kodiak's face. "I knew it!" He got up and ran for the house, praying he got there before somebody got killed.

Inside the house tension reached critical mass. Cyrena and Mildred stood in the dining room with no idea what to do. Even Ruth lay awake in front of the fireplace, watching.

Kodiak stood still, waiting for something to happen. Etorphine was deadly, but he had no idea how long it took to work. Was he going to suddenly drop dead right where he stood, or would he have time to grab Montagna and break his neck?

Montagna was smiling, and after a minute he said, "You can relax. It's just Ketamine."

Kodiak grunted something and charged at him, just as Ben rushed in and blindsided Montagna, knocking him headlong into the china cabinet. The glass shattered, and the ceramic figurines were all smashed upon the floor.

Kodiak dove into Ben and grabbed him by the shirt, thinking he was Montagna. Ben screamed, "No!" and put up his hands in defense. Kodiak quickly recognized him and held his punch.

When all the commotion broke in the living room and that fool Montagna was thrown into the cabinet, Ruth made her move on the cat. The cat couldn't find a way out of the house, so it fled upstairs, and Ruth followed. There were two bedrooms on the second floor and a bathroom at the end of the hall. Only one bedroom door was open, so that had to be where the cat had gone. Ruth crept to a linen closet and took out a pillow case. She carried it in one hand, drew the large Bowie knife from her belt with the other and wound her way into the bedroom.

She didn't need to turn on the light; her rattlesnake eyes were well accustomed to the dark. The room was simple in its set-up; a queen-size bed was positioned against the far corner under the window, with a nightstand beside it that had a telephone and bottles of prescription medicines on top. There was a chest of drawers directly across from the bed, and the room was all very neat and tidy, like a display in a furniture store.

The cat was under the bed. Ruth didn't have to see an animal to know its whereabouts. This was a special talent of which she often made grisly use, and the reason she was brought along on this trip. If necessary, she would be their homing device to track the Sasquatch through the woods.

The old hag cackled to herself as she went over to the bed and got down on the floor, the arthritic pain that plagued her back and legs gone – blocked out by her bloodlust.

The cat was backed into the corner. It hissed and growled at Ruth as she wriggled under the bed to get at it. The cat screamed and Ruth swung wide with the knife, trying to force the cat out of its corner. She felt the blade graze against the fleshy part of the cat's haunch as it hissed and howled in pain.

Ruth worked her way farther under the bed, groaning with the effort.

ह।

As Montagna lifted himself out of the rubble of the china cabinet, his feet slipped from under him. He instinctively put his hands out to catch himself, only to feel fragments of broken glass cut into his palms.

Kodiak grabbed Montagna and hoisted him up. He was about to smash him in the face when Ben intervened again. "Don't, George!"

"Come on, Kodiak..." Montagna spat blood from his cut lip and glared at Kodiak, ready for a fight.

"Shut up, Jamie." Ben got between them, facing Kodiak. He kept his hand pressed against Montagna just in case he had to take action to separate them again. "George, listen to me. This is completely out of hand. I don't know what happened in here, but I saw it coming. And I'll be damned if – "

"Forget it, Ben. This guy's got it coming. And if I haven't worked everything out of my system, then maybe I'll just mosey on up to the roof and go a couple rounds with old Norm..."

Cyrena and Mildred watched from the dining room. Finally Cyrena just shrugged in disgust and said, "I can't just stand around. I'll help you get this mess cleaned up, Mildred." They started for the overturned cabinet.

Montagna stopped them. "Just stay put," he ordered.

Kodiak gave him an icy glare and took a step toward him. "You want to finish what you started?"

Intimidated, Montagna stepped aside. "Get this mess cleaned up."

❧

Ruth got within grabbing distance of the cat. The cat hissed and clawed at her, but the pain in her hand only seemed to excite the vile hag. After several minutes of this game of cat and mouse (with the tables turned inexorably on the cat), Ruth grabbed its tail.

The cat sank its claws into her leathery hand and bit as hard as it could. Ruth screeched, and to get the damned cat off of her arm, she severed its tail with her knife.

The cat ran from the room, screaming and trailing blood across the hardwood floor.

Ruth grumbled some animal sound of frustration and spat, backing out from under the bed, holding the knife and the cat's tail in one hand. She didn't see Mildred. She only heard her suddenly screaming, "I'll kill you!" and was struck upside her head with the bristle-end of a broom. Ruth fell to the floor, dropping the knife and the tail. Everything was spinning as she felt around the floor to push herself back up, but Mildred hit her again, this time with the broom handle, and Ruth screamed out of fear and pain.

Mildred was livid, driven by the blind, hysterical rage of a protective mother. She had heard the cat's shriek when she was downstairs sweeping the broken glass, and ran upstairs to investigate. As she came up to the second floor hallway, the cat, minus its tail, fled past her. "I'll kill you! I'll kill you!" Mildred kept screaming the words, as though they would add to the full impact of her fury.

Ruth scrambled to her knees and grabbed the knife, and as an added insult, she made a special effort to get the tail and shove it into her shirt pocket before standing up. After the initial shock of the attack, the power of Mildred's blows diminished in intensity. This gave Ruth anchor to turn on Mildred and raise the knife.

The sight of the knife startled Mildred, and she hesitated from the shock. But when Ruth lunged at her, she instinctively thrust the broom handle into Ruth's gut, forcing the hag to double over and spit her dentures onto the floor. Mildred raised the broom over her head, but Ruth body-slammed her. They both dropped their weapons and rolled about, interlocked, on the floor.

Mildred tore off Ruth's bandanna, revealing her near-baldness. The part in her hair was abnormally wide, like a reverse widow's peak. Ruth grabbed Mildred's hair and banged her head repeatedly against the floor.

Kodiak, Montagna, Ben and Cyrena heard the ruckus and ran upstairs. When they got to the open bedroom door and saw the two old women wrestling on the floor with all the strength of two third-grade boys, Montagna began laughing hysterically. Kodiak and Cyrena rushed into the room and broke up the fight, a feat not easily done, because the two women wanted to kill each other in the worst way. Kodiak lifted Ruth off of Mildred. Cyrena helped Mildred to her feet, holding her back from going for Ruth's throat.

Kodiak shouted, "Knock it off!" The tone of his voice even made Montagna stop laughing. Kodiak's face was an expression of shock that almost looked comical, even though he saw no humor in what was happening. "What is going on in here?"

Mildred was crying. While Cyrena restrained her, she screamed, "She cut off my cat's tail!"

They all looked at Ruth, who's cold glare made everyone, except Mildred, unable to look her in the eyes.

"Is that true?" Kodiak didn't know what kind of answer to expect, but he was more concerned about letting this animal-woman loose than anything the old hag might say.

"It's in her shirt pocket!" Mildred screamed.

Ruth, pinned within Kodiak's arms, just growled.

Kodiak looked at Ruth's shirt and saw a spot of fresh blood on the pocket, but he couldn't see inside it. If he reached in, Ruth could wrench free, and he didn't want to deal with that. "Ben...?"

Ben stood in the doorway, his face stunned white from shock. He glanced at Kodiak, then shook his head slowly as he looked back at Ruth. He looked like he was going to be sick.

Kodiak said, "Cyrena, would you...?" He gestured to the shirt pocket with his eyes.

Cyrena hesitated.

Mildred hissed through her clenched teeth, "Let me..." Cyrena knew she couldn't let Mildred go, or she'd go right for Ruth's eyes. "I can't..."

"What a bunch of wimps." Montagna laughed as he picked up the broom and placed it against a wall. "I believe this belongs to Mama." Then he knelt down and picked up Ruth's knife. He debated picking up her teeth, then thought better of it. He stood in front of her, and she watched him with a baleful glare, the way a wild animal looks at its enemy. Montagna lost his smile and reached into her pocket. He lifted out the cat's wriggling tail and dangled it in Kodiak's face. "The prosecution rests." Montagna dropped the tail on the floor.

Mildred let out a heartwrenching sob.

"Jamie! Jamie!" Norm was calling over the radio earphones that were hanging around both Ben's and Montagna's necks. "Jamie! Can you hear me? I see it! *I can see it!*"

Everyone stopped and looked through the bedroom window at the dark woods. Somewhere outside, beyond where they could see, the Sasquatch had returned and Norm spotted it. Montagna pushed past Kodiak and Ben and walked to the door, putting the radio headset back on. "Where, Norm?"

Norm was still on his belly, lying on the garage roof, looking at a spot in the woods through his rifle scope. All he could see was one leg and part of the foot, but there was no mistaking what it was. "If he steps out a little further, I can let him have it."

"Just take it easy," Montagna said. "Dave, can you see it?"

Dave was closer to the woods, literally with a bird's eye view. He was also looking through his rifle scope, but couldn't find it. "No!"

Inside the house everyone was watching Montagna as he spoke to the two outside. He ordered Dave, "Lower your voice. Now listen, both of you. Just lay low and let him come into the yard. *Don't jump the gun.* I want at least two guns on him." He took off his headset and complained, "I can't believe it finally shows up, and all I got are those two dumb-asses out there!"

Ben was caught up in the heat of the moment. "Maybe we can sneak out back and flush it into the yard?"

Montagna retorted, "You can flush that idea."

&

The animal could sense something was different from the previous nights it had come here. Mildred's place was the first human habitation it had encountered after having traveled hundreds of miles from its home canyon, and although it was curious, it was still cautious. When it had finally come down from the hills, it had watched her feed the cat in her front yard, and so became interested in the food.

When Mildred had become aware of it, she had offered it food, and so it had become less wary – at least enough to keep coming back to see what else might be offered.

It would have been here earlier this evening, but it was distracted by the pack animals, and it felt compelled to investigate them. After satisfying its curiosity there, it headed for Mildred's place.

There were other humans here tonight. There was a man on the roof, another on top of the telephone pole, and another who had gotten up from behind the bushes and gone into the house. After a brief period, a fourth man came running from the back of the house and also went inside. There were some loud noises, and the creature hesitated. Its instincts urged it to run, but its curiosity and prior contact with Mildred had bastardized its senses. So it chose to stay and see what was happening.

&

Dave was sweating and trying to keep his hands from shaking. He still couldn't see the animal. The scope's field of vision was frustratingly narrow. He lowered the rifle and tried to see with his naked eye, but he could only make out the fringe of the trees caught in the glow of the front porch light. He spoke into his radio, "Norm, I can't see anything. You have him in your sights?"

Norm spat. "Just his foot, kid. I'm real tempted to go ahead and see if I can't stick him, anyway."

Montagna cut in, "Forget it. If we blow this when we're so close..."

Downstairs Montagna was pacing around, trying to decide the next move. He was inwardly grateful to be inside, and wondered just how close that thing was to where he had been hiding only ten minutes before. The thought made him shudder, and he felt nauseous again. So far, nobody seemed aware of his fear, but he felt a panicky need to save face. Especially in front of Kodiak, who he knew was just itching to take everything over. But he didn't dare go outside himself and risk screwing things up. He said, "All right, Ben. Go out through the back and creep around to the front of the house. Do not go beyond the front corner. I want you to wear the goggles and wait until you actually see it. You're going to direct the assault. If we blow this and it takes off, run after it!"

Ben's eyes were wide with excitement. He was nodding anxiously, waiting for Montagna to finish so he could get out there. "I'm going."

Kodiak was surprised Montagna was sending Ben out. Montagna had gone to such efforts to exclude Kodiak from actively participating in the hunt, it seemed odd that he would so willingly give Ben the driver's seat at this critical juncture.

Something suddenly occurred to Montagna. "Ben, here..." He tossed Ben his air rifle. "You may have the best shot."

Ben nodded again and went out the back door through the kitchen.

Montagna went into the dining room and spoke into the radio. "Norm, Ben's coming out. Don't go mistaking him for another Sasquatch and shoot him in the ass."

"Up yours." Norm was tired of Montagna and his snotty, condescending attitude. His right eye was getting tired, and the scope even drifted off target a couple times. When it did, he had a hell of a time relocating the foot. There's gotta be some way to draw this thing out, he thought. But even Norm knew that if he fired at it and missed – which was more than likely – the animal might take off for good.

He looked down and saw Ben standing at the corner of the

garage. "Just follow the direction of my rifle barrel, and you should spot him."

Ben waved acknowledgement and looked in the indicated direction. At first everything was just a tangled mass of tree branches and foliage. But the goggles didn't magnify things the way the rifle scopes did, so he had a better field of vision. He spotted the Sasquatch standing between two trees. He gasped.

Norm heard him and let out a short laugh. "He's something, ain't he, Tyler?"

Ben was frozen with amazement. It almost looked like a man in a sophisticated gorilla suit, except there was a subtlety to it that could not be faked. It was in the way its eyes scanned the area around it, its mouth slightly agape, its tongue rubbing against its lower teeth out of nervous contemplation. Ben forgot he had the rifle.

Montagna sat at the dining room table, listening. Nothing more was said after the last time Norm spoke. "Ben, what's going on? Do you see it?"

A long pause, then, "God, yes..."

"And?"

"It's real." Ben let out a loose giggle. *"It's real, Jamie!"*

Montagna rubbed his face. In the excitement of the moment he forgot that his hands were cut, and he smeared blood over his nose and cheek. "I know it's real, Ben. Emory Pittman knows it's real, too. Are you in a position to shoot it?"

Ben suddenly remembered the air rifle and hoisted it into position against his shoulder. He lifted the nightvision goggles and sighted the Sasquatch through the rifle scope. It was easily within range, and he lined its torso up in the cross-hairs. Then he thought about what Kodiak had said before about Jamie and Norm looking to exploit this creature. He could deliberately miss, but then Jamie and Norm would probably beat the hell out of him. Ben wasn't afraid of them. Not Norm, anyway.

"Do it, Ben..."

Mildred was in the kitchen with Cyrena. She felt trapped by Montagna, Norm, and that disgusting hag, Ruth. First that creep

Montagna threatened to break her cat's neck unless she told him the truth about the Sasquatch. Then the old witch went after the cat, cutting off its tail for some sick trophy. Now they were out there, ready to stick the unsuspecting Sasquatch with tranquilizer darts, after which it would be imprisoned in some zoo, or dissected for the sake of scientific research. And she felt so guilty about having lured the hapless animal into this trap. No. This was where she would have to take action.

Mildred said to Cyrena, "Would you excuse me, dear? I have to take out the trash." Mildred went into a closed pantry and took out a fire extinguisher. She pulled the pin and marched into the living room.

Ben placed his sweat-slickened finger on the trigger and took aim at the center of the animal's chest. He started to squeeze...

Ruth was hunkered near the front door. She turned to see the fire extinguisher's nozzle pointed in her face and... *SHHOOOOOOOOMMMMMM!!!!!!* Ruth was knocked through the screen door, stumbling out onto the porch, enveloped in a cloud of white CO_2 powder. Mildred followed her out and let her have it again.

Ben fired the rifle, but because of Mildred's distraction, he missed his target.

The animal felt the surge of air as the dart narrowly missed its head. It took off into the woods.

Montagna jumped up and screamed at Mildred. He came around the table and ran for the door.

Fearing Montagna was going to attack Mildred, Kodiak grabbed the head from a broken ceramic polar bear and followed quickly after him.

On the garage roof old Norm saw what was happening to Ruth. He aimed his air rifle at Mildred's back.

Montagna ran past Mildred and Ruth, shouting, "Run after it, Ben!"

Ben pulled the nightvision goggles back over his eyes and ran after the Sasquatch. He had a pretty good idea in which direction it had gone, but the thing moved like lightning.

Kodiak came out behind Montagna, saw Norm aiming his rifle at Mildred, and hurled the piece of the ceramic polar bear at him. It smashed into Norm's head, shattering with a loud *CRACK!* Norm dropped on top of the roof. Kodiak didn't know if he was knocked out, and he didn't care.

Cyrena rushed out behind Kodiak, and for the second time that night, they pulled Mildred off of Ruth.

On the telephone pole Dave saw the Sasquatch break from its place among the trees and run for the woods. He drew a sight on it with his rifle and squeezed the trigger just as something huge and black entered into his scope's field of vision. To his horror, Ben let out a sudden yelp, and when Dave looked down, he saw Ben fall to the ground. The Sasquatch kept running.

All Dave could think about was how Montagna had told Norm not to go mistaking Ben for the Sasquatch, and that's exactly what he just did. Dave, shaking, clambered down the telephone pole.

A fog had come in, cutting visibility considerably when Montagna reached Dave, who was on the verge of panic. "Jamie... it's Ben... He's hurt."

Montagna flushed with anger. He had to force himself to keep from slapping Dave. "Now what?"

Dave started to catch his breath and said, "I... I shot him."

Montagna debated going after the Sasquatch. Between the fog, the moonless night, and half the team being incapacitated, he thought better of it. Besides, the Sasquatch was a night creature, and this was its turf. If it was aggressive, it would easily have the advantage over them in an attack. He thought he heard Kodiak say, "Don't forget, you're also a coward," but when he turned, no one was there. He realized that he was hearing things.

Kodiak called to them from somewhere toward the north, and Montagna and Dave followed the sound of his voice. They could see the beam of a flashlight in a small clearing directly ahead. Kodiak was kneeling down beside the unconscious Ben, holding the tranquilizer dart that struck Ben's leg.

Cyrena helped Mildred catch her cat, which had taken refuge

under the couch in the living room. It had lost a great deal of blood, so it was fairly easy to handle when they finally caught it. Mildred wrapped the cat in a towel to disable it from clawing her. Cyrena loaded Mildred and her cat into Ben's jeep for the drive to the veterinarian back in Red Fern. At the very least, it was an excuse to get away from this place for a few hours.

On the front porch Norm used a dish towel to beat the CO_2 dust off of Ruth, while holding a cold can of beer to the bruise on his head.

❧

By six-thirty the next morning Ben had slept fitfully for hours. He felt a little sick after first waking up, but as the effects of the Ketamine wore off he felt good enough to get some food down and prepare for the trek into the woods. Dave professed sorrow for what happened, and Ben forgave him. He said he understood how, in all the excitement, such an accident could happen. Still, he couldn't shake the feeling of malevolence he had experienced last night as Dave stared down at him from the telephone pole.

Everyone got into Norm's wagon and left to get the horses. Kodiak decided to stay behind and wait for Cyrena to come back from the vet.

An hour later Cyrena and Mildred pulled up in Ben's jeep. They were both exhausted from the long drive. The cat had to be left with the vet for observation.

The house looked even worse in the light of day than it did the previous night. The cat's spewed blood had dried on the floor, and the cabinet was ruined; the glass was broken and the intricate woodwork had been smashed to pieces. Mildred sounded defeated. "I think I'm going to be sick."

Cyrena put a comforting arm around her and helped her to the couch.

"I hate those horrible people. Those pigs."

Kodiak and Cyrena both felt like dirt and wanted to leave out of shame.

Mildred looked at Kodiak with red, bleary eyes. "I guess I'm lucky they didn't kill me when I ruined their attempt to catch it."

Kodiak said, "I wouldn't have let them touch you."

Mildred smiled. "They've gone after it, haven't they?"

Kodiak said, "Yeah."

"I would never wish for you to be alone with them, but... do you think you can stop them?" Mildred implored him.

Kodiak said, "Yeah, I can stop them."

"Besides," Cyrena said, "he won't be alone."

Kodiak turned to Cyrena and said, "Like hell."

Having been a school teacher much of her adult life, Cyrena was not prone to giving in. "You can't rely on Dave, and even with Ben you'd be outnumbered."

Kodiak said, "Which is exactly why you're staying here. Look, I didn't realize just how dangerous Jamie Montagna is."

"He's right." Mildred said to Cyrena. "Those men are evil. And that old woman..." She shuddered.

"It'll be a few days before they know for sure if they're gonna catch that animal. If they don't, they're likely to swing back this way to take their frustrations out on Mildred. I'd feel a whole lot better if you and she went into Red Fern and stayed close to the ranger station."

Cyrena leaned toward Mildred. "Do you have a friend who can drive you into town?"

Kodiak said, "Of course she does. You."

Cyrena turned to Kodiak. "You have two choices. You can stay here with us and let them go their merry way. Or you can go after them with me at your side."

"You forgot door number three. I'm going alone."

"So, you'll go after them while I wait here, wondering if you're in trouble? What about Ben? He's my friend, too, and I'm not going to sit back and let him be victimized by those slobs. No, George. There is no door number three."

⁊▲

Two horses were left at the clearing when Kodiak pulled Ben's jeep alongside Norm's wagon. Cyrena untethered the horses, and they mounted up. Kodiak hadn't said much to Cyrena since they left Mildred's house. She was adamant about joining him, and while he was extremely concerned about her safety, he was secretly glad to have her company. Mildred had agreed to go to Red Fern. She didn't believe Montagna and the others would come back, but she didn't want to be on the receiving end of such a surprise.

Kodiak looked at the fresh hoofprints that covered the ground, and on the opposite side of the road they found the medium-sized footprints left by the Sasquatch. "Looks like he's been through here. They'll be following his path," he said.

The way the tracks were laid, it appeared that the creature had come back to the horses and llamas after the incident at Mildred's before proceeding into the canyon.

Cyrena said, "He seems awfully curious, when you consider how cautious these animals usually are."

Kodiak nodded. "That's what worries me." He turned his horse in the direction of the footprints, and they followed the mixed tracks of the Sasquatch and the other horses into the woods of Olympic National Park.

❧

The going was much slower than Montagna had anticipated, and his patience was wearing thin. The ground cover was thick with ferns three feet high that were so dense along the route they were traveling they only made three-quarters of a mile in two hours. Another problem was Ruth. She was leading the pack, following the Sasquatch's path through some animal sixth-sense that took them off the main trail and slowed their progress considerably. She would ride ahead about a hundred feet, stop, dismount her horse and spend the next ten minutes scrutinizing some minuscule detail among the plants or on the ground that would probably evade even the most experienced bloodhound.

But he had to admit, although her manner was highly peculiar, she had a talent for uncovering evidence of the creature's passing that he and Norm – who were both experienced trackers – couldn't hold a candle to.

They were traveling under a canopy of three hundred-foot-tall western hemlocks that blocked out the daylight save for a scattering of light shafts that penetrated the forest like swords driven by a magician into a wicker basket. They were insignificant as ants in a primeval world virtually unchanged from the dawn of time. A world of greens and browns, daubed with minute patches of red and yellow, orange and blue, all enveloped in an otherworldly mist.

The forest was alive with the cries of birds and the smell of pine that was heavy on the air. Their eyes weren't wide enough to take it all in.

The air at this level was pure, and it managed to clear Ben of the hungover feeling he had been unable to shake off since waking up. His leg still hurt, and there was a severe bruise where the dart had struck him, but he was feeling so good, so alive, that none of the previous night's activities bothered him.

He was still savoring the image of the Sasquatch in his mind. It was real. After more than twenty years of searching, putting up with people and their idiotic jokes and accusations of fakery, he finally saw one. He finally saw the face. And it was a beautiful face. Its skin was gray, lighter than its black fur, although Ben only saw it through green-tinted goggles. Its eyes were the most captivating. They were wide, and held the innocent curiosity of a juvenile animal. He would reflect on the image of that face every day for the rest of his life, even if they never caught up with that animal again.

Dave was sullen and still feeling dejected. He felt that he now must look like a fool in Cyrena's eyes for what he had done to Ben, and he knew everyone else thought he was a loser, too. Nothing about this heaven on earth could ease the badly distorted persecution complex he bore all his life.

※

Kodiak and Cyrena were three miles behind Montagna and the others, but they rode at a leisurely pace, since they were not in any great hurry to catch up with them. Their path was easy enough to follow, as the horses and llamas trampled a passage through the ground ferns and often left their calling cards behind in steaming piles.

Kodiak asked her, "How long have you been a teacher?"

"Eighteen years." Cyrena's mind was on the conversation, but she couldn't take her eyes from the wilderness that not only surrounded, but enveloped them.

Kodiak said, "The world's toughest profession. Some of the greatest loves of my life were teachers. Although they never knew it. Their ignorance of my affections also reflected in my report cards."

She laughed, then said, "It is a tough job. Believe me, we earn these three month vacations. But I wouldn't trade it for anything. I love my students."

"So, how did a nice girl like you get caught up in all this Sasquatch stuff, anyway? You just don't seem the type."

"I saw one of Ben's ads in a Seattle paper about six years ago. I called out of curiosity and managed to get him to give a talk on cryptozoology for my class. They ate up his every word. I have to admit, I was fascinated, too."

Kodiak said, "What got you to join his group?"

"He gave me a copy of your *Hunt for the Living Gigantopithecus*. He called it the bible."

Kodiak shook his head, embarrassed by the overzealous description of his book.

Cyrena continued, "Anyway, I read it and the whole thing seemed entirely plausible. I think it was when you took it out of the realm of being a monster and simply explained that it's a perfectly normal animal that I was sold."

They rode in silence for a short while. Then Cyrena asked, "Why did you leave the Park Service?"

"I didn't care for their schizophrenic policies. On the public side, they talk a good deal about preservation and the like. But behind the scenes, they're motivated by greed.

"I used to work in Yosemite. There was a time it was two separate valleys. After the earthquake that decimated San Francisco in 1906, one of the geniuses that headed the Forest Service made it his personal project to secure a water source in Yosemite National Park by flooding the Hetch Hetchy Valley. Due to that act of supreme stupidity, the public was so outraged that private citizen organizations ultimately got this place established. Because the Park Service tried so hard to sell out these forests, it was one of the most heated and drawn-out battles of all time. And it's been fought over and over for more than fifty years. It wouldn't surprise me in the least if all these old growth forests vanish within our own lifetimes."

After a short, thoughtful silence, Cyrena brought up the subject of their Sasquatch. "So, did you see it last night?"

੨੩

"No, I didn't see it," Montagna was obviously irritated as he rode alongside Dave. They were thirty feet behind Ruth who was leading them up a trail near the top of Tshletshy Ridge. "What did you see?"

Dave shrugged. "I saw something dark. I thought it was the Sasquatch and ended up hitting Ben."

They had been riding for six hours now and had made considerably better time once they cleared the Montane forests of the lower Queets Valley. None of them had slept at all the previous night (except Ben), and the ride was beginning to wear them down. Montagna decided once they were on the opposite side of the ridge they would set up camp beside the first river, lake, or creek that would be adequate for fishing, as well as a source of water for the animals.

Dave was still feeling low, thinking about Cyrena. After she had talked to him the other day he had grown very fond of her, although he wasn't ready to admit being in love. Then she seemed to snub him whenever that damn Kodiak was around. He didn't want to see Norm and Jamie hurt her, but if it came to that, he might take what he felt was his due.

The trees had thinned out along the spine of the ridge. The air was thinner and the sun was hot, draining them of stamina. Ben looked haggard again, having not fully rid himself of the effects of the Ketamine hydrochloride. Ruth popped another pill under her tongue. As they reached the vista, they looked down upon the great canopy of an even bigger rainforest that filled the canyon below like a massive green punchbowl encircled by a giant crown of gray mountains.

જ

"And where in the hell have you been?" Montagna watched Kodiak and Cyrena ride into camp. It was a little past five o'clock, and camp had been set up in a clearing beneath the cover of two gigantic silver firs, just off the Queets River, one hundred feet from a multi-tiered waterfall. There were four igloo tents, and the boxes of supplies were set off to one side, with the most pertinent ones opened up.

Kodiak smiled at Montagna and asked, "What's for supper?"

Montagna was irritable, and his whiney voice made him sound petulant. "Ben, Norm and Dave went fishing. If they don't catch anything, then it's powdered chili and peanut butter sandwiches."

Dave was in better spirits after they set up camp, and hiked half a mile upstream with Ben and Norm, where they found a deep pool that had been dammed off by some beavers. They saw several good-sized trout swimming in the crystal water.

Ben filled his canteen and after capping it off, got down on his belly and started drinking with deep, wonderful gulps. He was suddenly distracted by Dave's and Norm's laughter, and when he looked upstream he saw Norm standing on a large boulder, urinating into the river.

They caught plenty of fish, so much so that everyone could eat their fill. Ben fried it up, and everyone just helped themselves as it came off the pan.

Earlier that evening Ruth had taken off on her own and returned with the carcass of some poor animal she tracked down and clubbed to death. The thing was unrecognizable after she butchered it and shoved it onto a spit over the fire. It looked so grotesque, that nobody was interested in asking her to share.

After dinner the sleeping assignments were passed out. Montagna announced that Cyrena would share a tent with him, and after the obligatory laughter, he admitted that he was kidding. He would share a tent with Dave. Ben would share with Kodiak, and Norm would share with Ruth (since nobody else could actually manage to sleep in her company). Cyrena would have a tent all to herself, and everyone accepted this arrangement.

Kodiak and Montagna were standing beside the fire looking at the scraps of food on the ground: fish bones, scatterings of the Hostess cupcakes they had for dessert, and what was left of the thing Ruth ate. "Don't you think we should get some of this stuff cleaned up? It may attract bears," Kodiak said.

"Yeah, it might. And it might also attract our elusive friend. And right now, that's all we have to hope for, because until he shows up, we're screwed," Montagna stated.

"That animal's long gone, Montagna."

"Not according to Ruth. And Norm swears by her. He says she can smell a rat's fart from twenty miles away."

"That's one on old Norm," Kodiak said. "Rats don't fart."

"I'm being facetious." After a long, uncomfortable silence, Montagna said, "I know you don't like me. I know I haven't given you much reason to. But we are on the verge of making the greatest scientific discovery since the *Coelacanth*. Doesn't that mean anything to you? Are you that jealous of not being the only one to bring it in?"

Kodiak shot him a sidelong glance. "Where do you get off calling this travesty a scientific expedition? You're in this for the money and nothing more."

Montagna seemed troubled. He paced back and forth, contemplating something, then said, "You remember I said something about working for the State Department, a liaison of sorts? Well, that's not entirely true."

Kodiak said, "Now why doesn't that surprise me?"

"I work for the National Security Agency. The branch I operate is funded by people in the private sector, like Emory Pittman. You'll also recall I told you that I have a personal interest in things cryptozoological. That is true, but it goes well beyond a personal fascination.

"A few years ago, when the Soviet Union fell apart, some of my contacts within the KGB sold me information that documented an experiment that was carried out by their scientists involving the Russian equivalent of the Sasquatch..."

Kodiak said, "The Almas."

Montagna nodded. "That's right, the Almas. What they had done was to create a hybrid species: part Almas, part *Homo sapien*..." Montagna let this information sink in.

Kodiak slowly turned on him. "Wait a minute. Is this what you were talking about on the ride out here, that business with Zana?"

"That's right."

"Montagna, if Zana existed at all, I guarantee she was, at most, a relic species of *Homo sapien*. *Cro-magnon*, at most. Not even Neandertal. Any so-called hybrid children she may have born were *strictly human*."

Montagna's eyes became wide, almost manic, as he said, "That's what I thought, too! But back in the late seventies and eighties, the Russians were finding the bodies of these dead Almas out in their forests. They had died from radiation poisoning, because the stupid Russians had been dumping all their radioactive waste into rivers and lakes throughout the mountains. These creatures had either been drinking the water, or eating the fish they found dead on the river banks.

"But I saw the film of these things they had laid out in their laboratories. They were apes, Kodiak, *just like the Sasquatch!*"

"Okay, even if they did have these dead Almas in their labs, how did they manage to create a hybrid species?"

Montagna explained. "The Russians discovered that sperm cells are still viable even after they have died. Through test tube fertilization and gene splicing, they bred twenty-two of these hybrids to experiment with a new type of soldier. A soldier with the physical strength, agility, and the instincts of an animal, but with the cognitive abilities of a human being.

"When the Soviet Union faded out, the new government wanted the project stopped, and they ordered the extermination of these hybrids. A Russian General named Belikov was brought out of retirement to hunt them down and kill them.

"Last year I went to Russia and smuggled the last surviving member of this species into the United States. He's everything they set out to create!"

Kodiak had no doubt in his mind that Montagna was psychotic. He was starting to fear that Montagna was actually becoming unglued right before his eyes. He said, "And where is this hybrid now, Jamie?"

Montagna shook his head. "I don't know. He has to remain hidden, because he doesn't look normal, you know, like a human being looks. Emory Pittman was going to let us use his Sasquatch for genetic material so we can breed one of these hybrids for ourselves. And according to your own research, you said the North American species would appear to be the largest of all of them reported throughout the world."

Kodiak never thought the information in one of his books would come back to bite him on the ass, but there it was. He didn't say anything.

"I still want to go after this animal, and I need you to do it."

Kodiak still didn't know what to say.

Montagna felt that he might have laid this on Kodiak a little too heavy-handed, so he tried to lighten the mood. "So, what's the word on you and Cyrena? You getting sweet on her, or something?"

Kodiak didn't answer. He threw a stick into the fire and went to his tent. Ben was already asleep, looking like a monstrous caterpillar in his sleeping bag, and snoring loud enough to wake the dead. "Terrific," Kodiak muttered to himself as he took off his boots and laid back on top of his sleeping bag.

Cyrena was in her tent three feet away. He heard her whisper, "Good night, George."

"Good night, Cyrena."

The Capture

s a species the Sasquatch are transient by nature, never settling in any one place for long. They have no specific migration patterns and, like many other wild animals, make no use of caves. Any time they do bother with shelter, it is temporary at best.

They do, however, have certain territories they favor, and the juvenile Sasquatch had come to this canyon after being separated from its parents when it was five years old. It managed to survive the next three years in the same manner as its adult counterparts. Being omnivorous, the creature fed from the abundance of foliage available to it in the woods, or preyed upon smaller animals. This Sasquatch found particular enjoyment in rolling over large rocks to remove small, hibernating rodents from their nests underneath and eating them by the handful.

Oftentimes the Sasquatch would come upon the carcass of some large animal and roll in it to leave its scent. This was one reason so many witnesses reported them as having a "foul stench." Another reason was that, being bipedal animals, when the Sasquatch would urinate, the urine would run down their own legs and become matted in their fur.

The Sasquatch watched the camp all day, and in the evening, when the only light was from the fire, it came closer to watch the humans as they ate their dinner. It also watched the pack animals, still intrigued by them. But it knew instinctively that, if the animals sensed its presence, they could panic and draw unwanted attention to it. So the Sasquatch stayed away from them.

After everyone finished their meal, the fire slowly dwindled. The creature saw the scraps of food on the ground, and the bones from Ruth's kill. It would wait for the people to go away. Then it would make its move.

Dave climbed onto the sturdy lower branch of a western red cedar, ten feet off the ground. There were some smaller branches beneath that wouldn't support his full weight, but if he had to scramble down they'd make an adequate ladder. He was wearing the nightvision goggles, and everything glowed phosphorescent green. The weather was a little cooler than he was used to, so he wore a lightweight parka and cradled the air rifle in his arms as he watched the camp.

More specifically, he was watching Cyrena's tent. Once again she had turned his feelings around. During dinner she had come over to him and brought him some fish and a can of beer. She smiled at him and stayed to talk. This surprised him, because he thought she would be on the other side of the camp talking with Kodiak and Ben, who were both watching Ruth-less as she gorged herself on the animal carcass she had dragged into camp. Cyrena had asked him some more about his hobby, and they both talked about their jobs. He was a boxboy at a Seattle supermarket, but was hoping to make cashier before long, then assistant manager. As he talked to her he was nervous, probing and squeezing the pimples on his face, trying to keep his eyes on her face, and not her chest.

He wondered if she was sleeping now. He felt like he was keeping guard over her, making sure Norm didn't sneak out of his tent and saunter over to hers. He felt bad for ever wanting to rape her, and when they got back to Seattle maybe he would even ask her out to dinner.

The sudden crack of a stick somewhere in the dark startled him, and his throat seized up. The rifle almost slipped from his trembling hands, so he held it against his chest and looked around to see what caused the sound. The horses and llamas stirred slightly in the clearing by the river, then seemed to settle back down. There was no sign of any Sasquatch. He scanned the area once more, then sighed lightly.

His thoughts went back to Cyrena. Was she thinking about him? He hoped so, even though he thought it unlikely. He tried to live by the old expression: hope for the best, expect the worst. And the worst was what life seemed to always have dealt him.

He was gawky-looking: too tall and too skinny, with frizzy blond hair, a bad complexion and crooked teeth. He looked dimwitted, but he wasn't, and that's what made people's writing him off at first glance so painful. But he was guilty of not even trying to change things, choosing instead to draw upon old experiences, savoring the pain and poison of past victimization and torment. If he thought about them long enough, his hatred could keep him warm on cold nights.

There was another sound, closer now. It could have been someone, or something, walking under the trees. He heard it on the pine needles that covered the ground, and he scanned the area again, and still saw nothing. But when he looked down, his heart skipped a beat. He gasped. The Sasquatch was standing directly beneath him, looking up at him with eyes that glowed demonic green in the nightvision goggles.

Dave snapped the air rifle into position but started to slip off the branch. To keep from falling, he let go of the rifle and it seemed to drop a hundred feet in slow motion before it clattered to the ground at the Sasquatch's feet. The animal jumped back, then looked back up at him. Dave watched as the Sasquatch picked up the rifle. He could have shouted for the others, but that would just scare it off, and he wasn't sure they'd get a third chance at it. All he could do was wait and hope for an opportunity to get the rifle back. Despite his conscious effort to remain calm, Dave was scared. It wasn't as big as he'd heard they could get, and it showed no aggression, but he didn't like being alone with this thing – especially if it could climb trees.

The Sasquatch looked the rifle over, held it by the barrel and hit it against the ground several times. It bit into the stock, lost interest and dropped it back on the ground. It looked back up at Dave, who didn't move. After a brief observation, it turned back around and headed for the woods.

Dave scrambled down the tree and grabbed the rifle in a near panic. As he watched the creature amble away, he felt like Roger Patterson as he rushed to get his movie camera out of his saddle bag to take those incredible few seconds of film. But Dave didn't have a camera.

He steadied the rifle in his shaking hands and tossed the nightvision goggles aside, opting for the rifle scope. He aimed at its back and squeezed the trigger.

The creature let out a startled squawk and stopped in its tracks. It didn't fall. It turned around and faced Dave. If it was hit, it showed no sign of the drug taking effect. It growled and started to walk toward him, not in any more of a hurry than when it was walking away, but there was a terrible sense of fury. It swayed a little as it came at him, but it did not deviate from its course.

Dave was too stunned to move. He was shaking and felt too disoriented to remember which way the tents were. When the creature opened its mouth and grunted at him, Dave screamed. "NORM! JAMIE! IT'S OUT HERE! HELP!"

This worked. Startled by the outburst the creature turned back and ran toward the woods. But now the tranquilizer was starting to work, and it was unable to run. It moved at a partial trot, teetering a couple times, dragging its feet along the dirt as it vanished among the trees.

Norm and Montagna ran out of their tents, with Ben and Kodiak bounding out of theirs. Dave was pointing toward the trees, his eyes wide, and shrieking, "I hit him with the tranq! He's already starting to slip!"

Norm had a flashlight, a big industrial model with a beam that shone a hundred feet. He led them toward the trees, following the sloppy path left by the Sasquatch. Judging by the footprints, it was going down fast. They should find it fairly easy, and they knew it. They were emotionally charged and ready for anything.

The animal had never experienced anything like this before. It was confused, angry and terrified. The initial strike of the dart stung very badly, and the Sasquatch pulled it from the small of its back. When it saw Dave standing back there it wanted to retaliate. But its head suddenly felt strangely light, and everything was spinning. It wanted to sleep, but knew it would be vulnerable to its enemies. It had to get away.

The animal moved for the shelter of the forest, but it could hear them close behind, and its legs didn't want to carry it any longer. It knew it was going to sleep soon, but its will to survive pumped enough adrenalin to keep it moving. It would do whatever it could to defend itself.

Suddenly, white light, worse than looking straight into the sun, was shone in the Sasquatch's eyes, blinding it. It let out a miserable squeal of protest.

They found it! The ape had fallen to its knees and was clutching a large pine cone when Norm shone the light in its face. It bared its teeth at them and half-heartedly threw the pine cone.

Norm laughed. "Fish in a barrel."

Dave's voice was shaking. "Don't go near him!"

"Just shoot him again," Norm said.

"No!" Ben shouted, sounding as nervous as Dave. "That would kill him!"

"This'll fix him." Montagna walked over and knocked it across the head with a tree branch. The creature turned to bite him, but Dave came up just as suddenly and kicked it in the abdomen with the point of his cowboy boot. It yelped like a hurt puppy, but lunged for Dave like an attack dog, baring its teeth and snapping.

Norm cracked its head with the flashlight and then all three of them were beating and kicking it like a gang of thugs. The creature shrieked from fear and pain, but could not do anything to fight back, or escape. It whimpered, covering its head with its long arms and bringing its knees up against its chest.

Kodiak stepped in and grabbed Norm by a handful of his greasy hair and threw him back. He tripped Dave, and Ben stepped on Dave's chest to keep him down.

Montagna swung back with the branch to hit the animal again, but Kodiak grabbed it away from him and shoved him back. "That's enough!"

They all got up and stared at Kodiak and Ben like children who had been cheated out of dessert.

The Sasquatch was lying face-down on the ground, unconscious. Dark splotches of its blood looked like black tar in the moonlight. They finally captured Emory Pittman's Sasquatch.

ça.

Montagna, Norm, and Dave worked on assembling the cage that would be used to transport the animal back to Emory Pittman's estate. Kodiak, Cyrena, and Ben took the Sasquatch's body measurements as it lay unconscious with a steel chain fastened around its leg. The chain was bolted to a tree.

Based upon an admittedly cursory examination of the Sasquatch, it appeared its wounds were superficial. No bones had been broken, nor did its skull bear evidence of fracturing.

Kodiak drew up a diagram of the animal that featured its proportions and body measurements for his own reference:

SEX – Male.
AGE – Juvenile, possibly 5-10 years, based on gorilla.
TOTAL BODY LENGTH – 70 inches.
HEAD (crown to jaw) – 13 inches.
SHOULDER WIDTH – 27 inches.
ARMS (shoulder to middle finger) – 37 inches.
LEGS (inseam) – 32 inches.
NECK (circumference) – 30 inches.
CHEST (circumference) – 44 inches.
WAIST (circumference) – 38 inches.
UPPER ARM (circumference) – 18 inches.
UPPER LEG (circumference) – 24 inches.
FOOT LENGTH – 12.5 inches.

It was absurd that at this, *the pinnacle moment* in the history of the worldwide search for this animal, nobody would have a camera. Emory Pittman strongly stipulated that the capture not be publicized. To ensure that no photographs leak out, Montagna had made a thorough and secret search through everyone's belongings, confiscating any camera equipment.

Ben was speechless, staring at this creature about which so much myth and folklore had surrounded for hundreds of years. It was not to be feared, but admired. Upon the initial glance, its face did resemble a gorilla more than any of the other anthropoid apes, but not exactly.

"George, look at this..." Cyrena had knelt down beside the Sasquatch and was studying its profile. The animal had a protruding nose. Looking at it straight on, the nostrils were flat and wide, but from the side, the nose was its most prominent facial feature, sticking out just a little beyond the muzzle.

"That makes sense," Kodiak said. "There's been some speculation in scientific circles that the development of the nose played a major role in mankind's ultimate venturing throughout the world. The theory is that a protruding nose conserves moisture that would otherwise be expelled through a flat, ape-like nose. This kept the nose cooler than the rest of the body during times of physical exertion, such as traveling into the open grasslands away from the forests, thus allowing it to retain moisture that would keep the brain from literally over-heating.

"No known species of ape has ever done what this guy has done," he said, admiring the unconscious Sasquatch. "If eye-witness testimony and physical evidence are any indication, then *Gigantopithecus* has spread to nearly every continent on the planet, second only to us. And his nose does lend credence to the theory."

Ben's voice was dreamy as he looked at the animal. "Look at his head. Just like the ones in Tibet." In 1953 the existence of two relics had come to light during one of many expeditions to the Himalayas in search of the Yeti. They were scalps. According to the Tibetan monks, they were Yeti scalps. The first was discovered in a monastery in *Pangboche*, the second in another monastery located in *Khumjung*.

They had been cut from the skulls, just above the ears, and were conical in shape. So much so, they almost looked like torpedo shells, except for a protuberant crest that ran vertically from above the brow to the top of the head. The age of these relics was said by the monks to be roughly three hundred and fifty years.

The scalps were considered sacred, and the members of the expedition were not allowed to take them from the monasteries. They were, however, given a single hair which, upon examination by one of the foremost experts in hair identification at that time, proved to be of an unknown species possibly related to bears, or primates, but not humans.

Then a third Yeti scalp surfaced at a monastery in *Namche Bazaar*. This one had been manufactured from two pieces of hide that were cut from the shoulder of a *Serow*, a species of Tibetan yak, and sewn together from the inside. They were placed over a mold of the Yeti scalp and set out to dry in order to replicate the other scalps. This caused a furor over the authenticity of the first two scalps, and many people wrote them all off as fakes.

However, while the shape of the scalp could be replicated, the hair follicles and hair tracts could not be imitated. When compared to known anthropoid apes, the Yeti hair patterns came remarkably close in similarity, without being totally identical, to the gorilla.

The Sasquatch that now lay before them bore the same tall, almost pointed shape to its head as the Yeti scalps in Tibet. Its hair was black and covered a greater portion of its body in comparison to the other anthropoid apes. Its facial hair came within inches of its eyes, and covered its chest – another physical trait seen in the Patterson film.

Its teeth were bigger than a gorilla's of comparable age, except for the maxillary cuspids, or canines, which were shorter and blunter.

Although the animal's skeletal structure showed evidence that it did walk erect like a man, the rest of its features were strictly simian; particularly its hands, which measured ten inches long, possessed a non-opposing thumb, and lacked a thenar pad beneath the thumbs. Its fingers were a lighter color than the skin of its face, like the fingers of a heavy smoker; a nicotine tinge, almost copper.

The palms of the animal's hands and the soles of its feet were covered with exceptionally thick pads of compressed fat that not only insulated them from the extreme cold and the harsh environment, but tended to give their surfaces a smooth, almost creaseless appearance.

The most striking characteristic of the animal's foot was its heel, which projected farther back from the ankle than a human foot. This would allow proper weight distribution for such a heavy animal – something also seen in the Patterson film.

In two hours the titanium cage was fully assembled. It was eight feet long and three feet in diameter; big enough to accommodate the animal without giving it too much room to move around. It was designed to be carried between four or six horses, depending upon the size of the captured beast. Once the Sasquatch was inside, the two end pieces would be bolted in place.

Montagna and Norm walked over to where the others were measuring the creature, and Norm panned his flashlight over it. He was laughing and half-drunk from the six pack he had put away after beating the animal senseless. "Look at that, Jamie. Why do you suppose he's got such a little wiener?"

Montagna looked at the creature's genitalia. "I remember reading something that said apes have smaller dicks in comparison to humans. You must have some Sasquatch in you, Norm." Everyone laughed, except Norm who spat. Then Montagna said, "Let's get him into the cage."

Ben, Norm, and Dave helped Montagna lift the slumbering

animal off the ground by its arms and legs. Despite its slim build, the Sasquatch weighed more than two hundred and fifty pounds, and its backside dragged across the ground as the four men hauled it to the cage.

Kodiak stood among the shadows of the trees, watching to make sure the idiots didn't harm the Sasquatch any more than they already had. He held the clipboard to his chest and was pretending to write on it, but his thoughts were elsewhere. If they could have read his mind, they would have killed him.

It took them another ten minutes to get the creature inside. They were all panting for breath and sweating profusely by the time they were able to bolt the end pieces onto the cage. Montagna reached in between the struts and bolted the leg chain to the cage.

Kodiak continued to watch... and wait. His night was only beginning.

&

The sun wouldn't be up for six more hours. After the adrenaline of the capture had worn off and the alcohol started kicking in, Montagna and the others decided to call it a night.

Kodiak and Cyrena stayed up and watched the Sasquatch. They weren't happy about the turn of events, but it was still far from over.

And they both knew what was going to happen next.

Cyrena said, "What I still don't understand is how they were planning to get him out of the park. It's illegal to kill or remove any wildlife. Even if it's something like this."

Kodiak held a lug wrench in his hand and said, "Emory Pittman's got one of his lackeys camped out in a Winnebago somewhere out here. When he gets word from Montagna, they'll rendezvous at a certain place, load the cage into the camper, then it's off to Arizona."

"Looks like they have it all figured out."

Kodiak nodded, then said, "Listen, why don't you go on ahead. The less you have to do with this, the better."

"But he's so drugged up he can't go anywhere on his own," Cyrena said.

"I'll bring him to the gully on one of the horses, and we'll stash him there till he comes around on his own. By then Montagna and the others will be after us, so we may have to stay hidden for a few days."

"This is really scaring me, George."

"We'll be all right. Now get out of here so I can get started."

She looked at him with those wide green eyes, unable to mask her fear for what would happen to him if he got caught. "Please be careful." She leaned over and kissed his cheek. Then she smiled, and reluctantly headed into the woods.

On their ride into the canyon they discovered a gully that was partially covered by a deadfall and some undergrowth. Cyrena was going to hide there until Kodiak could arrive with the Sasquatch. She wanted to help with the animal's release, but he absolutely forbade it, not daring to risk her safety.

Under a three-quarter moon, as passing shadows of incoming storm clouds accumulated above, George Kodiak was finally alone with the Sasquatch. In twenty years of researching this phenomenon, basing his theories on frustratingly little physical evidence – footprints, stray hairs and ever so often fecal matter – here he was face to face with the living *Gigantopithecus*. And he was about to release it.

He waited long enough for Cyrena to get well away from the camp, then he started to loosen the first bolt that was fastened to the end piece near the creature's feet. The metal creaked as the titanium plate parted from it. He stopped and looked over at the four dark tents. There was no sound, so he continued.

He removed the first bolt. He started on the next one and realized the struts were so close together that he would have to remove at least six of them before he could get the animal out. This was going to take at least ten minutes. Ten minutes more than he wanted to spend on this task.

Two bolts removed. Ten to go when he heard a noise from behind and turned around – Dave Bovard kicked him just over his right eye with the pointed tip of his boot. Kodiak fell back. The lug wrench flew out of his hand and hit the ground some twenty feet away.

"Norm! Jamie! He's trying to cut it loose! Hurry!" Kodiak got up and slammed Dave into the ground. The kick to his head was more severe than it felt; he was dizzy and staggered around. He could taste his own blood coming from the wound over his eye into his mouth. He punched Dave twice in the face, then he looked up and saw Montagna and Norm coming at him – fast.

Dave crawled up on his hands and knees, so Kodiak kicked him in the gut, and he flopped hard to the ground with a satisfying *"Umph!"*

Before Kodiak could turn back to face the other two, he was tackled by Norm. They both went down. Norm's ugly ape-face was right in Kodiak's, blowing fetid breath as he screamed and pummeled Kodiak with his fists.

Kodiak hardly felt the blows, but he was concerned that Norm might try to bite his nose off to disable him. He backhanded Norm across the face, and though the move felt completely inadequate to Kodiak, it must have worked, because it bloodied Norm's nose and stunned him long enough for Kodiak to throw him out of the way.

As soon as Kodiak was free of Norm, Montagna came at him with the lug wrench positioned to smash down on his head. Kodiak rolled to the side and was struck on his left shoulder, blinded by white lights of pain as Montagna hit him again.

Montagna swung down a third time. Kodiak grabbed the wrench with his right hand. They struggled for control of the weapon for what seemed like minutes. Kodiak was lying on the ground, still reeling from Dave's kick to his head, and holding onto the lug wrench. He couldn't understand why Ben hadn't heard the commotion, but he had no way of knowing everything that had just transpired took place within eighteen seconds.

Kodiak realized that he must have had some strength left, as Montagna was having difficulty holding onto the wrench. As they continued to struggle for the weapon, Montagna placed both hands on the wrench and pressed his left foot against Kodiak's chest. Kodiak let go of the wrench and sent Montagna flailing several feet back. Due to the momentum, the wrench flew from Montagna's hands, and he had to scramble across the ground to get it.

Kodiak came up behind him and hoisted him to his feet by his shirt collar, nearly strangling him. With one punch across the mouth, he knocked Montagna back to the ground and went for the wrench.

Montagna landed hard on his tailbone, and he cringed from the excruciating pain. Norm immediately ran over and attempted to help him up, but the pain was so severe Norm had to lay him back down and go after Kodiak himself.

Kodiak still couldn't see very well and, because of this, lost precious time feeling around blindly for the wrench. Just as he grasped it, Norm tackled him, and they both went down, rolling around and struggling. By some good fortune, Kodiak got a firm hold on the wrench, and he jammed it hard into Norm's side.

Norm gasped, forcing up another lung oyster that stuck to the stubble on his chin. He crawled away like a crab, holding his arm against his injured side.

Kodiak saw Montagna coming at him again, and he threw the wrench as hard as he could – hitting Ben square in the chest! Ben went down like a bag of wet cement, and Kodiak realized he made a terrible mistake. He spotted Montagna really coming at him and reached into his back pocket...

Dave shouted to Montagna, "He's going for something!"

Distracted by the warning, Kodiak turned toward Dave, and Montagna kicked him in the testicles. Overcome by crippling pain, Kodiak withered to his knees and several playing cards dropped out of his hand onto the ground. He fell down on top of them as Montagna, Norm, and Dave started beating him as mercilessly as they had beaten the Sasquatch.

The fight was over.

Just before he blacked out completely, Kodiak heard Norm hawk up a loogie and spit on him.

Norm's nose was swollen and bleeding, and his side hurt like hell. As far as he could tell no ribs were broken, but he'd have a hell of a nasty bruise tomorrow. He had to admit Kodiak put up a good fight. He kicked Kodiak again, and Montagna pulled him back. "He's had enough."

Norm glared at Montagna, then said, "I say we kill him. Ain't that right, kid?"

Dave looked almost as bad as Kodiak, except that he was conscious. "Yeah... kill..." Dave had been knocked senseless, and Norm would have felt bad for him, if he hadn't thought it was so funny.

Montagna picked up some of the playing cards that were scattered on the ground and looked them over in the moonlight. "That's weird."

"What?"

"These cards are marked, but the markings make no sense. And they're not even hidden. Look." He handed a card to Norm who scrutinized it. The cards were marked with dark smudges and streaks along their edges. Not all of them were marked, but the ones that were just looked sloppy.

Norm shrugged and tossed them on top of Kodiak. "Who cares. What I want to know is, are we gonna kill him?"

Montagna said, "No."

Norm persisted like a petulant child. "We don't have to do it, Jamie. Let's let Ruthie have a go at him. She won't leave much behind..."

Montagna sighed with impatience and said, "No. We aren't gonna kill him."

"Then what are we gonna do with him?"

Montagna looked around and saw that hardly any significant damage had been done to the cage and the Sasquatch was still unconscious. "We'll tie him to a tree and leave him here while we get the Squatch to Pittman. He'll be a little worse for wear, but maybe he'll be a little humbler, too."

"I'd still like to kill him," Norm said, disgusted.

"Forget it. Take the kid back to camp and get him cleaned up. I'll take care of this fool. Then maybe we can get some sleep. I want to leave at daybreak."

Ruth-less

A s near as he could deduce by the position of the moon, Kodiak guessed that it was about two in the morning when it started to rain. Not hard, but steadily, and it was cold, especially because he was tied to a tree without any kind of protective covering. In a flash of lightning he saw somebody heading toward him from the direction of the tents, so he closed his eyes and braced himself for another beating.

"George." It was Cyrena. She was as soaked as he was. He could tell by her eyes that he must look pathetic, at best, and he felt that way. He had a massive headache and his right eye was swollen shut. He knew the cut above his eye was open because he could feel warm blood still oozing over his eye and down his cheek. "I'm going to cut you loose," she said, and took a pocket knife from her jacket.

Kodiak shook his head. "I'm no good for riding. Besides, if we just take off... they still have that." He nodded toward the cage that held the Sasquatch, which was now underneath a plastic tarp that Montagna had covered it with before going to bed.

Cyrena urged him. "I can't leave you tied to this tree. And if they find out I'm cutting you free, they'll beat the tar out of me, too. And we both know they won't stop there."

"I know. That's why you're gonna... gonna cut me loose. Then you're gonna ride out of the canyon... Alone."

There was an edge of wariness to Cyrena's voice when she asked, "What about you?"

"Cut the horses loose. All of them. Llamas too. Get rid of them."

"Why?"

"I can't ride. At least... without horses, they can't carry the Sasquatch out. That will give me time..." He stopped to catch his breath.

"I don't like the sound of this, George. Time for what?"

"To come back... to come back and kill them."

"No. That's going too far. I can understand your wanting to let the animal go. I'm all for that. But killing them..."

"They'll make it inevitable."

Her eyes were hard on him. He sensed a harshness to them that would make most people look away. Then she said in a cold, deliberate manner, "You're the boss." She got up and briskly walked to the clearing by the river where the pack animals were. She vanished in the darkness, and the only sounds were the falling rain and the rushing river. Then he heard the trotting of the horses and the llamas as they scurried past him, heading back the way they had come into the canyon through the woods.

Cyrena returned, looking far more cautious than before. "I don't want to stick around long enough to find out if the horses made enough noise to wake them out of their drunken sleep." She cut the ropes, and he started to get up. The circulation in his legs had been cut off while he was tied down, and he lost his balance. She caught him, and he leaned on her shoulder. "Thanks. Remind me to kick your ass for not getting the hell out of here when I told you to."

"I'll remember that the next time you need me to save your butt."

"Touche'." He winced from the pain in his crotch and leaned on her for support as they headed away from the campsite, into the dark.

≈

At seven-thirty in the morning Norm tore into Montagna's tent, raging, "Kodiak's gone! He took the horses and Cyrena with him!"

"The Squatch?"

"It's still here."

Montagna let out a tremendous sigh of relief. "Oh, thank God." He climbed out of his sleeping bag and suddenly cringed from the pain of his fractured tailbone. It felt like somebody had struck him on the backside with a sledge hammer. When he finally got all the way up he said, "What was that about the horses?"

"Kodiak took them all. The llamas, too. She probably cut him loose and they rode off together. Now how the hell are we supposed to get the Sasquatch outta here without the horses? We sure as hell can't carry it."

Montagna was limping as they went outside. The pain had subsided a little as he walked over to the river where Dave was standing, holding the end of the steel cable that was used to hold the pack animals. It had been untied from the tree. "The horses were let go," Dave said.

Montagna looked at Norm. "That boy's got a bright future. So what do you suggest, old buddy? We can't catch up with them, and we can't carry the cage on our shoulders. And I seriously doubt it would walk on a leash."

"You're in awfully good spirits, considering," Norm stated, still fuming.

"What do you want me to do, Norm? Everything you're whining about are set backs. We still have the Squatch, and that's as good as gold."

"So what do we do, wait? What about Pittman's geek with the Winnebago?" Norm asked.

"No can do. Not until we move the Squatch to some place the Winnebago can get to. We have nothing to worry about. What's Kodiak gonna do? He's worse off than we are, and how do you feel?"

Norm pulled up his shirt and looked at the ghastly purple bruise on his side. It hurt just to look at it. "Yeah, I suppose that's true." Norm then became subdued in thought. "No, Kodiak don't strike me as the type to go running for help. He likes doing it himself too much."

"Whatever. Here's what we're gonna have to do. Somebody's gonna have to stay here and guard our prize while somebody else hikes back to get more horses."

"That's a hell of a hike, Jamie."

"Not necessarily. I can have Pittman's boy meet me with the Winnebago once I get to a main road."

"So you'll go?"

"I don't trust Ben and Dave enough to stay here with the Squatch, so I guess the only real choice is Dave and I make the hike while you, Ben, and Ruth stay here."

"You're no good for a walk like that, Jamie. Hell, you're walking like an old man ever since you took that fall last night. Tell you what. What if I go with the kid? That way we can head out right away."

Montagna rubbed his sore butt and nodded. "I think you may be right, buddy. Just let me contact Pearl on the radio and arrange a rendezvous point, okay?"

ॐ

By noon Andy Paul managed to replace some fence posts and was heading back to the office for some barb wire when his assistant met him halfway there. "Got a call for you from Jim Crichton."

"Okay." Paul went to the office, slipping twice on the muddied ground without falling. He wiped his face with a bandanna and picked up the phone. "Yeah, Jim."

"How you doing, Andy?"

"Oh, can't complain. Not too much, anyway. This a social call, or is something up?"

"I just got a call from Ken Ohler at the Hoh Rain Forest Visitor Center. He says about half a dozen llamas were rounded up outside of their campgrounds this morning. He knows you're the only one around with llamas, so he had me check it out. You rent out any llamas recently?"

Paul said, "Yeah. About that many, along with seven horses, to that group of folks out there Bigfoot hunting."

"Hmm. Do you think there might be trouble?"

Paul considered this. He was worried for that sexy little gal who rented the animals and thought about telling this to Crichton, then thought, hell, he was more than capable of checking things out himself. "No, Jim. I know what must have happened. Those damn llamas like to chew through the ropes. Now I told those people to use a cable to tether them, but they probably didn't. I'll go take care of it."

Crichton had known Andy Paul for more than twenty years. Paul knew these mountains as good as any ranger and could have been a ranger if he so chose. "Okay, Andy. Just give a call if you need any help."

"So long, Jim. And thanks." He hung up the phone and sat down on the desk, thinking. He didn't believe that line about the rope being chewed through, because he gave Cyrena the section of cable himself. And he didn't believe they came across Bigfoot and paid the ultimate price. But he also didn't like that punk Dave who was with her the day she rented the animals.

131

That was it. He'd put his stallion in the truck, grab his twelve gauge shotgun and ride into the woods to see what had happened to those people.

ò≥.

It took Kodiak and Cyrena the rest of the night to go the three and one-quarter-miles to the gully where he planned to stash the Sasquatch while it recovered from the tranquilizer. It suited their purpose perfectly; it was cut seven feet into a granite wall and well hidden by undergrowth.

It was just after daybreak, and the morning sun barely shone through the coastal fog like a dull silver dollar. Cyrena saw that the gash on Kodiak's forehead was still oozing blood. It needed stitches, but she couldn't think of any way to close the wound. To relieve the pain in his crotch, Kodiak made much of the trip leaning on Cyrena's shoulder. He pulled away from her support and hobbled over to the hundred-foot trunk of a long-dead cedar pine, kicked off a slab of bark and tossed it near her feet. It was swarming with big black ants, and she stared at it, not understanding what it was for.

Ten minutes later he was sitting in the gully holding the two sides of the cut together with his fingers, while Cyrena knelt before him, holding one of the ants with a pair of tweezers. With its mandibles wide open, she brought the ant up against his skin. It bit down and closed part of the wound. She pinched off its body, leaving the head in place, where it joined four other ants that sacrificed their heads to suture Kodiak's wound.

When Cyrena finished closing the wound, Kodiak lay down on a bed of moss and fell asleep almost immediately. His sleep was fitful, his face belying the pain he still suffered from the previous night's beating.

ò≥.

Ben decided to go fishing. He hiked three miles upstream, not so much to find a good fishing spot, but to get the hell away from Montagna, Norm, and the others, and to get rid of his depression. Walking was the best way he knew how to do it, short of a good stiff drink. Finally, he came to a small brook and sat down to rest.

He wasn't really interested in catching anything, but he baited

132

his hook with a couple salmon eggs and cast his line into the water.

When he had gotten up this morning, Kodiak and Cyrena were gone. So were the horses and llamas. There was nothing keeping him here now, but he was depressed that they would take off without him. He knew they hated Norm and Montagna, but he wasn't like those guys. He and Cyrena had always been friends, and he was hurt to be left behind. He figured Kodiak was pissed at him for his participation in the Sasquatch capture.

What a lousy trip this turned out to be. Here, they had become the first people to capture a Sasquatch, to actually prove that *Gigantopithecus* still existed, and Ben Tyler was miserable. He could hardly breathe, because his chest was still sore from being hit with the lug wrench. Nothing was broken, but he had a nasty bruise, and taking a deep breath was asking for punishment. He almost laughed when he thought of what had happened the past couple of nights: first Dave mistakes him for the Sasquatch and shoots him with a tranquilizer dart, then Kodiak mistakes him for Montagna and throws the lug wrench at him. The way things were going, he was probably going to end up dead before this trip was through.

He popped the tab on a can of beer he brought with him, took a drink and continued to brood. It was definitely going to rain again, but he was too depressed to bother covering himself.

&.

Jamie Montagna was sitting on a crate looking at the radio transmitter in his hand. Old Norm was standing beside him, becoming exasperated. "How come that guy ain't answering?"

Montagna shrugged. "Don't know. I know I'm on the right frequency. He should be on the alert."

"Yeah, well daylight's wastin', and I'm getting tired of waiting on this fool."

"About all else I can suggest, buddy, is that you and the kid get started, and I'll radio Pearl where to meet you."

"All right, Jamie." Norm spat and went to get Dave while Montagna made another attempt to contact Emory Pittman's man in the field.

Dave was looking at the ground, scrutinizing it when Norm walked over to him. "You ready to go, kid?"

"You know something, Norm. I don't think they rode out of here."

Norm laughed. "That's crap. They'd have to be complete damn fools to – "

"Look at this..." Dave knelt down. "I followed the animals' tracks as they came from the meadow and right through here. Even though the rain washed away most of the tracks, you can see Kodiak's dragging one foot, 'cause it dug in a little deeper."

"So?"

"So, his tracks continue away from the direction the horses went."

Norm's face brightened as he realized what Dave was saying. "Kid, you feel like doing a little hunting?"

After Ruth got up, it seemed that she didn't care one way or the other about the animals being gone. She passed on breakfast and walked down to the river where she found a large, flat rock. She lugged it back to her tent, and setting it down on the floor, placed a nickel on it and began to flatten the coin with a jeweler's hammer she carried on her belt. She was turning it into one of the tags that hung from the pelts she carried with her.

As she hammered and flattened the nickel into an oval tag, she hummed the Indian song that she learned as a child.

వ

Ben reeled the fish in. It was the same fish he'd reeled in twice already, and he was thinking maybe this time he'd just go ahead and eat it. But he didn't. He removed the hook from its mouth and tossed it back into the brook.

"Hi, Ben..."

He dropped his fishing pole and turned to see Cyrena standing behind him. "I thought you'd be back in Red Fern by now. Or at least damn close to it." There was a coldness in his tone that made it clear to her his feelings were hurt and he was in no mood to be messed with.

"We never left."

"I don't see George."

"I'll take you to him. When you see him, you'll understand why we took off like we did."

134

"So where the hell have you been?"

Even talking to him over the radio, Ron Pearl wanted to slap Montagna across his snotty face. "For your information, fart-head, I've been cooped up in this damn camper for four days waiting to hear from you. It was a beautiful day, so I took a hike. How's the fishing? You catch anything?"

"As a matter of fact, we did. Just a small steelhead, but worthy of mounting." This was an open CB frequency, and speaking in code was essential. The fishing trip was in reference to the Sasquatch hunt.

Pearl suddenly forgot about Montagna's irritating manner and became very excited, almost like a kid. "You're kidding! My God, really?" He started to laugh.

"Don't overreact." This was an absolute order, and Pearl suddenly felt foolish. His reaction could easily raise suspicion to unwanted ears.

Pearl cleared his throat, trying to imagine what the animal must look like. "Sorry, it's just that this is the kid's first time fishing. He must be thrilled."

"As we all are," Montagna said with an intense lack of enthusiasm. "Any word from friend Pittman?"

"Nothing for two days. But then I'm not supposed to call till we have some news. You ready to be picked up?"

"Not exactly. A couple of the guy's are coming out to meet you. Norm Cocke and Dave Bovard. They left about an hour ago, so if you head south for about fifteen miles you should come across them."

"Okay, sounds real good. Guess I'll be seeing all of you soon." Pearl set the radio transmitter down and sat back, smiling at the anticipation of seeing the captured Sasquatch.

He immediately grabbed up his cellular phone and dialed Pittman's private line. The voice on the other end sounded pained and discomforted. "Yes?"

"Mr. Pittman? Ron Pearl, sir."

A painful-sounding grunt, then, "What news have you got, Pearl?"

"It's a boy, Mr. Pittman. Congratulations."

Emory Pittman was lying on his belly, propped upon his arms, with a pillow under his pelvis as Dubbins, in surgical gloves, gently wiped fecal matter from his exposed buttocks. Pittman was smiling at the news Pearl was giving him. "Outstanding."

The surgical incision along Pittman's hip was enflamed and swollen to the point where it looked like the staples were going to pop loose. It looked painful, but Pittman was never one to complain about physical adversity. Even at the age of eighty-three he still had a physique that put many men half his age to shame.

Dubbins wiped the last of the crap from Pittman and started to apply cream to his hemorrhoids. Dubbins must have struck a nerve, because Pittman suddenly smacked his hand, knocking the tube of ointment across the room. "Damn you!" Then Pittman turned back to the phone. "No, not you. That idiot, Dubbins. The man's not fit to wipe his own ass, let alone mine."

Dubbins' face flushed with anger. This abuse had become a regular thing lately. Throughout their years together there had been abuse: physical, verbal and emotional assaults. But they had always been tempered by the gentle side Pittman had kept concealed from most others who knew him. Pittman had often gone to great lengths to make Dubbins feel special. To feel loved. But lately, he had been a monster all the time. Even before the accident that smashed his hip and the surgery that still wasn't healing.

Dubbins gently rolled Pittman off the pillow and onto his back, fighting the temptation to roll him onto the floor.

On the phone Pittman chuckled, but his face winced from the pain of being moved. "Yes, Pearl. Very good. We'll see you in a few days." Pittman hung up on Pearl and glared at Dubbins. There was going to be hell to pay. Again.

❧

The gully was only half a mile from the brook where Ben had been fishing. He had to admit it was so well hidden that anybody who came looking for them would have a hard time spotting it.

Kodiak was in the back, in almost total darkness. Once Ben's eyes adjusted he could see what Kodiak looked like, and he repressed a gasp. He didn't realize just how bad the beating was that Kodiak had been subjected to. And what were those black dots on his forehead, he wondered.

Kodiak looked at him with his one open eye. "Ben."

"George... How bad is it?"

"It looks worse than it is. By the way, I'm sorry I hit you with the lug wrench last night."

Ben rubbed the sore spot on his chest. "Forget it." He looked at Cyrena. "Why didn't you ride out on horseback and get him to a doctor?"

"This was his idea. He wants to go back to free the Sasquatch."

Ben knelt down in front of Kodiak. "Yeah, I can see how you'd be real effective."

"Don't write me off yet, Ben. I told you, it looks worse than it is."

"What are you thinking of? Why is it so important for you to free this animal? Can't you see it's too late? I just don't get you, George."

"I thought you were supposed to be good at reading people?"

Ben stared at him. "I suppose you do have some pretty good reasons, even though I think you tend to leap before you look. And I guess I have to admit, as much as I love being involved with the first real capture, the idea of Jamie and Norm taking credit for this does make me want to puke. So have you got a plan? And I do mean a realistic plan."

"Yeah, I have an idea."

"And does this idea have room for one more person?"

"Actually, I was hoping to count on you, so I made room for two."

Ben smiled sarcastically. "Very funny, smart ass – "

"Be quiet..." Cyrena hushed them up, and they all watched a stream of urine cascade down from somewhere above the gully. It was Norm.

Ben shook his head and whispered, "What is that guy's obsession with peeing?"

Kodiak had left a trail that was easy for Norm and Dave to follow, but they lost it two miles along the way, then came upon Ben's tracks that brought them almost to the gully. Norm was standing atop the deadfall that overhung the gully, and as he relieved himself he saw something two hundred yards away, barely visible between the giant columns of trees; a man on horseback. But it wasn't the horse that drew Norm's attention – it was the bright, curly red hair that covered the guy's head.

Dave was looking at Ben's fishing pole that lay on the ground some fifty feet from where Norm was standing. On the ground between here and the brook, clear footprints had been left that led in a specific direction for Norm and him to follow. But Ben's footprints weren't the only ones. Someone else had been there, someone who wore a much smaller boot than Ben: Cyrena.

She hadn't ridden out of the canyon, but was hiding somewhere with Kodiak, waiting to strike back at them, probably during the night. They were probably getting it on right now in some cave. She was probably letting Ben slip it to her, too. Dave hated her. Norm was right: she was a whore. And the first chance he got, he was going to do it to her. This would take some serious planning, because he didn't want to have to wait for Norm and Jamie to finish with her before he got his turn. He would have her first, for a couple of days. Then maybe he'd let Norm have her, then Jamie. And maybe even Ruth-less.

Dave was giggling when Norm walked back over and said, "What's so funny?"

Dave stopped laughing. "Nothing. What's up?"

"You ready for a good time?"

"You found them?"

Norm brought the machete with them when they left camp, and it looked like they were going to get to use it.

୨⋆

Andy Paul rode over Tshletshy Ridge and into the canyon as fast as the weather and the wet terrain would allow. He came to the Queets River and followed it for another thirty-five minutes after Norm had spotted him. Paul located the campsite in the clearing and knew it must belong to the people he was looking for, but he stayed well away from it until he could figure out what might have happened.

He rode around the clearing, taking care to stay out of sight, hoping above all else Cyrena was safe. He kept his shotgun across his lap, just in case he had to ride in and play hero.

He turned to make another pass when something flew from beyond the nearest tree and hit his horse between the eyes. It was a rock, and it connected hard enough to send the horse rearing up, throwing Paul from the saddle, and when he slammed down on the ground, he almost bit his tongue in half.

Two men came out from behind the trees. The first was that creepy punk, Bovard, who was carrying a machete and looking at him with complete hatred. Dave walked over to Paul, pressed his foot against his chest and rested the tip of the machete on his throat.

The other man was much older and looked like one of those museum sculptures he'd seen of a Neandertal man. He took the horse by the reigns, picked Paul's shotgun up from the ground and started laughing. His laugh sounded like the grinding an automobile makes in false ignition.

ॐ

They agreed upon Kodiak's plan, although Ben had some doubts about what Kodiak said he was going to do with his playing cards. Kodiak said, "We have to take them by surprise. The sooner the better."

Kodiak told Ben about Montagna's twisted hybrid idea, and Ben became angry at Montagna and Norm and was anxious to get things underway. He wasn't sure he could wait until dark. "It's gonna feel good to give those guys the beating they deserve."

Kodiak shook his head, saying, "We may not have a chance for that. On the other hand, we may have to put them out of commission so we have an adequate opportunity for success."

While Cyrena was on their side, she didn't care for the elation she knew they felt at the idea of beating the crap out of Montagna and Norm, and remained silent during the first part of their conversation. However, she did speak up when Ben said he wouldn't mind reading their obituaries. "I hope to God, for your sake, it doesn't come to that," she said.

Ben finally took his leave. It was more than a three-mile hike back to camp, and it would be dark soon. The walk would be good for wearing down his anger, and that way Montagna wouldn't sense anything when he got back.

ॐ

They walked into camp single file: Andy Paul, looking pale and scared, with Dave behind him still holding the machete in a ready position, and Norm bringing up the rear, riding on the horse and carrying the shotgun.

Jamie Montagna was sitting on a fallen tree trunk, drinking a cup of coffee by the fire, when he saw them and stood up. "What the hell is this?"

Norm said, "We caught this one riding near camp. He was nosing around, and he had this." He held up the shotgun.

Montagna tossed the coffee cup away and walked over to Paul, looking him over suspiciously. "Who are you?"

Paul felt like a POW brought into an enemy camp. He knew he could kick the crap out of the sneering little weasel who stood before him, but the shotgun in Norm's hands made him impotent. "My name's Andy Paul. I don't want no trouble. I just came out to see if you folks were all right."

"I don't know you."

"The gal – the woman, Cyrena, she rented the horses and llamas from me. I got a call this morning that they were running around loose. I thought something might have happened."

Montagna nodded, but said nothing. He looked up at Norm. "Norm, let's have a talk."

Norm dismounted, handed Dave the shotgun, and tied the horse to the tree trunk. "Keep an eye on 'em, kid."

They went inside Montagna's tent. Montagna turned on him, saying, "What in the hell were you thinking?"

Stunned by Montagna's vehemence, Norm said, "What?"

"I sent you idiots to meet Pearl in the Winnebago! I sent you to bring back some horses so we could get the Squatch out of here. And you come back holding some cowboy prisoner?"

"I told you, he was spying on us..."

"Spying? This isn't Robert Ludlum! You heard what he said."

Norm was hurt and confused by Montagna's anger. "Even so, he would have seen the Squatch. Then what would we do? Especially since he was armed."

Montagna took a deep breath and exhaled steadily, calming himself. "He probably would have helped us, Norm. Now I gotta figure out what to do with him."

"Well, at least we got a horse," Norm said plaintively.

They came out of the tent and walked back to Andy Paul, who was looking at the Sasquatch. "My God... is that it? You really caught Bigfoot?"

"Right now, Roy, that's not your concern," Montagna said, using "Roy" as an aspersion. "I might just as well be God Almighty, because right now I got the power of life and death over you."

"Then just tell me if the girl is okay." He looked at Dave. "Cyrena, is she still okay?"

Montagna suppressed a smile. He was suddenly swept up by flashbacks from what had happened back in Russia. His eyes widened and his pulse raced as he thought about how thin the line was between sheer revulsion and sick fascination about death – particularly horrible death. It looked like they were going to get to have a little fun.

"She's great, Roy. Matter of fact, we got her tied up in one of those tents, naked as the day she was born, but a whole lot prettier, I'm sure. You sweet on her or something, cowboy?"

Paul was soaked with sweat, and his eyes bulged angrily from his skull as he looked at Montagna. He wanted to kill him, but didn't dare raise a hand against him. "You son of a..."

"You wanna... you wanna hear her scream?" Montagna almost started laughing, but maintained his composure.

Paul was shaking. "What kind of animal are you?"

"Well, Roy, I'm afraid we can't let you have Cyrena. But we do have somebody else here who can show you a good time. Isn't that right, Norm?"

Norm smiled. "Sure do." He cupped his mouth with one hand and called out, "Ruthie! Come on out, gal! We got something for you!"

Ruth's head popped out from her tent like a cat being called for dinner. When Andy Paul got a look at her he knew it was time to start praying.

Dave's skin flushed hot from a rush of testosterone as he got caught up in the excitement and the taste of frenzy. He whacked Paul across the back of his head with the shotgun, and Paul fell on his hands and knees. Norm said, "I think old Roy here could use some tenderizing, don't you, Jamie?"

Montagna kicked Paul in the ribs. Paul cried out and flopped to the ground.

Norm took the shotgun from Dave and, smiling, he said, "What about you, kid?"

Dave, eyes bulging and hands tremulous with vigor, picked the machete up from the ground, knelt down beside Paul, lifted his head by a handful of hair and pressed the blade to Paul's throat.

Norm said, "Whoa, kid, that's for Ruthie..."

Dave looked at Norm, then grudgingly tossed the machete away. Paul was whimpering. His face was covered with dust and some blood from his nose and mouth. Dave jerked Paul's head back hard and hissed, "This is gonna hurt real bad!"

The three men lifted Paul up and proceeded to beat the living hell out of him; something they'd gotten a great deal of practice in lately. They beat him senseless, but not to the point of unconsciousness.

Ruth did not take part in the assault. In fact, she seemed totally oblivious as she knelt down and sharpened her large knife, continually running her thumb along the edge to test its sharpness.

After the beating, they sat Paul on the ground and then tied his hands behind him over the topside of the fallen tree trunk. Then they tied his feet together.

Paul watched the old lady as she finished sharpening her knife and got to her feet, which was a major effort for her. She shoved the knife back in its case and stood in front of him, staring at him with those black-as-coal eyes. He wanted to look away, but couldn't. He saw she had what was supposed to pass for a smile on her face. Then she took her shirt off and dropped it on the ground.

Norm, Montagna, and Dave started laughing, and even Andy Paul couldn't believe the disgusting sight of her flattened, leathery breasts, like hound dog ears with Jujubees on the ends.

He felt like he was going to vomit. She hiked up her dress and was naked underneath. Paul turned his head away, and she came at him.

The others laughed hysterically as Ruth croaked the words, "You are dog. I am stink," and shoved herself into Andy Paul's face.

≈⋆

Ben's legs were searing from the workout he was getting on his walk back to camp. He was huffing in great breaths as he moved, but he was so emotionally charged about what was going to happen tonight, he was able to channel his physical pain into energy. He refused to slow down.

He was only a third of a mile from camp, hiking along a ridge above the widest part of the river, when he looked across and saw Ruth. She was crouched down on a large boulder, washing her knife in the water. Ben stopped to watch her, but she didn't look up at him.

Something she had caught his eye and he wanted to get a better look at it. It looked like one of the animal pelts she wore on her belt, except this one had bright, *curly red hair*. Ben grew cold and felt nauseous when he realized these weren't animal pelts at all, but human scalps!

He couldn't recall having met anyone out here who had curly red hair, and he would have remembered if he did. Had she attacked some other campers? As near as he could tell, there hadn't been anyone else in the canyon.

As Ben tried to figure the mystery out, Norm and Jamie appeared on the opposite side of the river carrying something in a plastic tarpaulin between them. It was big enough to be a human body, and there was blood dripping from one end. They were all involved.

Ben's legs turned to gelatin, and he almost fell down, but he grabbed onto a tree trunk for support and took cover behind it.

Norm and Montagna dropped the body on the ground, and Norm said, "Man, this guy's heavy."

Ruth sniffed the air like a dog and suddenly pointed a bony finger at Ben and screeched.

Norm and Montagna spotted him. Norm hollered, "Tyler!" and fired at Ben with the shotgun.

Montagna grabbed the shotgun from him. "Stupid idiot! We only have three shells left. Besides, he probably knows where Kodiak and Cyrena are hiding." Montagna waded into the waist-deep water, fighting the strong current and started making his way across the river.

Ben ran like hell, forgetting all pain and previous discomfort. In his mind he was a gazelle and there was no way they were going to catch up with him, even if it meant running all the way back to Red Fern. Of course he knew that was totally unrealistic, and his plan was to make it to the gully where Kodiak and Cyrena were still hiding. At the very least he had to warn them that Montagna and Norm were armed with a shotgun and they would have to change their plan considerably, or abandon it altogether.

Ben visualized Montagna coming out of the water and resuming the hunt. Depending on the strength of the current, the added weight of his wet clothes, and the fact that Ben had cold white fear in his favor, the odds were strong he'd make it to the gully before Montagna could catch up with him. God, he was scared.

His lungs burned and he needed to stop if only to catch his breath, but there was no way he was going to do that. If he was going to die today it would be from exhaustion and not a shotgun blast to the head.

In his panic he must have taken a wrong turn somewhere, because he suddenly found himself up against a wall of giant boulders at least seventy feet high. They weren't insurmountable, but they were covered with thick, wet moss and grass, making the task of climbing arduous, especially for a man of Ben's size and physical condition.

Ben looked around, debating whether he had time to backtrack, but decided against it. At least this area was well covered by a dense growth of trees, and he didn't think he had left any tracks between the ground cover and the rocks that surfaced the last two hundred yards. He was going to scale the rocks.

Montagna and Norm both set out after Ben. After Norm shot at him everyone knew there was no way they could let him live. When they took off across the river they left Dave with Ruth, ordering him to dispose of Paul's body.

Dave had no idea what they were planning to do with the body when they suddenly went after Ben, so he asked Ruth, "I don't suppose you know what they were gonna do with him?"

Ruth ignored him.

"Thanks." He looked down at the bloodied tarpaulin. It was so strange. He thought he should feel sick, or scared. Something. The picture in his head of Andy Paul's face, pleading with his eyes for Dave to do something to help him, while Montagna and Norm held him down as Ruth peeled back the top of his head, was titillating. Even now. Still.

Norm, Montagna and Ruth killed him. At least that's what Dave convinced himself was the truth. He didn't know why he hated the guy. He didn't even know him, except for meeting him at the stable. But Paul's boorish flirtation with Cyrena had made Dave feel jealous. And seeing him now prance into their camp thinking he was her knight in shining flannel just whitened Dave's mind with rage.

Paul was so big there was no way Dave could lift the body by himself, and it was obvious Ruth would be of no help. He could drag the body to some gorge and dump it there for the animals to finish off, but that left way too much risk of being discovered. He could bury him. But where? He would have to dig a pretty big hole, because there was no way Dave could stomach chopping him up. But then, maybe he wouldn't have to... "Hey, Ruth..."

ع

Ben was halfway up the boulder wall. He found he could tear away sections of slippery moss with his rock-climbing boots and lose very little footing. He lay face-down against one of the boulders, and the wet grass soaked into his shirt, feeling wonderful. He was getting his second wind and had not seen hide nor hair of Montagna and Norm in the whole half hour since the incident at the river.

But he was still far from home-free, and he wasn't worried just for himself. It would be dark soon and he had to get to the gully before Kodiak and Cyrena left for the camp. Of course, if he didn't make it, there was always the hope that with Norm and Montagna after him, they could free the Sasquatch unhindered. He looked up and saw that he still had at least thirty feet to climb, and the sky was growing dark. The storm clouds had gone, so at least he wouldn't get rained on.

ع

Dave went back to camp while Ruth took care of bundling the last of Andy Paul for disposal. He thought the old battle axe was disgusting, but she did have her uses. He was surprised that he didn't feel particularly bad about watching that big idiot cowpoke die the way he did. After all, he told himself again that he didn't actually take part in the killing. But he knew that, on some level, somewhere, sometime, there would be payback. Possibly jail time – if it were ever found out.

His psychotic mind began to waver. Maybe he should have done something to avoid being involved in this, like run away. But now he had crossed a line, and it couldn't have been any more real if it had been painted on the ground.

Again, Andy Paul's final, terrified gaze haunted his brain. But it still didn't repulse Dave. It made his testicles tingle in anticipation of danger – like having done something that could put you on death row. It was almost a thrill, if it weren't for that other sensation: the feeling of creeping depression rising from the cold depths of his belly.

He had the camp all to himself. Norm and Montagna were still out trying to track Ben down, and Ruth was chopping Andy Paul into little bitty pieces. He figured he'd give Ruth a couple hours to do her dirty work, then he'd go check up on her.

ॐ

Ben made it to the top. He was just about to pull himself over the last boulder when he suddenly heard Montagna below. "Wrong time, wrong place, Ben. Nothing personal."

Ben turned around and looked down at them. He was a sitting duck.

Norm was pointing the shotgun right at him.

Ben's fear was suddenly replaced with a deep sense of peace. He knew he was going to die. He rested his head on the rock and closed his eyes, preparing himself for what was about to happen. "May I have a minute to pray?"

Norm laughed. "Does he really think praying's gonna save him?"

"Shut up, Norm." Montagna was subdued. Almost respectful. "One minute, Ben."

"Thank you. And Jamie?"

"Yes, Ben?"

"I forgive you."

The Sentinel
of the Woods

odiak and Cyrena heard the shotgun blast, but from the considerable distance she thought it was thunder. Kodiak knew it wasn't, but saw no point in frightening her any more than she had already been. "The sun'll be down in a few minutes. When do you want to go?" She asked.

He was looking up at the sky, wondering about the shotgun blast. Who had shot at whom? Or who had killed whom? "No need to hurry. I want to give them time to settle in."

૨**ል**

Norm and Montagna came back to camp exhausted, emotionally as well as physically. All they wanted to do was eat dinner, drink some beer and go to sleep. Tomorrow was going to be an even more taxing day.

Dave was waiting for them, and they knew something was wrong. He was pale and nervous and looked like he was going to be sick. "I got something I got to tell you..."

Montagna was bushed and not in the mood to deal with another problem. "So, what is it?"

"It wasn't my fault..."

Montagna was fed up, and he reacted with anger, "Listen, punk, I'm not in the mood to deal with your fidgety little – "

Norm cut in. He liked Dave and didn't want to see Montagna berate him. "Jamie, take it easy. Can't you see the kid's freaked out about something?" He addressed Dave. "What is it, kid?"

"Ruth. It's Ruth. She's... Ruth's dead..."

Norm freaked. He grabbed Dave by the shirt and Dave started crying. "What are you talking about? She's dead? How? HOW!"

Dave just sobbed like a baby and would have dropped to the ground if Norm hadn't held so tightly to his shirt, screaming in his face. "I'm gonna kick your ass if you don't explain to me – "

Montagna was back in control. He wrenched Norm off of Dave and worked on calming Dave down. "Now take it easy. We need to know what happened. Where is she now?"

"I took her... She's in... she's in... she's in her tent..."

Norm ran to the tent and went in.

Montagna sat down beside Dave. "Take it easy, kid. Just take a few deep breaths and fill me in on what happened. Was it Kodiak?"

Dave stopped crying and inhaled several deep breaths. Finally he could speak coherently. "I left her by the river after you and Norm went after Ben. I didn't know what you wanted me to do with the cowboy's body, so I asked her to chop him up and then I was gonna bury the pieces. I thought that's what you'd want..."

Montagna nodded. "That's fine. So what went wrong?"

"I couldn't take watching her do it, so I came back here till I figured she'd had enough time to finish. Then I went back to check on her..." A sob escaped him, then he calmed himself again. "She was in the water, face down. I went to her and saw she was dead. She was all stiff and white... Anyway, I guess she'd had a heart attack, or something. It looked like natural causes."

"It must have been. She's had a bad ticker for years. I can guess what happened. It takes a lot of physical strength to cut apart a body. The strain probably wore her heart out. Norm's an idiot for bringing her along, anyway. What about the other body, the cowboy?"

Dave shook his head and wiped his eyes. "Gone. The tarp was tangled in some rocks like he'd fallen into the river and got separated from it. I couldn't find him."

"All right. That sounds okay. You didn't do anything wrong. Don't worry about Norm. I'll deal with him."

"Thanks, Jamie."

Norm walked into the tent, saw Ruth's stiff, curled body and gagged back a sob. "Oh, Ruthie... Ruthie..." She looked like one of those mummified bodies found in peat bogs after two thousand years. He knelt down beside her and looked her over, searching for any signs of foul play, even though he had to admit her death was probably from natural causes, and long overdue. It didn't make him feel any less saddened. Nor did it stop him from taking her Bowie knife and tying it to his boot. After all, she wasn't going to need it anymore.

He looked her body over for anything else he might want when he noticed the flattened nickel still lying on the rock. There was something engraved on it: a name. He liked this because she used to write the names of her victims on these coins when she scalped them. Apparently she was planning to do someone else after Andy Paul.

He picked the nickel up and held it close to his eyes so he could read the scratchy letters.

Montagna and Dave heard Norm scream, then pounding violently on something inside the tent. They both stood up, but only Montagna ran inside.

Norm was kicking Ruth's body as hard as he could, attacking her much worse than he had Kodiak, or the Sasquatch. This sudden change of attitude surprised Montagna, to say the least. He screamed at Norm to stop. Norm finally stopped and looked at Montagna, his face flushed with rage.

"Norm, what the hell's going on?"

"Look at this!" He tossed the flattened nickel to Montagna, who looked at it. "Read it!"

Montagna shook his head, not really surprised by what he was seeing.

"She was gonna do me! She was gonna do me!"

Montagna held the nickel in his hand, looking at the words scrawled upon its hammered surface: NORM COCKE.

❧

The camp was eerily silent well into the night. Norm had been completely freaked out by the revelation about what Ruth-less was going to do to him and was now sullen and self-pitying. Montagna left him alone to stew in his own juices, and Dave stayed by Montagna, still scared from Norm's reaction to Ruth's death.

Montagna whipped up a light meal of canned stew that he and Dave ate while Norm just drank beer after beer, staying by himself and cuddling the shotgun.

Breaking the silence, Dave spoke just above a whisper. "You think he'll be all right?"

Montagna sighed. "I suppose. I think he's more pissed off about

Ruth planning to scalp him than he is about her dropping dead."

"So, how are you planning to get the Sasquatch out of here?"

"Huh? Oh. We'll hook one end of the cage to the horse like a travois till we reach the Winnebago." Montagna got up and went over to Norm who was sitting on the fallen tree trunk in front of the fire. "Norm, I wanna call it a night, but somebody has to stay up and guard the Squatch."

"I'll do it." Norm barely muttered.

"I want to get an early start tomorrow..."

"I said I'd do it. Leave me alone."

Montagna understood Norm's anger, but he still felt hurt by his attitude. "All right. Just be sure to call for help if something happens."

Norm held up the shotgun. "Got all the help I need right here. Go to bed."

Norm let the fire dwindle until it extinguished itself. After the storm clouds had passed, the air was cool and the moon was three-quarters full, bathing everything in a pleasant blue glow.

But he wasn't thinking about the dark. His mind was on Ruth.

That evil, sadistic, useless old hag was going to do him. Him. Had their relationship for the past fifteen years been a joke? Was she planning to do him the entire time, or did she know she was dying and decided to take him on a whim? And how was she planning to do him? He'd seen old Ruthie take some big dudes, and all by herself. She may have been a little too old to handle that guy Paul completely on her own, but in years past, Norm had seen her do it. And she always took their scalps.

He saw her do a woman once. A meter maid in Seattle who ticketed Norm's wagon. When Norm came out of the store, old Ruthie had her tied up and gagged in the back of the wagon. They drove her out to his place in the woods and used her very, very badly for a week. Of course, Ruth added the meter maid's scalp to her collection. He was hoping that 'holier-than-thou' Women's Libber Cyrena would be next. He was looking forward to that, and in some ways he felt more bitter that it wasn't going to happen. But he was still alive, as was Cyrena. Cy-re-na. It almost sounded like siren. Norm almost chuckled as he wondered if she squealed like a siren. If he could get Kodiak out of the way, she'd be his for the taking. Then he'd make her squeal. Maybe as a tribute to Ruth-less he'd take Cyrena's scalp. Maybe as another tribute to old Ruthie, when he got back home, he'd cut Letitia's filthy, smelly scalp off, too.

There was a sound – something moved just beyond the trees. It wasn't that Norm let his guard down, but he was thinking so much about Ruth he imagined her as a ghost coming at him from the darkness. Norm Cocke wasn't usually given to irrational fears, but he was scared of ghosts. He'd never seen one, but just talking about them made it difficult for him to be alone in the dark. He had to get his mind off the subject, to get away from the mental picture he had of Ruth's dead body curled into a semi-fetal position, hardened with rigor mortis. And the more he tried to get his mind away from that image, the more difficult it was. He felt for her knife, which was still tied to his boot, and he felt minor relief that at least she wouldn't be able to get him with that.

Another sound – from behind. It was the horse. It got loose and was running away from the camp. Then it dawned on him...

As Norm got up, a form emerged from the darkness in front of him: Kodiak stepped out from behind a tree and with a deft flick of his wrist threw something straight into Norm's left eye and cut it open. Before Norm even felt the thing in his eye, Kodiak rammed a knee hard into Norm's crotch, knocking the fight out of him. He grabbed the shotgun out of Norm's hands and tossed it away. He slammed Norm face down into the ground twice, knocking him out. Satisfied that Norm was out for the duration, Kodiak looked at the tents to make sure nobody else heard the ruckus.

He found the lug wrench lying on the ground near a stack of boxes beside the closest tent. Again he checked the tents for any stirrings, until he felt safe enough to continue.

The Sasquatch was awake. Due to all the excitement earlier in the day, Montagna had forgotten to dope the animal. Kodiak and the creature were now staring at each other. He knew releasing this animal was right, and he felt good for the first time since this trip began.

When he put the wrench to the first bolt, the metal creaked from the release of pressure. The Sasquatch growled at him and bared its teeth. Kodiak remained still, knowing if he made any sudden moves the animal would react. This job would be so much easier if only the animal were still doped up.

Kodiak looked back at the tents, his mind reeling. This was his last chance, unless he just went ahead and killed Montagna, Norm and Dave. Then he'd have all the time in the world. But he didn't want to do that. He had killed plenty of people in Korea, and several more in his capacity as an undercover agent for the Department of Fish and Wildlife. While he wasn't afraid of any man, he took no pleasure in taking another's life, which was why he had tossed the shotgun away.

The creature screeched. It screeched loud and hard.

Dave came out first, running right at Kodiak. "I knew you'd come back – *OOMPH!!!*" He was struck suddenly across the mid-section with a tree branch, and when he doubled over, Cyrena hit him again across the back of his shoulders.

She staggered back when Dave hit the ground. He wasn't unconscious, but he was hurt enough to stay down on his hands and knees until he regained his senses. He made a sudden lunge for her, but she jumped back out of his reach, and he fell back on the ground. She couldn't bring herself to hit him again, so she grabbed up a handful of dirt and threw it in his eyes. He screamed and rubbed furiously at his eyes with his fists.

Montagna bolted out of his tent, and Kodiak shouted to Cyrena, "Get the hell out of here!"

Cyrena ran back to the woods as Montagna jumped over Dave like a hurdle, and dove into Kodiak. They slammed into the cage, which flipped on its side. Kodiak stood up, and Montagna punched him in the face. The blow hurt, but it was not sufficient to slow Kodiak down. He drew back his fist to hit Montagna, but Montagna slammed into him and they became interlocked.

The entire time the Sasquatch had been in the cage, it had been lying on its back. When the cage flipped on its side, the Sasquatch leaned farther over and toppled the cage face-down.

Montagna bit Kodiak's left pectoral muscle and drew blood. The pain was excruciating, but finite enough to fuel Kodiak's own rage. He grabbed Montagna by his ears, trying to pull his head back, but Montagna just bit harder. They staggered backward until they tripped over the unconscious Norm, and they went down.

Montagna was dislodged, left with only a bloody piece of Kodiak's shirt hanging from his mouth.

Kodiak pressed his hand against the wound on his chest, recalling what Ben had said about Montagna fighting dirty.

Instantly, Montagna jumped back on his feet and charged at Kodiak again, shrieking like a lunatic...

Dave cleaned most the dirt out of his eyes and looked around wildly. Completely ignoring Montagna and Kodiak, he found and followed Cyrena's footprints into the woods. He was going to get her. Finally. If it took all night, he was going to find her, tie her up, grope her, and then rape her. Just as he had always visualized it. She would be his first, his way, in the woods, where nobody could hear *him* scream.

He kept running, cringing from the pain in his belly and across his shoulders. Nothing seemed broken, and his rage insured that the pain would not stop him from reaching his goal, his obsession.

When Montagna came at him, Kodiak struck him hard across the mouth, sending him reeling to the ground. Before Montagna could re-orient himself, Kodiak grabbed him by a handful of the hair on the back of his head and hurled Montagna face-first into a tree with a CRACK!

The Sasquatch, now on its belly, pushed its hands through the bottom bars and lifted the cage off the ground. It began to drag itself away from the human action, toward the precipice above the waterfall, where there was a twenty-foot drop to the river.

Kodiak was watching the Sasquatch from the corner of his eye. Hopefully, all he would need to do is keep Montagna distracted long enough for it to break free of the cage on its own.

The Sasquatch grabbed the titanium bars and with its superior strength was able to bend them apart.

Montagna turned on Kodiak and put up his fists. His face was covered with splotches of blood that were black in the moonlight, but his eyes were wide and they seemed to glow, as did his teeth when he grimaced at Kodiak. "Come on! Let's do it! You know what I did to Ben! And when I'm done with you, I'm gonna do Cyrena!"

Kodiak didn't put up his fists. He just stood in front of Montagna with his arms at his side. He then lifted what looked like a playing card, and with a snap of his wrist, he threw it at Montagna...

The card shot through the air like a Chinese throwing star and struck between the knuckles on Montagna's right fist. It pierced his skin and stuck out by its corner. Montagna was dumbfounded by this – it defied logic – but it also drew his attention away from Kodiak.

Kodiak grabbed one of the bundled CO_2 rafts and hit Montagna in the face, smashing his nose. He struck Montagna's torso and threw him across the clearing, sending him smashing into the cage.

The Sasquatch was already halfway out of the cage, but was still wedged between the bars when Montagna slammed into it. The Sasquatch *yelled* with a noise that sounded almost human; a cry of rage that, had anybody heard it in the forest, they would have fled for their lives. It grabbed Montagna with its free hand, biting into the top of Montagna's head. Montagna screamed, wrestling furiously to get loose. But the Sasquatch's teeth were sharper than they looked. He could feel the skin on top of his head being ripped open as the Sasquatch's jaws locked down like a pit bull.

Kodiak watched in stunned disbelief.

Finally, Montagna grabbed the bottom of the cage and flipped it away from himself, sending the cage – and the Sasquatch – over the precipice.

Kodiak ran to the edge of the waterfall, ignoring Montagna, who was face-down in the dirt, with trails of fresh blood oozing across his bald pate like a bad comb-over.

Kodiak watched as the cage hit the rocks and disappeared in the phosphorescent cloud of white water. He ran to the deep pool of water beyond the waterfall and jumped in, still holding the CO_2 raft, and landed in the deepest part of the river, clearing the rocks.

The icy water almost gave him a heart attack. When he came up for air the cage bumped up against him, and he grabbed it.

Montagna steadied himself on his knees and had to fight panic when he saw how much blood was dripping down from his injured head. He reached up and felt loose pieces of tattered skin, some the size of a nickel.

He spotted Kodiak in the water below and remembered seeing the shotgun on the ground during the fight, and he went for it. He came back to the precipice over the river and tried to get as clear a view of Kodiak as the moonlight would allow.

The blast narrowly missed Kodiak, but some of the pellets struck the cage, and he released it. He took a deep breath and dove back under water, out of the shotgun's range.

Montagna pumped the shotgun, but waited before firing again. He had one shot left, and it had to count. There had been four shells in the shotgun before the incident with Ben, and the rest were in the horse's saddle bag: the horse that was now gone. He watched the river, waiting for Kodiak to break the surface, his finger caressing the trigger, playing with it, itching to shoot...

Kodiak swam with the current, keeping his arms out before him to prevent hitting any rocks and to feel for the cage. He had to come up for air, but he knew Montagna was waiting for him to pop up. Ignoring the immediate need for oxygen, he fumbled with the raft until he found the triggering mechanism and pulled it open. The CO_2 tank filled the raft with an explosive *HIIISSSSTTTTT!!!!!!* The raft tore from Kodiak's grasp.

When the raft broke the surface Kodiak saw the angry flash of the shotgun high above, heard the ear-shattering *BOOM!* and felt the water spray on impact. Montagna missed again.

Kodiak came up for air and swam past the shredded remains of the raft.

Montagna threw the shotgun at him, screaming with rage. Everything was gone: Kodiak, Cyrena, and most important, the Sasquatch.

Behind him Norm stirred into consciousness. He was moaning.

Montagna dropped onto the ground beside Norm. He had come across Ruth's red bandanna and was gently daubing at his throbbing, bloody head. The pain was too severe to wipe, and he didn't want to risk tearing away more skin, so he folded the bandanna diagonally, wrapped it across the top of his head, and tied it under his chin, like a babushka.

Norm, still with the playing card sticking from his left eye, looked up at Montagna. "Ruthie... Ruthie... You look like crap..."

WHACK!!! Montagna cold-cocked Norm across the mouth, sending him back into unconsciousness.

જ

The sun came up but wasn't strong enough to burn off the shroud of coastal fog that filled the Queets Valley. In his crazed pursuit of Cyrena, Dave Bovard had become hopelessly lost. The thin air left him gasping for breath, and he had to double over to relieve the cramps that developed in his sides from running so hard. He spat, trying to dispel the feeling of having a wad of packaging tape in his mouth.

He had come so close to grabbing her. Just another couple of inches and he could have pulled her back by grabbing a handful of her hair. He would have pulled her head back so hard it probably would have snapped her neck. But she had gained speed and outdistanced him again.

He would still have her. Of that he was dead certain. She was a few years older than he was, and he had strength on his side. Women like her had no real capacity for effective self-defense. Besides, what was she – a middle-aged, divorced school teacher who tagged along on this trip to break the continual boredom of an otherwise uneventful existence. If she was looking for a good time, he was going to see that she got one. He'd ram a good time into her. That's what he had in mind for her. Someplace where nobody could hear her scream. Then he'd kill her.

The gray fog turned white in the daylight, but it was still impossible to see more than twenty feet in any direction. Everything was just shadows. Suddenly the fear of being lost started to sink in, and Dave had to hug himself to keep from shaking. There were wild animals out here. Just the other day he saw tracks belonging to what looked like a whole pack of wolves. What if there were wolves around now? Or bears? He couldn't block out the mental image of the juvenile Sasquatch after he shot it; the way it turned on him, its eyes wide and staring like a crazed animal. Then it started walking toward him... He changed the picture in his head to what he was going to do to Cyrena when he caught her. He got another erection.

He started walking. Hulking shadows on all sides offered no comfort and no familiarity, until he was close enough to make out the bark pattern on the trees through the fog. Even being lost, he knew he wasn't far behind Cyrena, and at least he was something of a skilled outdoorsman. But she was running blind, and if he was this scared, she must be coming completely unglued. Maybe she'd even be glad to see him.

Something moved.

Directly ahead, no more than thirty feet. He only caught a glimpse, but in that moment he saw enough of her long brown hair to eliminate his growing fear. Then she was gone. He picked up his pace, keeping a steady eye on the swirling patch of fog that she moved through. He stopped to listen.

She was still ahead, but not moving. She must have sensed his presence and taken refuge behind a tree. He went up a fifty-foot embankment for a better vantage point, found a rock, hefted it weightily in his hand, then discarded it for a bigger one. He held the rock and squatted down, peering down into the white, cloudy soup for any sign of movement from her.

Cyrena knew Dave saw her when she passed between the trees. She slammed up against the trunk of a pine and held her breath, trying to come up with some plan of action that would get her out of this mess. The fog was still too heavy to run through. She could easily trip and fall. And if she broke a limb, Dave would be on top of her in seconds and a broken limb would be the least of her problems.

She looked around for a weapon. During their stay in the gully Kodiak told her anything could be a weapon so long as you kept your wits about you. Well, looking around now she didn't see anything she could use, and as for her wits, she seemed to recall losing those several miles back.

When some time had passed and he hadn't heard any other sound, Dave knew he had Cyrena cornered. Since she was scared, there was no sense in attacking her outright. He'd much rather draw this out and play with her. Savor her suffering. He cupped his mouth with his left hand, holding the rock in his right, poised to throw and hollered, "Cy-re-na! I know you can hear me! You know there's no point in running anymore! Come on out!"

She had no weapon, no plan, and no serious hope for escape. But she did refuse to let him believe he intimidated her, which is exactly what he did. She reached into her pocket and took out one of the playing cards she found on the ground back at the camp. Of course there was no way she could do what George did with it. She shoved it back into her pocket and yelled, " Come and get – get me!" Despite the waver in her voice, she sounded confident and unafraid, but God only knew she sure didn't feel that way. She knew exactly what Dave had in mind for her, but she was going to make sure he suffered in the attempt.

Dave smiled, deciding he couldn't waste any more time, as the fog was starting to thin, and he had to take advantage of its cover. The landscape around him was becoming clearer, and the natural colors were coming through.

The image of Andy Paul's horror-stricken face filled his mind again. But instead of remorse, or dread, it confirmed to him that there was no turning back from what he had already done. Cyrena was now just sweet icing on the cake.

He grasped the rock firmly and stepped into the open. He saw her between the trees fifty feet below. An easy target. In high school he was offered baseball scholarships by several major colleges, and everyone who knew him expected that he would make the major leagues. His arrest in his senior year for dealing drugs ended all his hopes of college and a career in baseball. Through all these past years, his throwing arm remained strong. So when he threw the rock, it went straight for home...

But the thrill of the hunt, and what would follow, turned suddenly to icy terror as he realized his intended target was not who – or what – he thought. Just as the rock arced downward, the head of hair rose up to a full height of *nine feet.*

Dave froze, his eyes filled with horror, his body numb with sick dread as the rock hit with a dead solid *THUD!* Everything seemed to stand perfectly still for several long moments.

Then the animal reacted.

Cyrena feared the worst when she heard nothing more from Dave. She anticipated him tackling her at any second, but nothing happened. She heard the smack of the rock against something no more than thirty feet from where she was standing. Then she heard a startled grunt; something that sounded like the angry snort of an enraged bull.

Dave Bovard screamed.

It was truly *Gigantopithecus.* What stood below Dave was a monster with shoulders four feet across and a chest like two concrete slabs. It stood upright like a man, and was covered with dark hair like the juvenile. When the rock smashed into the back of its head, the beast whirled around and looked right at him.

Dave urinated in his pants. Even though he was on a rise fifty feet above the Giganto, its expression of rage and total ferocity paralyzed him. The beast rushed up the hill at him, bellowing with a roar like that of an angry baboon – only much more powerful.

Dave drew in a breath and regained something of his senses. His panic instinct drove him to turn and run. As the Giganto raced after him, it let out another ferocious roar, and its intensity almost made him break into wracking sobs. Even so, he was somewhat heartened by the fact that it sounded a little farther away than when the animal had come within grabbing distance of him at the top of the rise.

His footfalls felt awkward and clumsy, with his torso thrust so far forward he felt like he was going to stumble and fall face-down. There was no trail for him to follow, and the uneven terrain only jarred and slowed his progress. But something kept him going. He knew just by the size of the monster's legs its strides would equal several of his own, but his will to survive compelled him forward.

Behind him the Giganto ran at a pace comparable to a wolf. This animal didn't charge on all fours like the other great apes, but was running similar to a man, with its arms thrust forward, as though pulling at the air. The thick, solid slaps of its feet hitting the ground came up fast and loud behind Dave, and he could hear it panting in vicious grunts as it kept after him.

Dave lost all control and screamed, "Get away from me! Get away! Help! Help! Jamie! Norm! Help me!" As he ran down a minor slope he saw his path was blocked by a nurse log: a fallen tree trunk upon which several newer trees grew feeding off the decay of the deadfall. Normally, it would be a beautiful sight, but to Dave Bovard it might as well have been the electric chair.

He came up against the dead trunk, which was twelve feet high, and he grasped a section of bark that immediately broke loose under his weight as he tried to pull himself up. He heard the thunderous steps of the pursuer coming up fast behind him as he tried to scramble up the side of the deadfall again.

He almost made it halfway up, when his leg was suddenly grabbed by the huge paw.

Cyrena came out from behind her tree and saw the Giganto rush up the fifty-foot embankment in four easy bounds, then run after the screaming Dave Bovard. As much as she hated Dave for terrorizing her, she felt greater terror for what would happen if that animal got hold of him.

She couldn't hold back her tears as she ran after them with the futile hope of doing something to prevent the oncoming disaster. By the time she clawed her way up the loose layer of dirt, she had lost sight of them both and could only hear Dave's screams echoing from a good distance away. She got to the top of the rise and continued on, refusing to stop to catch her breath, or wipe her eyes as she followed the animal's twenty-inch footprints through the woods.

Dave never lost consciousness. When the Giganto dragged him off the tree, he lay on the ground looking up at the monstrous ape as it roared. This thing bore little resemblance to the juvenile Sasquatch. True, they were of the same species; both were bipedal, and had the same facial features and conical head. But the sheer size and brutishness of this animal eliminated any connection to the innocent, wide-eyed curiosity of the juvenile.

The Giganto never gave him a chance. Its face was almost a caricature; eyes hideously wide, lips drawn back bearing huge teeth. It held both Dave's feet in one hand and lifted him off the ground...

Cyrena stopped a hundred feet from where the Giganto lifted Dave off the ground by his feet and... *WHAM!!!*

She staggered back, all the breath forced from her lungs as if it had been she who was struck. The monstrous ape lifted Dave again and slammed him into the ground like a wet bag of cement. She clenched her eyes shut at the sickening crunch of almost every bone in his body being shattered.

Dave was dead after the first blow, but the Giganto was still far too enraged to have completely vented its anger. It lifted him off the ground a third time and slammed him down again, spraying the surrounding flora, and itself, with his blood.

When it lifted his body for the fourth time, he looked like a wet rag. *WHAM!!!*

ॐ

Norm was crying. When he finally came around, Montagna pulled the card from his eye and saw just how serious the wound really was. His eye was split open and leaking blood mixed with clear *vitreous humor*. Montagna didn't want to disinfect it, because he was sure that the pain would be excruciating. He barely managed to keep from throwing up as he gently wiped the skin around the eye, and then covered it by wrapping a gauze bandage around Norm's head. The pain was unbearable for Norm, who kept blubbering like a little child.

Montagna paced around, frustrated by his inability to ease his friend's suffering, or to just shut him the hell up. Norm's bawling was really starting to gnaw at him. "For God's sake, Norm! Is it really that bad? I mean, isn't there some way you can just block it out, or something?"

Norm turned on him. "I'm blind! I can't see a damn thing! I am totally blind!" As a reaction to the destruction of his left eye, Norm's right eye went into *sympathetic ophthalmia;* hysterical blindness. Norm's tone softened and he said, "Please, Jamie, get me out of here. For God's sake, please get me to a doctor. *Please!"*

This created a dilemma for Montagna. While he felt some pity for Norm, he was totally incapable of feeling any empathy for him. Norm's pleas only made him feel put out. "Norm, what's done is done. Your eye's been cut open. There's no doctor in the world who can save it for you."

Norm burst into louder sobs, sucking in deep breaths between bawls.

Montagna really wanted to beat the crap out of him just to shut him up, but he relented. "And whatever's going on with the other eye, well, it's just gonna have to take care of itself.

"I'm not saying this to be mean, or heartless. I'm just trying to toughen you up, buddy, because our work here isn't finished. What we gotta do is find the kid. We have to find Bovard, because we can still salvage this mess.

"First of all, we can forget about Pittman. He's not interested in a dead Sasquatch. But the rest of the world is. So what I figure we do is, we get Bovard and we cruise on downstream in the raft till we find where the Sasquatch washed up. Then we take the body back, and we make our fortune."

Finally, Norm calmed down enough to listen to what Montagna was saying. "Jamie, I'm hurting something terrible. I don't think I can stand much more of this, and them pain pills ain't kicked in at all."

Montagna knelt beside him, held him by his shoulders and spoke calmly. "And just imagine what the newspapers will say about you. How you continued in the face of physical adversity after what Kodiak did to you. You'll be a hero, Norm. A rich hero."

Norm sat quietly, tears trailing down the right side of his face from his undamaged eye.

Montagna watched him, stifling the urge to kill him, which he was certain he would do if Norm started that bawling again, or if he refused to continue on the hunt. "All right, Norm. I'm gonna give it to you straight, because we're tight and always have been. I'm going after the body. Now, between Bovard and myself, we can help you make it through the woods and we won't mind being slowed up, if that's what it takes. The choice is yours. You can come if you want, or we can leave you here with a load of provisions and firewood so you'll be safe until we get back."

Norm shook his head, bewildered. "You call yourself my friend? Jamie, I'm suffering here! Don't you understand that? I can't go with you. And if you leave me... Even with enough provisions, how the hell am I supposed to defend myself if something comes cruising around looking for a bite to eat? I'm helpless!"

Montagna said nothing.

Norm knew the answer couldn't be any more clear. "All right, Jamie. You win. But I ain't gonna help you pack."

Montagna smiled and slapped Norm's shoulder. "Good man."
He got up and set about packing things for the trip.
Norm started blubbering again.

ॐ

Cyrena was shivering. Not from the morning cold, which had
burned off with the fog, revealing the true, vibrant colors of the
Olympic Forest in all its majestic glory, but rather she was shaking
from what she had seen happen to Dave Bovard only ten minutes
ago.

She had fallen on her backside, unable to draw breath as the
Gigantopithecus kicked the lifeless sack of Dave's body. Satisfied that
there was no fight left in him, it turned its face skyward and roared,
its sound carrying on the wind, reverberating throughout the
canyon. Then it looked around, a couple of times right in her
direction, but the Giganto didn't seem to notice her, and it lumbered
off into the woods.

It seemed like several minutes before Cyrena could breathe, and
she even thought she was going to die of asphyxia when she
suddenly gasped in a breath so loud she thought the giant ape
might hear it and come back to kill her. But it didn't.

She sat on the hard ground, feeling the pebbles and pine needles
sticking into her backside and legs, but she didn't have the strength
to get up. She had to see what was left of Dave; not out of any
morbid curiosity, for she didn't have any, but she had to make sure
he was dead. She didn't believe he could have survived that
thrashing, and he was probably dead after the first strike, but she
knew it would be inhumane to leave him there if, by some miracle,
he wasn't dead.

She was crying from the terror of what she had witnessed, and
the senselessness of it. She knew what Dave had in mind for her if
he had caught her and in all reality, the Giganto probably saved her
life. But she wasn't capable of the same hate and disregard for life
and dignity that the others possessed. Besides, Dave may have been
a punk kid who needed to have his butt kicked, but she certainly
didn't feel he deserved to die, especially not like this.

Cyrena struggled to her feet, holding onto the nearest tree trunk
for support until the rubbery feeling left her legs. She looked over at

Dave who lay about thirty yards from where she was standing. He had no form; just a lump about six feet long wrapped in his jacket and pants and covered with blood. She closed her eyes and walked carefully across the small open area between the trees.

She prayed that Kodiak would show up so he could look at the body instead, and she also hoped it would be Kodiak who showed up before Montagna and Norm, as they would surely finish what Dave tried to start.

And what about Norm? She still couldn't believe what Kodiak had done with that simple playing card. She had seen a magician do something similar once. He threw ordinary playing cards across a stage and got them to stick into a plank of wood.

She finally came upon Dave's earthly remains and saw that he was very clearly dead. Cyrena turned away from what was left of him and threw up.

She ran from the place where Dave had been killed. She ran in the opposite direction that the Giganto had gone, and hopefully in a direction away from where Montagna and Norm were camped.

After about a mile she spotted a column of smoke rising above the trees more than a hundred feet ahead, and her heart leaped into her throat from fear. It could only be a campfire, and this far out it could only have belonged to Montagna and Norm. She hated being alone like this in the wilderness and continued her silent prayer that Kodiak would show up.

But for now she only had herself to rely on.

Being this close to the camp she'd have to make a quiet retreat, or they'd hear her and come running. As she turned to leave, a powerful hand reached from behind and pulled her aside. Before she could utter a cry, another hand covered her mouth and turned her around to face – Kodiak.

When he was sure that she recognized him, he let go of her.

She stepped back just to orient herself to what was happening and got another shock – Kodiak was naked. "Oh, my God..." She turned her head, embarrassed.

"May I borrow your jacket?"

"Huh?"

"Your jacket. I'd like to cover myself up."

"Oh, my God... yes. Yes, here..." She took off her jacket and handed it to him while still looking away.

He tied it around his waist. "Thanks. You can turn back around."

She did, and her eyes went automatically to his groin, which was covered by her jacket. She then saw the brutal wound on his left pectoral muscle where Montagna had bitten him. "Dear God, what happened to you?"

"Come on." He led her to the fire, and she saw his clothes were all laid out on rocks, drying out. "I went into the river last night and had to get out of my clothes before I caught pneumonia. I'm glad you're okay. How'd you manage to lose Bovard?"

Her expression became twisted with anguish as she sat down beside the fire, her eyes becoming wet again. "He came real close to getting me. He must have followed me for a couple of miles, but just when I thought he had me... he was attacked..."

"Attacked? By what?"

She shook her head, her eyes wide with tears streaming down her face. "A Sasquatch."

"Ours?"

"Oh, nooooooooo. It had to be the biggest thing I've ever seen! It was easily nine feet tall."

Kodiak searched her face for the source of the anguish that wrenched her. "Tell me exactly what happened."

"Oh, God. It was... it was *enraged*. I don't know what he did, but it went after him like a mad dog. And he kept screaming. He sounded almost like an animal himself, that terrible screaming...

"I followed them. I thought if I could help him get away from it, but... When I got there it had him by his feet and was slamming him into the ground.

"I went over to make sure he wasn't... It's stupid, but I had to make sure he wasn't still alive, or something."

"He was dead," Kodiak said, as if he had seen it for himself.

Cyrena nodded, closing her eyes and letting out a weak cry. Kodiak sat beside her and took her in his arms, holding her close to him. For the first time since this nightmare began, she felt safe. His powerful arms and thick chest gave her tremendous comfort. She revelled in it like a little girl and let her tears flow freely.

Kodiak just held her, taking the same kind of pleasure he knew all too little of in his own life.

An hour later he put his clothes on. They were warm and dry, but felt stiff the way clothes always do after being left to sun-dry on a flat surface. As he pulled on his T-shirt she admired the shape and definition of his muscular frame. He was not a young man, but he hardly looked his age; about fifteen years younger, closer to her own age. He put on his flannel shirt and rolled up the sleeves. He turned to face her and a shadow of cold anger altered his features. "You interested in doing something that'll screw those guys good?"

She stared at him, clearly undecided. The things that had happened out here were so far beyond her own scope she felt sick. She sat down on the ground and all she could say was, "I don't want anyone else to die."

Kodiak hadn't realized until now how hard this was for Cyrena. He knelt down before her and placed his hands on her shoulders, looking at her with as much compassion as he could muster. "I'm not talking about that. Last night the cage went into the river with the Sasquatch. I went in after it, but I lost it before I could get it out of the cage. Chances are it drowned."

She said, "If that's true, then isn't it useless to them?"

"A dead one's just as valuable as a live one. I want to find the body and bury it somewhere Montagna can't get his useless hands on it to exploit it."

She considered this, a shadow of sadness clouding her gentle face. "That's what it's all about with these guys, isn't it? Exploitation."

"For Montagna it is. And right now he's looking just as hard for that body as we should be."

"But even if he doesn't find it, won't he just go after another one?"

"If he does, the only one he's likely to run into is the one that killed Dave. And I can't say I'd feel real bad about that."

꒰ꕤ

They could only take one backpack, so Montagna was especially selective about the items he chose. Dehydrated food packs and canteens were obvious, as were the first aid kit, and a flashlight. He packed a tent, their sleeping bags, a nylon rope, a can of lighter fluid, a butane torch, the machete, and the last two six packs of beer.

The radio was too cumbersome to bring along, so Montagna

destroyed it.

He placed the backpack on Norm and the bundled CO_2 raft on himself, along with two aluminum oars. He used the nylon rope to tie around each of their waists so he could guide Norm. Their plan was to take the Queets River downstream until they found the place where the cage and the juvenile Sasquatch had washed up. Montagna put out the campfire, and they headed for the river. But first they would have to find Dave.

Norm whimpered most of the time, and openly cried on some occasions, but what really infuriated Montagna was Norm's incessant whining for Montagna to slow down. The rugged and totally unfamiliar terrain caused him to continually lose his footing, and every time he stumbled the rope would cut into Montagna's waist and bring him down, too. "Please, Jamie, this is killing me. We gotta take a breather. Please."

"We are only a mile and a half from camp! All right. All right." Montagna untied the rope from his waist, and they both sat down. They had to move inland, because the river's edge had proven impossible for Norm to make in his present condition. While they no longer had visual contact with the river, Montagna wasn't concerned about missing the body. His plan was to go down to the river and backtrack what they had passed while Norm rested.

As Norm sat on a rock, pulling burrs from his hands, he continued to moan. "Hey, Jamie?"

Montagna was curt. "What?"

"How's about one of them beers? And you think maybe we should change this bandage?"

Montagna opened a can of beer and shoved it into Norm's hand, spilling beer and foam.

"Hey, take it easy, would ya'? You know Kodiak did this as much to you as he did to me."

Montagna looked out at the woods. "How do you figure?"

"I'm slowing you down. I know you could've offed me, or left me for the wolves, or something. But you didn't. You're a true friend, and you're being made to suffer because of it. Because of Kodiak."

Norm was no sage, but Montagna liked his way of thinking. He no longer felt guilty about being angry at Norm. "Thanks, buddy. What do you say you polish off that cold one and we make tracks?"

For the first time since his injury, Norm managed a chuckle. "Well, actually, it's more like a piss-warm one, but I think I'll manage." He up-ended the can and guzzled the beer.

Montagna was thinking about Kodiak. Kodiak didn't like him, and he should have wanted to kill him for it. But he still had that sick desire to like him, and be like him.

A fly on a leaf next to his face caught his eye. It was a green fly, and green flies were drawn to decaying meat. He looked at Norm whose blindness prevented Montagna from sharing this discovery. "Norm, I think we may have struck pay-dirt."

Norm lowered the beer and belched. "Huh?"

"Look, I gotta check something out. Can I leave you here for a while? I won't be long, I promise."

"Just give me another beer, old buddy."

Montagna hastily shoved the rest of the six pack in Norm's hands and took off.

About twenty yards farther east the green flies began to swarm; the source of decay was nearby. There was no way the Sasquatch's body could have washed this far inland. It must have been dragged up here by some predator. He felt exhilarated. He was going to retrieve the creature's body, and he wouldn't have to drag Norm through the whole canyon after all.

He came to the bottom of a fifty-foot slope and stopped cold, staring at huge footprints that went all the way up. This was no juvenile, but rather a beast of monstrous proportions. Montagna's heart sank as he realized this bigger creature must have come across the carcass of the juvenile and carried it away.

Nonetheless, he climbed up the rise and followed the twenty-inch footprints that went farther east. Judging by the length of its stride, he determined that the animal had either been running, or was twenty-seven feet tall.

As he followed the tracks, the swarm of green flies became so heavy he had to constantly wave them away from his face. Then just fifty feet away he saw the source to which the flies were drawn, and where the huge footprints stopped.

There was a body lying before a gigantic nurse log, but it was not the juvenile Sasquatch. It was Dave Bovard. Montagna walked over to the body, fascinated by the unreal gruesomeness of it. His body was literally flattened. His arms and legs were splayed out, but they had no angles, as the bones were pulverized under the flesh, giving him a loose, ragdoll look. He never would have recognized it as Dave except by the clothing; his head was smashed like a hard-boiled egg that had been slammed against a kitchen counter.

The twenty-inch footprints left a very clear indication of where the animal had gone after killing Bovard. Montagna studied the prints, totally disregarding Dave. He tried to conjure up a mental image of what this massive animal must look like so he could get some idea of how he was going to confront it. Taking it alive was a ridiculous idea, especially with blind Norm slowing him up. But all he needed was a couple of pounds of flesh tissue, maybe some marrow from one of its bones. He formulated an idea. And Norm would be of considerable help.

Montagna smiled so broadly his face hurt.

The Twenty-Inch Footprints

T he cage had washed two miles downstream from the waterfall, throughout the course of which it had been torn to pieces among the rocks. The largest section remaining was the end piece where the leg chain was bolted. It was entangled in a shrub between some large rocks on the bank, making it inaccessible from the shore. Kodiak waded knee-deep into the icy water and tore the ragged sheet of metal from the bush.

Cyrena was farther downstream searching for any indication of what had become of the juvenile Sasquatch.

"Anything?" He had to holler to be heard above the roaring water.

"No. Whatever happened, it either got away, or the body was washed farther downstream!"

He came over to her, his eyes scanning both sides of the river.

"You think they could have gotten to it first?"

Kodiak shook his head. "No. Even if Norm was feeling up to getting around, which I seriously doubt, there's no indication that anybody else has been around here. There are no footprints, and if they did find the body, there sure as hell would have been some sign of them having dragged it away."

She asked, "You think it could have gotten away?"

He paused for a long time, then said, "That's a tough call. There's no way it could have gotten out of that cage before getting battered on the rocks. Considering the beating it would have been subjected to, it would have to have one hell of a constitution to survive. I hope it did."

"Yeah, well, if you got to see what they grow up to be like, you'd believe they're capable of surviving a pre-emptive nuclear strike," Cyrena said. "You wanna keep looking?"

He took another look around the river. "No. It's definitely not around here. Besides, the sun'll be going down soon, and we still need to find shelter."

"I don't know if I'll be able to sleep after I saw what that big one did to Dave."

Kodiak said, "I can practically guarantee Bovard did something stupid to piss it off. And he paid dearly for his mistake. We don't make those kinds of mistakes."

They made a small lean-to from pine branches, which would give them adequate protection if it should rain. They found blueberries, blackberries, and pine nuts in the area, and gathered them up. Kodiak made a paste from the inside of the bark of a pine tree, naturally rich in vitamin C. While it wasn't the most substantial or tasty meal either of them had ever eaten, it was sufficient nourishment.

They huddled together for added warmth after finishing their meal, and she tiredly laid her head on his shoulder. "You going to sleep soon?"

"In a while. I'd like to take another stab at the river tomorrow. See if we can't find that body. But we're not staying in this canyon another night. We'll hike to the Hoh Rainforest Visitor Center."

She smiled, watching the fire. "Were you ever married?"

She thought he ignored the question. Then he threw another stick into the fire and said, "Nobody in their right mind would have me." There was another pause. "What about you? I can't imagine anyone letting somebody like you get away."

She smiled again, warmed by the compliment and the security she felt by being with him. "Once, but it was a mistake. We were married right out of high school, and that was pretty difficult. What finally did us in was his inability to keep it in his pants whenever he was with other women."

"Idiot."

"Well, like I said, he was young. Not much younger than Dave... was. He had wild oats to sow, I guess, so we went our separate ways. I preferred not to have any hard feelings about it. At least that way I was better equipped to get on with my life."

"Any kids?"

"No."

They sat in silence for several minutes, just listening to the crackling fire. Then she asked, "What did you do after you left the Park Service, and how did you end up a cryptozoologist?"

"I joined up with the Department of Fish and Wildlife. I worked undercover going after poachers. It was probably the most rewarding work I've ever done. You run into a lot of people like Norm, and you get to put them away. Sometimes for a very long time."

"What made you give it up?"

"It seems like a long time ago. I guess it was. Fifteen years now. You ever hear of Hilary Fischer?"

"No."

"Well, he was big in the news after myself and a couple other agents busted him for poaching bald eagles. He would hide the bodies inside mounted bears and ship them all over the world. But when the axe fell, he turned us out and killed one of my friends. All hell broke loose, and he took off into the mountains. He was kind of a Claude Dallas; you know, became something of a folk hero on the lam.

"Anyway, after six months we weren't able to get a fix on him, so I got the idea that we spring an old enemy of his. I take it you're familiar with Russell Reid?"

"Oh, yeah," she said. "He was convicted of killing that federal marshal in 1978. Then he escaped, or did he die on the run?"

"He escaped. He and Fischer were bitter enemies back in the early seventies when Reid busted Fischer for poaching on Indian land. I knew Reid could get Fischer given the chance. I had enough clout with the boys in charge, so they let me pull Reid out of prison long enough to track Fischer.

"There was a lot of controversy surrounding the case against Reid. A lot of people believed he was set up by the government, and it looked like things were gonna reach a boiling point within a very few years. This gave the feds a chance to relieve some of the pressure.

"As it went, Fischer fled to Canada. The Northwest Territories. When Reid crossed the border after him, my ass was on the fire. It was up to me to get them both back." He paused, looking deep into the dwindling fire. "Anyway, when I came back, I turned in my badge. It was time to go. I'd seen so much wholesale killing of animals, and people, I was sick of it. There was even more government sanctioned killing going on than anything the poachers were collecting."

"So what happened with that case?"

"Fischer was gone. I could have had Reid, but it turned out old Uncle Sam wasn't through with him, yet. The plan was to set him up and kill him for trying to escape. Rumor was they were even going to take out a few bystanders as fodder."

"You let him go?"

"Yeah, but he doesn't know that. Matter of fact, if he ever saw me again, I'm sure he'd kill me."

They lay back and listened to the ambient sounds of the woods at night; chirruping crickets, mosquitoes, and the distant roar of a waterfall. Kodiak felt the numbing sensation of sleep starting to creep into his body and begin to overtake him. Then he heard another sound: light, gentle snoring against his neck. Cyrena had fallen asleep.

ใช้

Norm was starting to get some of the vision back in his right eye. The images were still badly fogged, but he could make out some shapes and differentiate light from dark.

Montagna tried to get up, but was stiff and sore from sleeping on the hard ground. The urge to urinate came upon him fast, so he ignored his discomfort and got up. Standing upon a boulder and squinting into the morning sun, he could see Mount Olympus rising above the green forest against the blue sky. For most others this sight would have taken their breath away, creating a bond between them and the Creator unlike anything they had known prior. But to Jamie Montagna it was just something to look at while he unzipped his trousers and pissed into a bush.

Norm was elated. The thrill of getting his sight back outweighed the pain from his wounded left eye. "And the best part, Jamie," Norm was saying, "I'm gonna get to see the look on Kodiak's face when I slit his throat with Ruthie's knife!"

Montagna needed to tune Norm out. His persistent rambling about getting his sight back and what he was going to do to Kodiak irritated him almost as much as when Norm was crying. But he needed Norm, because they were still on the track of the *Gigantopithecus* that killed Dave.

The animal had left a steady trail of prints for nearly three miles along the sandy bank of the Hoh River, about five miles north of the Queets, and they were making great time. Norm was now able to move quicker than before, but Montagna still had to use the rope to guide him along.

They spent much of the morning backtracking to where the prints left off. From there it was guess work, but judging by the terrain, and being this deep into the woods, Montagna surmised that the animal had no fear of running into humans here, so it would take the path of least resistance: a natural path twenty yards inland that was adjacent to the river.

There were a couple of times they had to climb over some large rocks, and Norm had to be especially careful. Once, he dislodged the gauze bandage that covered his eye, and Montagna caught a glimpse of it. All the blood had been washed away when he cleaned the wound. Now the eye was closed, leaking a steady stream of clear plasma. As Norm reattached the bandage, Montagna shuddered at the thought of what such an injury must feel like – and Kodiak had done it with a simple playing card! After Kodiak had gotten away, Montagna plucked the card from his own knuckle and tried to throw it. It simply drifted to the ground, spinning aimlessly.

"Why'd you stop?" Norm couldn't see that Montagna was looking up at a ragged cliff-face that they would have to scale in order to continue along their way.

"How are you for climbing, buddy?"

Norm shrugged. "Obviously nothing too rigorous, but I think I'm good for it. You still haven't told me what we're going all this way for, Jamie."

"We're following the river to find out where the Squatch's body washed up."

Norm was still confused. His right eye was directed at Montagna, but was unable to make visual contact, so it drifted about the perimeters of his face. "None of this terrain seems familiar to me."

"That's because you're blind. How's the eye?"

"The left one's throbbing real bad, but I think I can make out shapes with the other."

This wasn't what Montagna wanted to hear. The plan he was considering would work a lot better if Norm was still totally blind.

But he could also tell Norm was still a long way from getting any useful sight back, so he decided to go ahead.

≥●

Kodiak and Cyrena made breakfast from the last of the berries and pine nuts leftover from the previous night.

"It's about a twelve-mile hike to the Hoh Rainforest Visitor Center. You sure you're up for it?"

She smiled, looking angelic with the sun shining on her hair and into her green eyes. "For the chance to sleep in a real bed tonight, I'd hike a hundred miles."

"By the time we're through, it just might seem like it."

"You think we'll run into Jamie and Norm?"

"We won't be that lucky. You ready?"

They gathered up what few belongings they had and started on their way.

≥●

Montagna and Norm made it to the cliff-top in an hour. Norm's agility had improved greatly, and the rocks they scaled were all solid and fairly easy to climb. At the top a small scattering of trees were twisted into spirals from years of growing totally unprotected from the constant winds that buffeted them. Norm found a shady spot under one of the trees and laid back on the cool, smooth surface of rock.

Montagna looked down at a lake at the bottom of the cliff. It was a large body of turquoise water that turned indigo as the shallows disappeared to greater depths. In the water Montagna could make out a school of trout that swam parallel to the shore, then in unison turned sharply toward the deep water.

In the middle of the lake was an island; not a large one, but bigger than a mere sandbar. There was a beach directly across from where Montagna stood, but the rest of the island was made up of large granite boulders that rose from the dark blue water of the lake. The island boasted dense forestation, and was peaked by the three hundred-year-old cedar and spruce pines that were so common out here.

As his eyes followed the school of trout, he saw something else in the water: the *Gigantopithecus* was swimming toward the island.

Montagna rubbed his eyes and leaned forward for as clear a view of the animal as was possible. It was huge, just as its footprints attested, about nine feet long and dark. It was swimming like a frog, propelling itself forward with powerful sweeps of its long legs, while it held its arms out before it. This was unusual for an ape, as known species are incapable of swimming, yet this animal was clearly well-adapted to the water. This was a common phenomenon associated with Sasquatch activity by witnesses all over the world, for as long as people have reported seeing these animals. But Montagna was amazed nonetheless.

Montagna looked at Norm, who was sleeping. When he looked back at the Giganto it reached the island and was wading up the beach like a walking totem pole. In another couple of seconds it vanished into the woods.

Montagna went over to his backpack and starting grabbing the things he could use as weapons. The machete, the butane torch and the can of lighter fluid. Having seen the beast first-hand, he could understand the terror that must have filled Dave just before it got him. But Montagna's fears were overwhelmed by his desire to bring it, or at least a piece of it, out of the canyon. Naturally he'd have preferred it alive, but he wasn't an idiot.

Looking at these meager items, he wasn't sure what the exact steps would be, but he knew he had the most important element for his plan to work: Norm.

He woke Norm up, his voice quavering with barely contained excitement. "Norm! Norm, I found it! I found the body!"

Norm sat up, yawning and pressing his hand against the bandage over his wounded eye. "Where?"

"Get up." Montagna helped Norm to his feet, and they walked to the edge of the cliff. "Can you see that island? It's directly ahead, in the middle of the lake."

Norm sounded startled. "That's a lake?"

"Then you can see it? The island?"

"Yeah..."

"The body's lying on the beach. It washed up on that island."

"Oh, Jamie, we're screwed."

"What do you mean?"

"It's on an island, in the middle of a lake? How are we supposed to get over there?"

"I brought the raft with us – "

"Oh, no. You can count me out."

"Norm..."

"I mean it, Jamie."

"Norm, we're there. I'm looking at the body right now! Are you telling me after all the crap we've gone through, we're just gonna give it up?"

"Well, then leave me here. I'll wait while you get it."

"I can't do it alone. It'll be too heavy for me to move on my own."

"How do you know it's dead?"

"If you could see it, you'd know. Norm, don't do this to me. I swear to God, if we do this, by tonight we'll be back in town. You'll get to a doctor, and we'll be on the front page of every newspaper in the country!"

"Ain't it supposed to be illegal to kill one of those things?"

"Kill what? We found a body. There's no evidence that it died of anything other than natural causes. Besides, how do you like the sound of *Gigantopithecus-Montagna-Cocke?*"

"What?"

"That's what they'll call the new species. They always name it after whoever discovers it. In this case, it's us. You have to admit, it sounds a hell of a lot better than *Gigantopithecus-Kodiak*, doesn't it?"

"Yeah, but not as good as *Gigantopithecus-Cocke-Montagna.*"

The bundled raft was tremendously heavy, and Montagna's back immediately cramped up the instant he dropped it. He unconsciously rubbed his broken nose, remembering how hard the other raft was when Kodiak struck him with it. He tripped the CO_2 cartridge, and they jumped back as the raft erupted into full shape like an animal bursting forth from an egg. Montagna suddenly felt stupid as he recalled firing on the first raft when it shot up from under the river.

They waded into the lake with the raft. Norm shivered and exclaimed, "Man, this water's cold!"

Montagna was getting impatient again, but quelled the urge to yell at Norm and simply said, "Just start paddling. We'll be there in ten minutes."

At first their effort to paddle was clumsy, and they drifted in a circle. But after a couple of minutes, they managed to get synchronized and started heading in the direction of the island.

The estimated ten minutes lapsed into fifteen, then twenty-five. Norm did notice that without his eyesight his sense of hearing became more acute. But many of the things he heard he was so unaccustomed to hearing, he couldn't identify them. One sound he could make out, however, was the sound of water gently lapping on the shore of the island. They couldn't have been more than thirty yards from it.

He heard something nearby break the surface, or suddenly submerge beneath it, and the raft was slightly jarred. Norm grew wary. "Jamie?"

There was no answer.

"Jamie.... Jamie, say something."

No answer.

Norm reached out to where Montagna had been sitting. "Jamie! Jamie!" He felt along the raft but couldn't find him. "Dear God! Jamie! Jamie!" Norm was clinging to the raft like a lost child, scared and confused. He could feel it being helped along by the current. "JAMIE!!!"

Montagna climbed up one of the granite boulders that rose from the water on the west end of the island, well away from the beach where he left Norm. He carried the can of lighter fluid and the butane torch in a plastic bag and had tied the machete across his back. When he looked around he didn't see the Giganto anywhere, so he took the can of lighter fluid from the bag.

After drifting and paddling aimlessly for ten minutes, Norm could feel the ground under the raft. He laughed with relief. "Thank God... Oh, thank God!" He got out of the raft and pulled it ashore, where he flopped down on the sand and let the sun warm his body.

What in the hell had happened to Jamie? Had he suddenly drowned, or had something dragged him under the water? There was no logical explanation for it, and Norm was scared. Without the use of his eyes, he was unable to do anything for Jamie, and if the sight in his right eye didn't continue to improve, he'd be trapped on this island until who knew when. He cupped his hands around his mouth and yelled, "JAAAAMIIIIIIEEEEEEEE!!!!!!!!"

Montagna had to stifle a laugh when he heard Norm yell. It looked like Plan A was going to work. He was suddenly startled by the massive, dark form of the Giganto moving through the trees, heading in Norm's direction at a deliberate pace.

For the first time Montagna saw its face. In spite of what it did to Dave, he saw no menace about it. Rather, there was clearly an intelligence in its eyes; a type of wisdom that comes from a lifetime of surviving, for the most part, undetected. Now seeing its high cheek bones and intense, deep-set eyes, he was able to understand how people could actually mistake these animals as human.

He jumped down from the boulder and followed it.

Norm was on the verge of hysteria again. He had no idea what to do about his current predicament, and he could think of no way out. He cupped his hands around his mouth again and hollered, "Jaaaaaaaaamie!"

He heard somebody walking through the brush, and he turned toward the trees. He couldn't pinpoint it exactly, but he knew it was Jamie. It had to be. "Jamie?"

His eyes were screwed. He couldn't make out any details of the woods, he could only tell the dark black mass of trees set against the slightly lighter sky. But he could hear the steps; they were moving at a regular pace, not fast, but steadily in his direction.

Norm didn't say anything else. He would just let Jamie have his fun. In fact, he would let him get just close enough so he could knock him cold. Another sound, almost like a dog growling, and no farther away than the nearest tree. It sounded like something big. A lot bigger than any dog.

Norm grew pale and stood perfectly still. Whatever animal it was that was watching him right now was definitely malevolent.

It growled again, but didn't come any closer.

Norm started to cry.

Montagna lost sight of the Giganto as it went into the woods near the beach, right where Norm probably was. He set the can of lighter fluid on the ground and took the machete from his back. He stuck the tip of the blade repeatedly into the top of the can until he was able to tear three-quarters of it off, making it possible to hurl all its contents at once. With the machete in one hand, and the lighter fluid in the other, he headed for the beach. Everything absolutely depended upon Montagna's ability not to panic. And he was scared to death.

Norm was still facing the trees, trying desperately to make out the shape of the animal. He knew he could run for the water, but if this truly was an island, and not just a peninsula, then it was capable of swimming, and old Norm was a dead man.

He suddenly saw something moving away from what he assumed was a tree and move to another tree, still keeping its distance, still growling.

The *Gigantopithecus* studied Norm from about ten yards away. Ordinarily it went to great lengths to avoid contact with humans, having no interest in the species, but harboring a natural fear of them. It also remembered all too well being attacked the day before. Dave Bovard's rock had struck the animal hard, and it retaliated. But its head still hurt, and any confrontation with other humans was going to be met with the same hostility.

It knew Norm could sense it, yet it also seemed to understand that he was incapacitated in some way. He was incapable of knowing where it was. The Giganto decided to move in and deal with this man.

Norm heard the heavy footsteps coming his way. He saw a large, blocky form separate from the rest of the darkness that made up the woods. It was coming after him, so he ran for the water.

The animal roared as Norm splashed into the water and swam away from the island. He thought he was making good distance, when he was suddenly grabbed and violently hurled back on the beach.

The Giganto was only up to its knees when it caught Norm and was now coming out of the lake after him.

Norm got up and ran for the woods, praying that the closer he got, the clearer the trees would become. He narrowly averted slamming headlong into one tree, but scraped his hands on the bark. He could hear the Giganto coming up fast behind him, so he quickly felt his way past the tree, but almost ran into another one.

The Giganto roared. Norm screamed, probably exactly the same as Dave Bovard had just before he was killed. Montagna ran in the direction of Norm and the Giganto and... *WHAM!* Norm plowed into him and they both fell to the ground.

Montagna landed on his back and was splashed with some of the lighter fluid.

"Jamie!"

"Get off me, Norm!"

The Giganto broke through the foliage and stood over the two men. It stopped cold and stared down at them. It seemed confused by Montagna's presence.

Montagna felt humbled as he lay beneath this giant animal. He and Norm were completely at its mercy. If it wanted to kill them there wouldn't be a damn thing they could do about it.

But it didn't.

The animal towered over them, contemplating. It had either lost interest in the idea of killing them, or was discouraged by the fact that there were now two of them. It gave a hard grunt and turned to walk away.

Montagna pushed the whimpering Norm off of himself and got up. He came up behind the great ape and when it turned back around, Montagna threw the lighter fluid in its face. It staggered back, fiercely rubbing its eyes and squealing from the pain, when...

WHOOSH!!! Montagna touched it with the butane torch and a ball of gnarly yellow flame burst out several feet from the ape, igniting the lighter fluid that Montagna had spilled on himself.

The Giganto's huge arms swung around wildly as the animal screamed in intense, guttural agony.

It did not occur to Montagna that his chest was on fire. Seeing his only chance, he slashed furiously at the ape with the machete, trying to get the one blow that would at least cripple it until it burned to death. Only when the beast knocked him away, did he realize he was burning and threw himself down on the ground and rolled, trying to put out the fire on his shirt. He had seen people who suffered life-threatening burns, and it was something that always terrified him, so he kept rolling even after the flames were completely out.

The *Gigantopithecus* was not as fortunate. The fire completely engulfed its head and upper torso, and in its panic, it ran into the woods, shrieking like a devil and trailing flames behind it like streamers. It inevitably came to the boulders on the west end of the island and dropped into the lake, extinguishing the flames with an explosive *HIIISSSSSSSSS!!!!!!*

The Giganto did not reappear.

Montagna ran down to the beach, stumbling into the water until he was fully submerged. While the flames were extinguished, the skin of his chest, shoulders, and neck was covered with first and second-degree burns. The icy water felt good for about twenty seconds, then the burning sensation started again. He looked wildly around for the *Gigantopithecus*, certain that it had to be so badly wounded it could not have gotten far. There was no sign of it. Montagna was suddenly overcome with exhaustion and the effects of shock from his burns. He stumbled to the shore and vomited, retching so hard he felt like his ribs were going to crack.

Still dizzy and on his knees, he saw Norm making his way back to the beach. He coughed, "Bastard, Norm.... You didn't even try to help me!"

"What are you talking about, Jamie?"

"I was on fire! You didn't even lift a finger to help me!"

"How was I supposed to help you if I can't see you?" Norm did in fact see the flames. The terror of being hunted by the Giganto returned clear vision to his good eye. He saw the entire incident. "Besides, you could say I offered you about as much help as you were offering me when you used me as bait for that Sasquatch!"

Montagna shook his head. "We've got to go back across the lake."

"My God, Jamie. Don't you even have the decency to deny it?"

Montagna sat down on the sand and rubbed his tender, raw chest. "I left the first aid kit with the backpack."

"You didn't answer me."

When Montagna saw Norm walk over to him, he knew he was able to see again. "Norm, I don't think that Sasquatch'll be bothering us anymore. Okay?"

The red bandanna was gone, and Norm saw the top of Montagna's head all torn up and covered with scabs and tattered skin. "What in the hell happened to your head, Jamie?"

A horrifying thought suddenly chilled Montagna: What about the possibility of rabies? With his luck, he would be the only human being to come down with Sasquatch-related rabies. He stood up, fighting the wobbling sensation in his legs. "Let's go, Norm."

Norm looked warily at Montagna. "Where?"

"We're gonna find Pearl."

"Who the hell is Pearl?"

"Pittman's geek with the Winnebago."

"Is he gonna ride us into town?" When Montagna didn't answer, Norm flew into a rage. "I knew it! You're still gonna try to catch that damn Sasquatch!"

Montagna was calm as he tried to explain. "Norm, you do not understand the significance –"

Norm continued to rage. "Significance of what? Please explain that to me! Did you lose an eye? Were you set up to be eaten by that damn thing? The worst thing that happened to you is you got the top of your head scratched up! What, are you afraid the hair won't grow back? I got news, it was gone long before now!"

Montagna remained stoic, even though he was seriously concerned that Norm may finally have had enough and might actually attack him. "Norm, get in the raft. We are going to find Pearl, and then we are going to head into town to rebuild this expedition. Do you understand me?"

Norm was stunned silent. The only other time he had heard Montagna use that tone of voice was just before they killed Ben Tyler. He nodded. "Okay, Jamie..."

❧

Kodiak and Cyrena had followed the Queets River in a vain attempt to locate the juvenile Sasquatch's body. They then decided it was time to make the trek out of the canyon.

After five hours of hiking they came upon another creek, and Cyrena, exhausted from the trek and the merciless heat of the sun, took off her climbing boots and plunged into the water. When she came up, she let out a cry of sheer relief.

Kodiak removed his boots and jumped in after her. The water was only about four feet deep, but its flow was strong enough to carry them a hundred feet while they both just drifted along, feeling days of dirt and sweat wash away.

She climbed upon a large boulder and waited for him to catch up, then they both laid out under the sun. Their clothes were sopping wet, and they felt better than they had in days.

Empty Handed

orm was complaining about his eye again. He was afraid the dirty, two-day-old bandage might cause an infection, so he removed it. The sight of the vaginal-looking wound, still caked with dried blood and plasma, almost made Montagna sick.

"Please, Jamie. There's gotta be a quicker way out of this canyon. I gotta get to a doctor!"

"Norm, by tonight we'll be back in town, and I'll get you to a doctor! Please, just stop your belly-aching until we get there!"

"But it hurts!"

Montagna was getting furious, but still couldn't look at Norm's eye. "Norm, even if it is infected, which I don't believe it is, because you don't have a fever or anything else, it'll be treated tonight."

"I just want to get fixed up so I can get my hands on Kodiak. That's all."

Montagna didn't say anything. Even though he was no stranger to murder, and was clearly more predisposed to violence after recent events, he was still scared of Kodiak.

૨**ᴧ**

Kodiak and Cyrena had come to the bank of the Hoh River, where they picked up the scent of something that smelled burned and greasy.

They went another hundred yards along the river's edge when they saw something very large and abnormal-looking sprawled upon the rocks. They approached it cautiously, but it was clear that it could do them no harm.

It was the *Gigantopithecus*. It had been set on fire, and all the hair from its head, midway down its body and arms, was gone. What remained was covered with open, third-degree burns, and deep slashes from the machete. Its lips and eye lids were charred off, and its eyes were scorched white like a pan-fried trout.

It wasn't dead, but from the gurgling sound that came from deep in its throat, Kodiak could tell it had swallowed some of the flames that had engulfed it.

Cyrena was numb, almost in shock. "That's it... The one that got Dave..."

Kodiak's eyes were welling up as he stood over the animal. "The sons of bitches. They burned him."

The animal sensed their presence and made a feeble attempt to face them. It groaned miserably.

Cyrena held back a sob. "Why... Why would they do this?"

Kodiak didn't answer. He was looking around, then walked over to a large boulder and went about the task of forcing it up from the ground.

Cyrena watched him, her heart twisting inside her with sorrow and rage.

Tears rolled down Kodiak's face, and the bitter salt taste fueled his fury until he was finally able to pull the rock loose. He grasped it from the bottom. It was cold and damp with mud, and he could feel small, crawly things moving over his fingers.

He hoisted the two hundred-pound rock to his chest and walked back to the Giganto. He lifted the rock over his head, taking as careful aim as possible and slammed the rock down as hard as he could.

Cyrena wanted to turn away, but she needed to see that the rock landed squarely on the Giganto's head, putting it out of its misery quickly.

The rock came down hard, its dark, muddy underside cracking the giant ape's skull. They heard the low, deep whisper of its last breath escaping from its scorched lungs.

Kodiak stepped back, breathing hard from exhaustion and anger. As he stared down at the dead animal, Cyrena came up behind him and wrapped her arms around his waist.

He whispered, "I know you didn't want to see anyone else die. So if you like, I'll show you the way out of this canyon, because I'm going to kill Montagna and Cocke."

She didn't say anything. He could feel her tears forming a warm spot on his back.

He looked across the river and yelled as loud as he could.

"MONTAGNA! YOU'RE A DEAD MAN! YOU AND COCKE! YOU'RE DEAD!" The last two words echoed across the canyon in all directions: "YOU'RE DEAD! YOU'RE DEAD! UR ED! UR ED! UR ED!"

ع

Emory Pittman wasn't getting any sleep at all, and it was pissing him off. For some reason the thermostat had been turned up to ninety-five degrees, and that damned Dubbins wasn't answering his phone. He didn't know what was happening, but if there was a malfunction, Dubbins should have reported it. And if Dubbins was pulling something, he was surely going to pay.

Pittman may have been laid up with this broken hip, totally at Dubbins' mercy, but when he was back up and around Dubbins would be reminded of just who called the shots around here. Of course, after fifty-three years of faithful service, Dubbins was well versed in Mr. Pittman's intolerance for employee insubordination, and the usual procedures for straightening out said employee. Pittman preferred the cane for disciplining his manservant. It was the one thing with which he was truly generous. Once, he had even broken a cherry wood cane across Dubbins' back.

Pittman smiled at these sadistic memories, and the near unbearable heat made him think of more cruel punishments. Maybe this time he really would feed Dubbins to Mark Anthony like he was always threatening to do. Oh, that would be...

As Pittman lay in his bed daydreaming of all the cruelty he could and would inflict upon his gentleman's gentleman, he was distracted by the sound of the vault door opening. And then Dubbins walked in, looking at his employer in his usual stoic demeanor.

Pittman sat up against his pillows and glared at Dubbins, almost drooling at the thought of what he was going to do to punish him. "I've been trying to call you all day and night! Why haven't you answered me? Do you have any idea how hot it is in here?" Pittman was nearly screaming, but Dubbins simply stared at him through flat, vacant eyes, as he had for fifty-three years.

"I am sorry to disturb you, sir. But you have a visitor."

Pittman was incredulous. Was Dubbins serious? A visitor at this hour? "A visitor? What the hell are you talking about?"

"You have a guest. I suggest you prepare to receive them."

"What kind of crap is this? I'm not expecting anybody. Tell them to go to hell!"

Dubbins shook his head and clicked his tongue. "I'm sorry, sir, but I'm afraid I can't do that."

"Oh? And why not?"

"That would be rude. And I'm afraid your days of being rude are over." Dubbins let out an uncharacteristic giggle and started pushing the vault door all the way open. "I'm afraid, sir, your days of *everything* are over."

When the vault door was completely open, Pittman gasped and shuddered violently.

Mark Anthony was laid out upon a hydraulic lift that was specially built for transporting the reptile. He was unconscious, or dead, and Pittman was hoping – praying – it was the latter.

But he knew better, as Dubbins eased the lift into the room and lowered Mark Anthony to the floor and unfastened the straps that held him. Pittman watched everything with those blue-jewel eyes wide with disbelief and horror. "Dubbins... Dubbins... You... Don't do this..."

Dubbins stood back upright and for the first time since Pittman had known him, he was smiling. "You'll find the phones have all been disconnected. Probably why you were unable to get hold of me. I've also taken the liberty of changing the code to the lock, and as for the guns you keep hidden in here, including the German Luger you keep under your mattress that you didn't think I was aware of, I relieved them all of ammunition.

"Now, if you'll excuse me, Mr. Pittman, I have travel arrangements to make. But I will be watching the festivities from the closed-circuit T.V. in the game room. The big screen. So do put on a merry show. *I want lots of screaming.*" Dubbins bowed for what would be the last time and exited the room. Pittman heard the electronic locks jamming into place, and he knew that now it was Dubbins who had screwed him. And screwed him good.

Now he knew why the temperature was up so high. In order to guarantee Mark Anthony's cooperation, the temperature in his pond had to be lowered to where his body would shut down so that he could be handled. Once he was in the room with Pittman, the heat would revive him, and the odds were very high that all he had to eat in the past few weeks were a few scrawny chickens.

Emory Pittman was terrified beyond anything he had ever known in his life. He was trapped in here, not just because of the phones, the locked vault door, and his useless guns, but because his broken hip made it impossible for him to get out of bed. He looked up at the television camera from which Dubbins would be monitoring the scene, but decided pleading would be useless. If anything, it would just give the withered up old bastard the first real hard-on he's had in a hundred years.

He looked back at the slumbering Mark Anthony and saw the first sign of his impending doom; the reptile let out a great hiss, took in a breath, let out another tremendous hiss and slowly opened the two beady eyes set atop his huge head.

There was no defense other than to stay perfectly still. Between the stifling heat and his intense fear, Emory Pittman was swathed in perspiration that dripped from his domed head into his eyes.

Mark Anthony groaned and got up on his feet, looked about his new surroundings, and suddenly he spotted his prey.

Pittman looked into those cold, hungry eyes and felt his bowels opening up, filling his silk pajama bottoms. Mark Anthony sensed his fear and started ambling across the floor toward him.

"Oh, God." Pittman searched through his bed sheets and found the remote control for the revolving platform that supported his bed. He pressed down on the switch until his thumb turned white. The bed started to turn away from the alligator.

Mark Anthony followed him, picking up his pace from an amble to a deliberate surge. Pittman held the button down, but the bed continued to move at a pathetic crawl. He hit another switch and changed direction, but the platform continued to move just as slowly.

Pittman started crying. First just a little whimper that crept from the back of his throat, then quickly into open sobs of hysterical fear. The bed came to a three hundred and sixty degree turn, and Pittman looked up at the camera, screaming, "DUBBINS! DUBBINS! DUBBINS!"

Mark Anthony made his move. With a mighty thrust he threw himself upon the bed, dislodging the mattress and smashing the hydraulic platform under his tremendous weight. Pittman almost rolled into the huge, slavering jaws, but he drew away just as they crashed shut, narrowly escaping the razor teeth.

Pittman hit the floor, and his hip exploded in a violent blast of burning, crippling pain as the fracture re-opened. He screamed, and Mark Anthony lunged over the side of the bed after him.

Suddenly Pittman saw hope: the bathroom was on the far side of the room. It was a separate wing housed in black glass. If he could make it to the bathroom, he could lock himself inside and escape the alligator. He would have to crawl twenty-five feet across the floor, and up five steps to get in there, but what choice did he have? He scrambled like a lunatic away from the bed and Mark Anthony, and headed for the bathroom. He ignored the pain, and even managed to move a little faster when he heard the alligator's great bulk slide off the bed and hit the floor behind him.

Ten feet out, Pittman laughed and shouted, "Dubbins! I'll have your head!" But his luck was short-lived. In five easy steps Mark Anthony was on him, and his five-foot jaws slammed shut on Pittman's useless legs.

Pittman screamed at volumes he never before thought humanly possible, as Mark Anthony twisted his massive body and tore off both legs that were clamped securely in his mouth.

Pittman's mind died a little before Mark Anthony actually got him, which was Dubbins' whole idea. Now the thing that was Pittman pulled itself free of the alligator, minus his legs, and continued pulling himself toward the bathroom, spilling his life-blood in a river that led from Mark Anthony to a distance of seven more feet, where Emory Pittman finally shuddered in his death spasms. He then lay perfectly still, his blue-jewel eyes staring out from the brown, splotchy skin of his skull-like face.

ॐ

When they set out upon the river Jamie Montagna let Norm sit up front. Now that old Norm had his vision back, Montagna didn't cherish the idea of having his back to him, especially after he screwed Norm over on the island with the Sasquatch. Oddly, it didn't occur to Norm that maybe it was dangerous to have Montagna at his back.

It turned out that placing Norm up front was a mistake, because he smelled to high heaven. Nobody on this trip had the opportunity to take a real bath, but everybody had at least brought a change of clothes and had taken some time to wash in the river. Everybody except Norm, who had been wearing the same filthy clothes for a week. Come to think of it, Montagna had never seen Norm in any other clothes.

Thankfully, there was a powerful side wind that drowned out the desire for prolonged conversation, as well as blowing away the 'eau du Norm'.

Norm laughed, paddling the rubber raft through a narrow gorge. "You know, Jamie, I'm starting to feel pretty good! How much farther 'fore we're back in civilization?"

Montagna turned his head away to take a breath, then said, "Too far!"

Norm turned to him. "What?"

The raft suddenly shot down a ten-foot plume and disappeared in a cloud of white vapor. It was hurled violently upward to the cries of Norm's frenetic screams.

Montagna was almost hurled from the raft. He grasped the sides for dear life. But they were totally unprepared for the thrashing they were about to be subjected to; more than a hundred yards of white water rapids populated with ferocious-looking jagged rocks that threatened to tear their meager little raft to shreds.

Norm's bowels turned to water as he looked out at the hell before them. The raft felt totally inadequate as the water twisted and thrust the inflated rubber and canvas body towards the obstacle course of rocks.

Huge waves of frigid water pounded down upon them, threatening to wash them from the raft. The raft slid across large boulders and provided no barrier of protection for the two men as their legs and backs were relentlessly battered. God, there were so many ways to die; drowning, chief among them.

Montagna held tight to the raft, trying to see where they were being sent, but between the constant pounding of waves and total disorientation, all he could do was try to gulp in breaths of air before going under again.

Norm was terrified, screaming like a baby, clinging as fiercely to the raft as Montagna and whimpering with every wave that washed over them.

The worst of the rapids began to peter out where the gorge became wider and the water deeper. The rubber raft took a tremendous beating, but contoured with grace through the angry currents and banked off the rocks without major incident.

As the buffeting softened, Norm sat up and looked forward. "Jamie!" Directly ahead a large whirlpool had formed, and the raft was heading right for it.

"Jump, Norm!" Montagna jumped from the raft just as it slammed up against another rock.

Norm almost waited too long. When he jumped, he went straight into the water and was floating toward the whirlpool right behind the raft. He managed to kick towards an outcropping of rocks, and, just as he grabbed onto them and got a foothold, the raft was sucked into the whirlpool and dragged under the water in mere seconds.

Montagna looked across the river at Norm and thought, at least he won't stink anymore.

ða

It looked like Kodiak and Cyrena were going to spend another night in the forest, but, at this point, they didn't really care. They were like zombies; drained physically and emotionally, and far too tired to even consider going on tonight.

They had buried the *Gigantopithecus*. Between the two of them, they had dragged the seventeen hundred-pound body four feet into the river, then spent three hours piling as many boulders as they could onto its corpse, until there was no way anyone would ever see the remains. Even then, there would only be pieces of bones broken and worn away by the continual flow of the river.

When they finished, Kodiak looked at her and said, "Meet *Gigantopithecus-DeVarona*."

"What?"

He reached out his hand. "You still have your knife?"

She took her knife from her pants pocket and handed it to Kodiak. It was one of the deluxe model Swiss Army knives, with the saw blade.

Kodiak rolled away several large rocks that covered the Giganto's right foot and drew the largest knife blade. It was still sharp and sliced through the thick hyde around the dead ape's ankle fairly quickly. He sliced through muscle and sinews, then had to switch to the sawblade to cut into the cartilage in order to separate the bones of the foot from the ankle. The entire process took Kodiak half an hour, and when he finished, he was dripping with sweat.

The severed foot weighed thirty-five pounds. He wrapped it in his flannel shirt and carried the bundle under his arm as they walked away from the dead relic. "This puts us in more danger than anything that's happened so far."

Cyrena looked at the bundled shirt that was starting to saturate with blood. "Why?"

Kodiak said, "When I told you that I didn't want to be the guy who goes down in history as handing over the first sacrifice, I had other reasons. You think it might be a simple matter of showing up at some newspaper, or television studio with this foot, and that would lay everything to rest. Well, nothing could be further from the truth.

"By just coming out and saying we've got a piece of a body, chances are nobody will take us seriously, let alone come out to take a look. Odds are, somebody will try to con it out of our possession, or worse, kill us for it. Just look at Jamie Montagna and what he's done so far. No, we have to stash this someplace safe, until we can expose it to the media in a manner that guarantees our rightful ownership.

"Then there's all the controversy. You better be prepared for the wrath of those animal rights organizations that will accuse us of murder, as well as those who will be adversely affected by the effect on the economy, when the species is labelled as endangered.

"Of course, should we manage to weather all that, we will have the right to name the species." He stopped walking and smiled.

Cyrena lowered her head and said, "Good Lord."

"And now to find shelter." Kodiak dreaded the idea of having to build another lean-to, no matter how simple and flimsy. He was so tired, he just wanted to sleep. Then Cyrena said, "Maybe we can get a ride with them." She was pointing to a Winnebago camper that was parked between two huge trees. This in itself was not unusual, except that there were no campgrounds around for miles.

᠅

Ron Pearl was angry. He'd been stuck here in this Winnebago for two days now, waiting for Montagna's goons to show up, and there had been no sign of them. He didn't know how much longer he was going to have to wait before either going to look for them, or just leaving them altogether.

The fact was, he wasn't going anywhere. If they did catch a Sasquatch, as Montagna had alluded, then he would continue to be patient. That didn't quell the feeling that something was wrong. The fog was setting in again, and through the fading daylight it looked creepy, which made him wish he was back home where it was warm and spacious, with ceilings higher than seven feet.

Why hadn't Montagna contacted him on the radio? Was it broken? He suddenly had horrible images of the Sasquatch, ten feet tall, all hair and fangs, with glowing red eyes, getting loose from its cage and ripping everybody to bloody pieces.

Somebody pounded on the door of the camper, and he jumped. It had to be Montagna's people, he hoped.

Taking a deep breath to steady his nerves, Pearl got up and walked over to the door. He hesitated just a little before he pulled it open. Much to his surprise, it wasn't Norm Cocke and Dave Bovard. It was George Kodiak and some woman. They both looked like hell, and Pearl was definitely going to get to the bottom of what had happened out there. But right now, he was just glad that he could now get out of this Godforsaken wilderness. "George Kodiak."

"Mr. Pearl. Funny meeting you out here. How's Pittman?"

Pearl stood aside to let them in. "You mean, Montagna didn't send you here to meet me?" He saw that Kodiak was carrying something big wrapped in a filthy, blood-soaked shirt. It smelled like it might have been a dead animal.

Cyrena looked at Kodiak. "He works for Jamie?"

Kodiak nodded. "For Emory Pittman."

Cyrena's voice got louder, completely startling Kodiak and Pearl. "So he's working with Jamie and Norm..."

Kodiak said, "Yeah, I suppose you could say that."

Cyrena punched Pearl in his face. He fell back, his nose bleeding. Before he could react, she jumped on top of him and started pummeling him with her fists. Her blows were hard and effective.

Pearl was barely able to protect himself, let alone fight back. But when Cyrena grabbed a fistful of his hair, it came off – all of it. Ron Pearl wore a toupee, and when it came off, it distracted Cyrena. He kicked her.

She landed hard on her elbows and was almost struck again by Pearl's foot when Kodiak hauled Pearl off the floor and threw him out of the camper. She heard him thump into a tree as Kodiak shut and locked the door.

He helped her up. "You okay?"

She nodded, sitting on one of the beds and rubbing her elbows.

Kodiak started laughing. "You were gonna beat the living crap out of him!"

She looked at the toupee in her hand and tossed it aside. "It was Ben. The Sasquatch. And even Dave. I guess I connected him to Jamie and Norm, and everything just came out. I would have done anything I could to hurt him."

Kodiak stopped laughing. "Yeah, I know what you mean. Let's get going." He got in the driver's seat and started the engine, and much to their delight, Cyrena found the refrigerator was fully stocked.

&

"We finally made it." Norm's voice cracked with emotion as he and Montagna cleared the last of the woods and stared at the Hoh Rainforest Visitor Center. It was still two hours before the sun would set, but the temperature had dropped ten degrees, and they were still wet.

After the incident on the river, any realistic hope of finding Pearl and the Winnebago was gone. They could only hope to get to civilization before nightfall without catching pneumonia.

From here they could pick up a ride back to Red Fern.

Jamie Montagna could not believe how badly things had turned out. First Kodiak did everything he could to release their captured Sasquatch. Then came the business with Norm and his eye. Then finding Dave Bovard splattered like a cherry pie that was dropped from a rooftop. He felt like crying.

The Night the Red Fern Tavern Burned Down

n ten minutes it would be nine o'clock, and the girl could close the gift shop for the night. She hated the tourist season, because the work was boring, and the customers, mostly city idiots who wouldn't know a bear from their ass, were usually obnoxious. And she had been putting in longer hours than usual.

The customers she most hated were the ones who would come in five minutes before closing, screaming that they still had five minutes before nine, and they knew exactly what they wanted which, of course, they didn't.

When the bell over the front door jingled, she groaned inwardly and expected the worst. Two people came in; a man and a woman. They looked like they had spent the last twenty-four hours in Hell. The man was badly battered. His face was bruised, his right eye was swollen almost shut, there was a nasty cut on his forehead, and he was walking with a noticeable limp.

The woman was a mess, too, but not as badly beaten as the man. The looks on their faces made it clear they weren't your run-of-the-mill tourists looking to waste her time.

The man took something off a display rack near the door and brought it over to the counter.

"This do it for you?" she asked them.

"That'll do it." The man looked like he was ready to kill somebody, which made his purchase seem all the more bizarre; a deck of playing cards with a picture of Mount Saint Helens in full eruption.

&

Montagna and Norm went to the Red Fern Tavern and were sitting comfortably in a booth, sucking down depth charges.

When they finally arrived in town, Norm went right to a doctor, just a country practitioner, but capable of treating his eye. He asked Norm about what caused the wound, and chastised him for not cleaning it up better and allowing the dressing to get dirty. He also explained that while he was no specialist, the eye was gone.

Norm didn't answer any of the doctor's questions, took the prescription for antibiotics, and told the doctor to get screwed.

Their rooms at the Red Fern Lodge were still rented under their names, so they got cleaned up and put on some fresh clothes before heading to the tavern. Montagna had a Glock model 20 pistol with a fifteen-round magazine in one of his bags that was left in the room prior to going out to Mildred Hunnicut's place. He shoved it in the pocket of his windbreaker and then went to meet Norm for dinner.

They devoured two New York steaks each, along with baked potatoes, soup, and salad. Then they started in on the booze.

"Some trip, huh, Jamie?"

Montagna was preoccupied, thinking about how they had come across *two Sasquatches,* something that was totally unheard of, and then lost both of them.

"I'll tell you," Norm said after dropping a shot glass into his beer, "if I ever see that Kodiak... he's a dead man. And that woman, where'd she say she was from? Seattle, that's right. Yeah, I think I'm gonna have to look her up. Jamie? Jamie, are you listening to me?"

Montagna glanced at him and said, "Yeah. Kodiak."

"You're not listening to me." Norm belched and sat back. He raised his hand to get the waitress' attention and called, "Couple more shots and Old Milwauks." The waitress came over to the booth, and Norm thought she must be deaf. "Sweetheart, I said a couple more shots – "

"I got it. I was asked by a gentleman at the bar to deliver something to you..." She took a playing card from her apron pocket and set it on the table between them. She had no idea what it was about, and was even more confounded by the expression of terror that overtook both their faces at the sight of it. She figured it must have something to do with the fact that it was the ace of spades – the death card.

Norm grabbed her arm, squeezing off her circulation and baring his ugly, stained teeth. His one exposed eye was wide and crazed-looking. "Where is he?"

She tried to wriggle free, but was unable. "Let go of me – "

Norm raised his hand like he was going to beat her. "Where is he?"

Before she could scream, Montagna pulled Norm off of her. "Forget her. Let's find him." He felt for the Glock in his jacket, and they both looked around the tavern.

The place was packed with people: tourists, construction workers, locals, even kids. There was no sign of Kodiak – not that he'd be stupid enough to stand still for them. Montagna and Norm split up to circle the outer perimeters of the tavern.

Montagna, adrenalin pumping, kept his hand on the gun as he looked around for Kodiak, or Cyrena, ready to blow either of them away. Between the loud music and the other noise, nobody had noticed the row with the waitress.

Norm was on the other side of the tavern, anxious, trembling, looking through the sea of faces that all looked frustratingly the same under the dim lights and through just one eye. His white gauze eye patch and distinctive ape face drew more than a few stares. One face he did recognize was the waitress he had strong-armed at the booth. She was looking at him, pointing him out to the bouncer, some local boy who looked like he was on steroids. The bouncer nodded, acknowledging Norm, and started moving towards him with an agility that was alarming for somebody who looked so graceless. Norm cut into the crowd in an attempt to get lost.

He had to find Jamie. With the bouncer on his tail, and Kodiak lurking about looking to do him grievous bodily harm, Norm suddenly found himself voted least likely to succeed.

"Hey!" The bouncer was on his toes and spotted Norm in the crowd. He worked his way between bodies to get him. Norm looked for Jamie, but was hopelessly alone, so he pulled up his right pant leg and took Ruth's knife from the case tied to his boot.

"All right..." As the bouncer put his heavy paw on Norm's shoulder, Norm whirled around and – WHOOSH! He swung hard with the knife, aiming for the bouncer's throat, but because of his lack of depth perception, he only grazed the bouncer's cheek. But Norm was quick; he drew back and buried the blade deep into the side of the young man's neck. The bouncer screamed, dropping to his knees, as blood oozed between his fingers and down his shirt.

Dead silence filled the tavern. Somebody even pulled the plug on the juke box. The bouncer was on his belly, jerking in violent spasms, until Norm kicked him in the head and knocked him out.

There was a gunshot. People screamed. Children were crying. And everyone was looking at Jamie Montagna with his Glock pointed at the bar, where the bartender was slumped over with a gunshot wound to the head. Directly beneath the bartender a shotgun lay on the floor in a pool of his blood.

Montagna had complete control of the room, scanning the faces around him. "Everybody get at least twenty feet away from the shotgun." The crowd moved well away from the bar. "Anybody so much as moves to scratch his ass, I'll kill him. Norm, I'm gonna watch them. You find Kodiak!"

Norm wiped the knife on his khaki pants and shoved his way through the crowd. He looked at the waitress and pointed at her, saying, "I'm not through with you, either."

Montagna got up on a table with his back to the wall for a better view of the tavern.

Norm looked at every face he could, shoving people out of his way, looking under tables.

Montagna was feeling very sure of himself. He had complete control of the room and mentally chastised himself for ever being scared of Kodiak.

His self-satisfaction was short-lived.

WHACK! He jumped at the sound and turned toward the wall, where a playing card struck the paneling by his head. "NORM!" Montagna jumped off the table and crawled underneath it.

The crowd freaked out and ran like the outgoing tide for the exits.

In his panic Norm grabbed a ten-year-old girl and held her against his chest, holding the knife to her throat so hard that when she swallowed, the blade cut her.

Montagna stayed under the table, watching as people's legs

stampeded all around him. He spotted Kodiak's blue jeans and black boots, and fired three shots. A high-pitched scream followed, then a woman fell to the floor, clutching at her bloody, shattered legs. Two men reached down and carried her out of the tavern.

Norm was backed against the wall, surrounded by people waiting for a chance to free the girl, but there was no way they could get at her without jeopardizing her life.

But Norm had one major disadvantage: Kodiak rose up from the dark corner on Norm's blind side and struck him across the throat with the handle end of a pool cue. The girl tore from Norm's grasp and darted out of the tavern.

Kodiak stepped square in front of Norm and made quick work of him. A solid crack to his groin with the pool cue, and then Kodiak spun him around, repeatedly bashing his face into the wall, leaving a bloody imprint on the white stucco surface.

Satisfied that Norm was no longer of any consequence, Kodiak let him drop to the floor.

Montagna was on the other side of the tavern, beyond the bar that separated the lounge from the dance floor. Kodiak knew his little deck of playing cards wasn't going to do squat against a gun.

As the last of the customers ran out the door, the tavern was now empty except for Norm, the unconscious bouncer, the dead bartender, and Montagna, who was still under the table.

Kodiak took a kerosine storm lantern from a post at the end of the bar and removed the glass cover, exposing the wick. He didn't know exactly which table Montagna was hiding under, so he took a book of matches from the floor and lit the lantern, allowing the flame to take hold before he lobbed it into the lounge. It smashed into a booth, and the flames quickly spread.

No Montagna.

Kodiak grabbed another lantern, lit it and hurled it at the lounge. This one struck a table, and the flames engulfed it. No Montagna.

He grabbed a third lantern, watching the steadily spreading flames on the other side of the tavern. He struck the next match.

Montagna suddenly got up from under his table and fired several rounds to cover his flight as he ran for the exit.

BOOM! The floor exploded at Montagna's feet, and he stopped. Kodiak was in front of the bar, aiming the bartender's shotgun right at him. He pumped the shotgun hard for effect.

The last thing Montagna wanted was to give Kodiak another excuse to kill him, so he threw his Glock as far away from himself as possible and put up his hands.

Kodiak walked towards him, kicking overturned furniture and other debris out of his way. His eyes were shadowed, and his face looked like stone reflected in the light of the flames that were now threatening to consume the building.

Montagna remained frozen in his spot and looked at Kodiak's hands covered in the bartender's blood. When Kodiak came up close to him, Montagna could see his own horrified face reflected in Kodiak's eyes. "...Don't..."

Kodiak didn't shoot him. He drew back with the shotgun and brought the stock hard into Montagna's face, shattering his jaw and sending him crashing to the floor.

Montagna screamed, crawling on his hands and knees in a psychotic attempt to get away. His mouth hurt like the worst kind of torture, and he spewed blood and teeth through swollen lips.

The temperature had gone up drastically in the few minutes that the fire had been eating away at the lounge and was now spreading to the walls of the dance area.

Kodiak came up behind him and drove his foot into Montagna's crotch and flipped him on his back.

Montagna tried to scream, but gagged on his own blood. Kodiak pressed his boot heel into Montagna's jaw, forcing his head to the floor. He reached down and grabbed Montagna's testicles, vice-gripping them in his fist, and lifted Montagna off the floor.

Montagna made pathetic animal sounds as Kodiak tightened his grip and hoisted Montagna up by his waist.

Kodiak never heard the rangers storm into the tavern. They must have yelled at him to release Montagna half a dozen times, before one of them finally struck him across the back of his head and knocked him out.

Out of the Woods

odiak woke up in jail. His body protested angrily against his effort to rise, but he finally managed to crawl to what passed for a toilet and got to his feet. His head hurt, and there was a bump the size of a goose egg on the back of it, but he was lucid.

"Kodiak, you're free to go." Ranger Crichton was standing beside the open cell door, looking at Kodiak with mild disdain. "Can you make it?"

Kodiak just leaned against the sink, still trying to get his bearings.

Crichton turned to somebody out of Kodiak's view and said, "You want to give him a hand?"

Cyrena came in. She was cleaned up, wearing a blue flannel shirt and the khaki slacks that hugged her shapely hips and bottom. She went inside the cell and let Kodiak lean on her as they walked out. "Are you all right?"

Her soft voice was turning him on, and he knew he'd be okay. "All right enough."

Crichton went on ahead of them into the main office, and Cyrena led Kodiak down the row of tiny holding cells that lined the corridor. There were five cells, and they were all empty except for the next to last one, where Norm Cocke was being held.

He was in terrible shape; his face was badly disfigured and covered with scabs that made him look like a relief map of some foreign planet. There was an angry red welt on his neck where he had been struck with the pool cue, and he was glaring at them with his one good eye. It was a look of pure, cold hatred that even made Kodiak look away, if only for a moment. "Kodiak." He spoke with a lisp, because one of his front teeth had been knocked out.

Kodiak stopped, feeling for some absurd reason that he owed Norm a minute.

Norm walked up to the bars. "Know this. I am going to kill you. Jamie's not gonna let them put me away. Not me. Uh-uh."

Kodiak was confused by this remark and looked into the other cells. They were all empty. "Where is he?"

Norm spat, but because of his cracked, swollen lips and missing tooth, it was a pathetic gesture that ended up on his own shirt.

Kodiak grabbed him and slammed him up against the bars. "Where's Montagna?"

"Up yours!" The scabs on Norm's face cracked open when he yelled.

Kodiak shoved him back, as Cyrena gently urged him to keep moving.

As they walked out of the corridor, Norm shouted at Cyrena, "And you. I'm gonna find you too! You hear me? I'll find you!"

Ranger Crichton shut the door behind them as they came into the office.

Kodiak asked, "Why am I being released?"

Crichton debated how he was going to answer the question, then said, "Mr. Montagna's chosen not to press charges against you. So all you have to do is settle up with the owner of the tavern for damages."

Kodiak and Cyrena were astounded. He let go of her and took a step toward Crichton, who moved back out of reflex. "What do you mean, he's decided not to press charges? What the hell kind of place are you people running here? Doesn't it matter that he's killed three people? How is it he just gets to up and walk away from that?"

Crichton was uncomfortable, but wasn't going to lie. "I'm guessing you didn't know he's connected?"

"Connected? How?"

"He's government. While you were sleeping off your headache, he placed a couple calls to Washington, D.C., after which I caught all sorts of holy hell for holding him. A few hours later, a couple of feds came to collect him. I had no choice but to cut him loose."

"And what about that freak you have locked up back there?"

Crichton became less defensive. "Cocke's another story. He's strictly civilian, so he'll stand trial for the murders of Ben Tyler, the bartender from the tavern, and, once we find the body, Andy Paul. I don't think he'll do too much time in prison, though. After a couple of years, they'll hang him."

Kodiak was unimpressed. "Well, thank God for the American system of justice."

Following Cyrena's report of the previous events, a search of the area turned up Ben Tyler's body at the bottom of a seventy-foot ravine. He was dead from gun shot.

Crichton became indignant. "I didn't want to let Montagna go! It just turned out that way. But I can assure you of one thing, my friend. He sure as hell didn't let you go out of the kindness of his heart. He's gonna look you up again someday, and he's gonna have some payback in mind."

"You'll notice I'm not particularly concerned." He gestured Cyrena to the door.

"By the way," Crichton said, "I understand you people were out there looking for Bigfoot?"

Kodiak turned back to face him. "And?"

"Lots of people go looking for those damn things every year, but I never heard of it getting so badly out of hand. So tell me, was it worth it? Did you find anything?"

Kodiak looked at Ranger Crichton and decided he didn't like him. "Not a damn thing."

Crichton chuckled. "I didn't think so. You're gonna want to stick around for a couple days, Kodiak. We need your statement for our investigation."

Kodiak nodded. Then he and Cyrena left the ranger station.

Outside, the morning air was still chilly, but the sun felt warm, and the scent of pine was strong and intoxicating. Despite the wondrous surroundings, Kodiak preferred looking at Cyrena as she walked beside him. Her auburn hair shined in the daylight and smelled of almond-scented shampoo.

They walked arm in arm up the street until they came to the Red Fern Lodge. The adjacent tavern was burned to the ground. A work crew was busy removing wreckage.

"That's gonna cost you."

He looked at the building, thankful that nobody had been hurt in the fire. "I'll manage. At least the lodge is still intact, so I'll have someplace to stay while I'm stuck here. What about you?"

"I've still got a few weeks left of my vacation."

"Some vacation."

She smiled. "I don't know. It is an experience I wouldn't have wished on my worst enemy. It's certainly one I'll never forget. There is one thing. The rangers gave me Ben's personal belongings..." She dug into her pants pocket and pulled out a gold cigarette lighter. "I guess they didn't realize what it really was." She flipped open the lid and pulled out a tiny camera. "Ben always kept this with him. Any guesses as to what's on this film?"

Kodiak smiled as she gave him the camera. She said, "He'd want you to have this."

"The world will see these soon enough. And Ben's going to get the credit."

"That's nice, George. So, what will you do when you're finished here? Go back to Hell?" She suddenly laughed out loud because of how ridiculous the question sounded.

Kodiak just smiled. "I don't know. I was thinking of maybe heading back to Seattle for a couple of weeks. I always wanted to check out the Space Needle."

"If you need a place to stay, I know somebody who might be willing to put you up if you offered to show her how you do that card trick of yours."

He smiled and said, "I'll show you if you'll show me!"

She laughed. "Why don't we discuss that over breakfast? There's a nice little cafe down the street. It's got a great view of the mountains."

He pulled her close as they walked slowly down the street, away from the remnants of the Red Fern Tavern.

❧

Mildred Hunnicut went out on her front porch to watch the sun set behind the mountains, as she had for most of the last thirty-seven years. She sat on the porch swing, watching the sun's red fire sink slowly into the black walls of the forest. The air was getting cooler these days, and the sun was setting earlier. It would be Autumn soon. Then the snow would come and aggravate the hell out of her arthritis, but she would survive, just like she always did.

Larry jumped up on the swing and lay beside her after finishing his dinner. He survived losing his tail, but Mildred kept it bandaged even after the vet told her it was no longer necessary. She wanted to play it safe.

She heard about what had happened to the people who came to her house that night. Three of them died. Then the Red Fern Tavern burned down. She felt a pang of sadness, not only for the destruction and loss of life, but also because of what she had and then lost with her Sasquatch. There was an emptiness for what might have been, if nobody had interfered.

She thought fondly of George Kodiak and Cyrena DeVarona, and was relieved that they weren't among those who died. She felt there was something special between them, and she hoped that they knew it.

The sun went down, and the cold began to gnaw at her joints. She should go in, but she couldn't help but search the trees that surrounded her property, hoping for some sign of the presence she knew would not be there.

Finally, she convinced herself it really wasn't coming back. She stood up, looking at the plate of canned cat food in the center of the lawn. She had gotten into the habit lately of putting out much more food than the cat could eat. "I guess the raccoons and possums will enjoy it, huh, Larry?" She picked up her cat and went in for the night, closing her door to the outside world.

And the mountains.

Author's Note

The material in this novel is based upon documented research done by scientists and laypersons educated on the subject of cryptozoology – the study of hidden and unknown animals.

For information regarding the *International Society of Cryptozoology*, an organization dedicated to the scientific study of unkown animal phenomena and the implications of their possible discovery, please contact:

J. Richard Greenwell, Secretary
International Society of Cryptozoology
P.O. Box 43070
Tuscon, AZ 85733
Telephone/Fax: (520) 884-8369

Bibliography

1. Bord, Janet and Colin, *Alien Animals*.
    (Stackpole Books, 1981)

2. Ciochon, Russell; Olsen, John; James, Jamie,
    *Other Origins; The Search for the Giant Ape in Human
    Prehistory.* (Bantam, 1990)

3. Green, John, *Sasquatch; The Apes Among Us.*
    (Hancock House, 1978)

4. Heuvelmans, Bernard, *On The Track Of Unknown Animals.*
    (Hill and Wang, 1958)

5. Krantz, Grover, *Big Footprints; A Scientific Inquiry into the
    Reality of Sasquatch.* (Johnson Books, 1992)

6. Lien, Carsten, *Olympic Battleground; The Power Politics of
    Timber Preservation.* (Sierra Club Books, 1991)

7. James, Jamie, *Bigfoot or Bust.* (Discover magazine, Volume 9,
    March, 1988)

8. James, Jamie, *Stalking The Giant Ape.* (Discover magazine,
    Volume 10, February, 1989)

9. Waters, Tom, *Almost Human.* (Discover magazine, Volume 11,
    May, 1990)

10. *An Upstanding Ape.* (Discover magazine, Breakthrough
    Section, Volume 19, February, 1998)

THE KODIAK BOOKS

WHERE LEGENDS ROAM

If you enjoyed reading this exciting adventure from Lee Murphy and Defining Moments, then order additional copies today!

Call 1-877-996-3717
Or copy and mail this form with check or money order to:
DEFINING MOMENTS
P.O. Box 7037
Van Nuys, CA 91409-7037

Name _____

Company _____

Address _____

City / State / Zip _____

Phone Number _____

Number of Copies* *($12.95 each)* _____

Shipping / Handling *($4.00 for first book, $1.00 each additonal)* _____

California residents add 8.25% tax per book _____

Total _____

*Ask about our quantity discounts on orders of 10 copies or more.